"Okay, then. Here's the plan."

Hoops, Freckles, Tony and Terry all looked expectantly at Billy.

"If Sully and Lauren got to really likin' each other, then she'd give him the money and we won't have to leave, right?"

"But he *don't* like her," Freckles pointed out.

"So what?" Billy said. "That doesn't mean she can't *make* him like her. I got three older sisters, so I know how they do it."

"But why," Tony asked, "would *Lauren* want Sully to like *her?*"

" 'Cuz that's just how girls are. And even if she doesn't want him to like her yet, if we fix things right then she'll start wantin' him to. And when she does, he'll have to."

"Why?" Tony asked.

" 'Cuz she's pretty and rich."

"So what?" Tony said.

"So she must know how to make guys like her way better than my *sisters* do."

Dear Reader,

The books I enjoy writing most are humorous ones. And since I see Lauren Van Slyke and Jack Sullivan as an illustration of a "most improbable couple," I knew the only way to write their story was with a lot of humor.

Readers often ask if I draw on my own life experiences for my stories, and the answer is both yes and no. I'm not an ex-con, like Jack Sullivan. Nor do I come from a wealthy family, like Lauren Van Slyke. But I know Sully's dog, Roxy, and Lauren's cat, Killer, very well. They're patterned after my own dog, Miss Molly, and my cat, Yeats—who live together under a rather shaky truce.

The settings of *Sully's Kids* are also familiar to me in real life. Living in Toronto, just over the border from New York State, I've spent time in both the Adirondack Mountains and in New York City.

Of course, it's not the settings but the characters that make a story. And in the case of *Sully's Kids,* I really enjoyed Lauren and Sully as I wrote about them. Despite the fact that they start off without a single thing in common and a whole lot of strikes against any possible relationship, they muddle their way through to a happy ending.

I hope you enjoy reading how they do it.

All the best,

Dawn Stewardson

Dawn Stewardson
SULLY'S KIDS

Harlequin Books

TORONTO • NEW YORK • LONDON
AMSTERDAM • PARIS • SYDNEY • HAMBURG
STOCKHOLM • ATHENS • TOKYO • MILAN
MADRID • WARSAW • BUDAPEST • AUCKLAND

ISBN 0-373-70691-X

SULLY'S KIDS

Copyright © 1996 by Dawn Stewardson.

This edition published by arrangement with Harlequin Books S.A.

® and TM are trademarks of the publisher. Trademarks indicated with
® are registered in the United States Patent and Trademark Office, the
Canadian Trade Marks Office and in other countries.

Printed in U.S.A.

To all the readers who've told me they laughed while
reading one of my books. I hope you find
Sully's Kids is another of those.

And to John, always.

CHAPTER ONE

ON THE SIDEWALKS OF NEW YORK

IF THE WINO HADN'T lurched in front of her, Lauren would never have veered left and noticed the cat. When she did, she stopped dead. You *never* saw a cat on Madison Avenue.

Of course, she almost hadn't seen this one. It wasn't very big, really, not more than a kitten. And its dirty copper-colored fur blended perfectly with the dirty copper pipe it was huddled against—one of those grossly fat utility pipes that look as if they're growing out of the sidewalk beside a building.

She stood watching the cat for a few seconds, then told herself she'd better get moving. This was the kind of Manhattan morning that melted your makeup.

July could be brutal in the city, and today the temperature had already climbed into the eighties. The air was muggy, there hadn't been a break in the heat for over a week, and the city's stench had reached the impossible-to-ignore stage—all in all, not a good day to be lingering on the sidewalks of New York.

Besides which, the boss was supposed to set a good example. And in the three months since her father had convinced her to take this job she'd been late more often than not.

She started to turn away, then hesitated. Unless something unexpected had come up, all she had to do this morning was make a few phone calls. And she hardly had a staff of thousands to set an example for. There was only Rosalie, who at fifty-six didn't have the slightest interest in any example set by a thirty-year-old.

Besides, the cat looked so darned pathetic she hated to just leave it sitting there. If she did, it was bound to end up as road kill. Or was the appropriate term here avenue kill?

Whichever, she'd really rather it didn't end up dead. She took a couple of tentative steps in the little guy's direction—deciding it had to be a male because no self-respecting female would let herself get *that* disheveled.

He hadn't noticed her, so she called, "Hey, kitty," then glanced self-consciously at the people hurrying past. New Yorkers simply didn't stand out on the street calling "Hey, kitty." On the other hand, no one in the crush of humanity eddying around her could care less what anyone else was up to.

When she looked at the cat again he still hadn't twitched a whisker, so she edged closer and tried calling him once more. He finally looked at her, his yellow eyes unblinking. Then he looked to either side—unmistakably scoping out an escape route.

The sidewalk was solid human traffic, though. So if the cat made a mad dash for freedom, it would be foot kill before it even had a chance to become road kill.

She hesitated again, afraid that taking one more step would make him bolt, then she made her decision. Putting her briefcase down against the building, with a quick prayer that nobody would steal it, she dashed forward and grabbed the cat.

He let out an indignant yowl, but didn't scratch her.

"Good kitty," she murmured. "Good kitty, you're safe with me."

He eyed her for a moment, then apparently decided she was telling the truth and snuggled close—digging his claws firmly into her jacket.

She gazed unhappily down at him. Now that he was nestled against her off-white suit, she could see he was even dirtier and more bedraggled than she'd realized. His fur was covered with the dry, dusty kind of dirt that instantly rubs off onto whatever it comes in contact with. And apparently, it was especially attracted to raw silk.

Telling herself that's why dry cleaners existed, she retrieved her briefcase and started toward the entrance of the Van Slyke Building. To preclude a run-in with the security people she hoisted the briefcase in front of her, effectively concealing the cat, then breezed across the lobby and into an open elevator.

One of the advantages of being late was that the elevator was almost empty and nobody had pushed a floor below eleven. That made the trip up fast and uneventful—except that, halfway there, the cat began purring and kneading her jacket.

There wasn't much she could do to stop him when he was tucked under her left arm and she was holding her briefcase with her right hand. So by the time the doors opened on her floor, a patch of pulled threads and a gray area had developed over her left breast.

Rescuing the cat, she realized, was rapidly becoming an example of what her father referred to as "Lauren's little errors in judgment." But she could hardly abandon a cat in the hallowed confines of the Van Slyke Building, so she quickly carried it down the corridor to the Foundation offices and opened the door into the reception area.

Rosalie glanced up from behind her desk, her dark eyes coming to rest on the cat. She slowly pushed a strand of graying hair back from her brown face, then said, "You didn't warn me we'd be playing show-and-tell today."

Neither the Jamaican lilt in her voice, nor her expression, betrayed the slightest hint that she was teasing, so Lauren resisted smiling. She'd gotten used to playing Rosalie's game of deadpan humor, although it had taken a while.

"I found the little guy just outside the building," she explained. "And he looked so hungry I thought I'd call Nate's Deli and get them to bring over some milk and tuna fish."

"On rye or whole wheat?"

"Oh, I thought they could hold the bread. And the mayo and pickle, too. He strikes me as a no-frills kind of cat."

Rosalie almost smiled, but not quite. "Yeah? Well, he strikes me as a no-baths kind of cat. You haven't forgotten you've got a couple of appointments this afternoon, have you? That jacket isn't looking exactly fresh."

Lauren nodded, thinking how frequently Rosalie sounded more like her mother than her administrative assistant. But that wasn't entirely surprising, considering the woman had raised five children.

"And if you try to sponge off that dirt," she continued, "you'll only make it worse."

"I know. So I thought I'd run down to that one-hour cleaners as soon as I got the cat fed and cleaned up."

"Cleaned up," Rosalie repeated. "So now we're into more than giving him a free meal. Does that mean you're keeping him?"

"No... well, maybe. I don't really know. I haven't thought that far ahead. But it's not going to hurt to take him into my office and wash the dirt off, is it?"

"You mean in the executive washroom?"

Lauren couldn't keep from smiling this time. Rosalie's term for the minuscule bathroom off her office amused her. "Yes, I think the executive washroom's best. If I took him to the one down the hall, that snippy Karen Petroff would probably come waltzing in and tell me I was being inappropriate."

Rosalie finally smiled, too—a slow, sly smile. Then she said, "Do you know much about cats, Lauren?"

"Not *very* much," she admitted. Both her brother and sister had allergies, so her parents had ruled out pets before she'd even been born. But how hard could it be to deal with one small cat? Half the people in America had a cat. Or more than one. Why, in the apartment across the hall from hers, Jenny and Mark had three.

"I know cats aren't too crazy about water," she added, to show she wasn't completely ignorant. "But if I just put him in the sink and give him a quick rinse, that shouldn't be a big deal, should it?"

"I'll tell you what," Rosalie said thoughtfully. "Instead of having Nate's deliver, why don't we just let the voice mail handle our calls while I go get some cat food. And if I take your jacket with me, I can get it looked after, too."

"Thanks, but I don't have a blouse on under it, only a slip."

"Oh, well, you can wear this while I'm gone." Rosalie reached for the long fuchsia cardigan that always hung on the back of her chair.

"Ahh..." Lauren gazed at the sweater, wondering whether the bright acrylic nightmare was large enough to wrap around her three times or only twice. Her hundred-and-twelve pounds scarcely compared to what had to be Rosalie's two-fifty.

"You go put it on," Rosalie pressed. "Then give me your jacket. I'm not too crazy about cats, so I'd just as soon leave him to you and look after everything else. I shouldn't be long, though," she added as Lauren headed into her office to change. "I'll be back as soon as that dry cleaner does his thing."

SULLY HAD MURDER on his mind. Merely standing here, staring up at her family's name on the damn building, had gotten him furious at Ms. Lauren Van Slyke all over again. But as tempting as the thought of killing her was, he knew it was one he'd better forget about before he got to her office.

He turned and strode down the block a few hundred yards, telling himself that nothing was worth risking another stretch in prison. If anyone had ever *deserved* to be murdered, though...

Hell, he'd never had a single problem while Matthew Grimes was director of the Van Slyke Foundation. But now that Grimes had retired, now that this moronic family member had been put in charge, he was facing the worst problem he could have imagined.

"Damn woman," he muttered, turning and starting back the way he'd come. He'd been trying to figure out exactly where Lauren Van Slyke fit into the family, and his best guess pegged her as an old maid aunt—the sort that, in an earlier era, would have been locked away in somebody's attic.

But since this wasn't an earlier era, the relatives must have decided that making her director of their foundation would keep her occupied.

Of course, his best guess could be wrong. He really only knew two things about her for sure. One, she was a Van Slyke, which undoubtedly meant she was up to her ears in inherited money. And two, she wasn't exactly a straight shooter.

As soon as he'd discovered that, he'd begun suspecting she might be trouble. And sure enough, he'd been right.

When he reached the front of the building once more, he couldn't keep his gaze from drifting back up to those huge brass letters over the front entrance. The Van Slyke Building, they proclaimed. And the date, in smaller letters, told him it had been constructed in 1932. Obviously, the Van Slyke family had gotten through the depression years just fine. It made him wonder, not for the first time, exactly how much Lauren Van Slyke was worth.

When you'd grown up in a Bronx tenement, it was tough to even imagine coming from a family with enough money to have established a private charitable foundation, let alone have an office building on Madison Avenue.

Running his fingers through his hair, he told himself to get on with what he'd come here for. Then, taking a deep breath, he squared his shoulders and headed inside. The cool air was a relief. This might be the last place in the world he wanted to be, but at least it was air-conditioned.

As he started for the elevators, the security fellow at the desk sized him up with obvious disapproval. The guy probably figured anyone who'd walk in here wearing jeans and a T-shirt was a complete boor. But hell, he hadn't driven four hours through the early morning traffic to impress Ms. Lauren Van Slyke with his wardrobe. He'd driven down here to impress upon her that she was an idiot.

He marched into an elevator and pushed the button for eleven. When the doors closed and the elevator started upward, he began mentally picturing her—which was a little tricky, when he hadn't as much as spoken to her. She'd called Eagles Roost once, though, and talked to the boys' teacher. And according to Otis she had a voice like a chicken scratching. So she was probably a skinny old bat of a woman. As the elevator slowed and stopped, he began imagining himself wringing her scrawny neck.

Ordering himself to knock it off, he strode down the hall to 1117. A plaque on the double doors assured him this was the Van Slyke Foundation office and told him to please walk in.

He did, but all was silent and empty inside. Nobody was at the elegant reception desk and nobody was in the expensively furnished waiting area.

When he wandered closer to the sole door leading off it, he could see its nameplate read Ms. Lauren Van Slyke. He smiled, silently congratulating himself on having cornered the old bat in her cave. But there was no response to his knock.

Tentatively, he opened the door and peered in. The office, too, was empty—except for enough antique furnishings to make it look like a miniature museum.

So he hadn't quite cornered the old bat, after all. He would have, though, if she'd been here. He took a couple of steps forward and stood surveying the large office. Then, just as he turned to leave, deciding he'd better wait in the reception area rather than the inner sanctum, a woman shrieked, "Dammit!"

He turned back. It had been a most unladylike shriek, and unless the woman was invisible it could only have come from the closet.

But what in blazes was the old bat doing in her closet? Hanging upside down, waiting for nightfall?

"Dammit!" she shouted again. "Will you stay still? You're going to feel a lot better when I'm finished with you. I promise you will."

Good God. She had someone in the closet with her. But what the hell was she doing to him? There were some questions in life you just had to have answers to.

He quietly closed the office door against potential prying eyes—Lord only knew what he was about to discover—then walked over to the closet and called, "Everything all right in there?"

For a moment, there wasn't a sound. Then the closet door burst open, a wet weasel or something shot between his ankles—startling the hell out of him—and a teenaged girl who looked like a drowned rat was standing glaring up at him.

She was drenched from head to shoeless feet. Her hair was plastered to her skull, there were lines of mascara running down her cheeks, and the bright shapeless red . . . *thing* she was wearing looked like it had come straight out of a washer's spin-dry cycle.

Strangely, just seeing how wet she was gave him the sensation of not being quite dry himself. Then he looked down and saw there was a good reason for the sensation. There were a pair of little wet patches at the bottoms of his jeans, where the weasel had rushed between his legs.

"Who are you?" the girl was demanding. "And what are you doing in here?"

Instead of answering, he glanced over her head—which wasn't tough since she was only about five-foot-four—and tried to make sense of things. What he'd assumed was a closet was actually a tiny washroom, so maybe the girl had been washing her hair. Of course, that didn't explain the wet weasel, but—

"What are you doing in here?" she demanded again.

He wanted to ask her the same thing, but quickly thought better of it. It wasn't tough to read the look in her big blue eyes. She was mad as hell, and maybe a bit frightened, too. He took a step backward and slowly raised his hands to chest level, palms facing her, to show he meant her no harm.

"I'm sorry if I scared you," he said quietly. "But I heard you swearing, and I just . . ."

When her face flushed almost as red as that baggy thing she had on, he cut the explanation and said, "I just came in looking for Ms. Van Slyke."

"*I* am Ms. Van Slyke."

He stared at the kid for a moment, waiting for a punch line. When she didn't deliver one, he shook his head. "No, no. I'm looking for Ms. *Lauren* Van Slyke."

"I told you," she snapped, wiping water off her chin, "that's me."

"No, no," he tried again. This girl couldn't be more than eighteen, but maybe she was a niece or something—named Lauren after the old bat aunt. "It's the Lauren Van Slyke who's the director of the Van Slyke Foundation I'm looking for."

"And that's who you're looking *at*. But you'll have to give me a minute to find the cat. If I don't get him dried off, the air-conditioning will give him pneumonia."

SULLY IMPATIENTLY PACED across Lauren Van Slyke's office and stood staring down onto the rat race of Madison Avenue, wishing she'd hurry up and come back out of that washroom.

They'd captured her damn cat, although not before it had laid a slash that would have done a tiger proud down his forearm. But then, before he'd even had a chance to introduce himself, her secretary had arrived and taken the little beast into the reception area—leaving behind something dry for Lauren to change into.

So now that the *important* things had been taken care of, maybe they could get down to business. But only if she ever reappeared.

Just as he was deciding she was a human fly who'd crawled out the bathroom window and buzzed away, the door opened. He stared at her as she walked over to her desk, knowing he'd never have taken her for the same person he'd seen a few minutes ago.

The smell of wet cat had been replaced by the scent of a sinfully sexy perfume. If she'd been a different woman, it would have been an instant turn-on—particularly since it was obvious now that she was no teenager. She was, he'd guess, in her late twenties.

She'd washed off the mascara stains and had dried her hair enough that it was fluffed out, softly framing her face. It wasn't very long, but he liked its dark honey color.

He also liked the way she looked in clothes that fit. And the creamy-colored suit that had replaced the baggy red thing fit extremely well. The red thing had been concealing a surprisingly nice figure.

And she was wearing shoes this time around. High heels, which he couldn't help noticing made her legs seem longer and extremely shapely.

All in all, she was a very attractive woman. Almost beautiful even, with high cheekbones, regular features, the big cornflower blue eyes he'd noticed earlier, and a lusciously full mouth. But she was also, he reminded himself firmly, the enemy.

"So," he said, pacing back toward the desk as she sat down behind it. "Do you always bring your cat to the office for its baths? Your husband or roommate or whatever doesn't like you using the sink at home?"

"I don't have either a husband or a roommate. And the cat..." Her words trailed off and she focused on the scratch on his arm. "Oh, my," she murmured. "I'm sorry, I hadn't realized that was nearly as bad as it is. I've got some bandages in the bathroom if you'd like me to—"

When he waved off the suggestion, she said she was sorry again, then gave him a tentative smile and gestured at one of the chairs facing the desk. "Please sit down, Mr...."

Since the frantic, shrieking tone of her *dammits* had disappeared, she sounded nothing at all like a chicken scratching. He decided she must have had a sore throat the day she'd called Otis, because her voice was actually so smooth it made him think of a tall cool drink on a hot day like today.

"Mr....?" she said again.

"Jack Sullivan," he told her, sinking into the chair. "Sully to my friends."

He liked the way her face paled when she put his name into context. He obviously wasn't on her list of want-to-sees, and he was glad his visit was going to make her uncomfortable. She deserved to be.

"Ahh..." she murmured. "I'd never have expected you to drive all the way down from the Adirondacks."

So what *had* she expected? That she'd write him her kiss-off letter and he'd just go crawl under a rock? He dug the offending letter out of his jeans and tossed it onto her desk. For a moment, she simply looked at it the way someone might look at a sheet of toxic waste, then she reached for it.

Lauren only picked up the letter because Jack Sullivan clearly expected her to. She certainly didn't need to read the words she'd written a few days ago. She'd agonized over them so long that they were burned into her memory. But at least rereading them would give her time to organize her thoughts.

Dear Mr. Sullivan,
While the board members of the Van Slyke Foundation hold your work at Eagles Roost Lodge in the highest regard, I regret to inform you the Foundation will be unable to renew funding for the coming fiscal year.

My sincerest wishes for the continued success
of your program.

Yours truly,
Lauren Van Slyke, Director

She stared at the letter for a little longer, but when
she realized that having time to organize her thoughts
wasn't helping, she glanced across her desk at Jack
Sullivan again.

Now that she'd had a chance to look at him without water in her eyes, she'd realized he might have
walked straight out of a sexual fantasy. Not any sexual fantasy of hers, of course. She wasn't prone to
such things. But she could see he'd be the sort of man
some women would fantasize about.

He was tall and dark, and something about him
seemed as dangerous as all get out. In his early thirties, he had untamed hair so long it curled up at the
bottom of his neck, a straight nose, heavy eyebrows,
sensual lips and a shallow but intriguing cleft in his
chin.

On top of all that, he looked as if he spent a whole
lot of time chopping wood up at his wilderness lodge.
Beneath his blue T-shirt and jeans was a lean version
of Arnold Schwarzenegger's body.

Yes, even though she wasn't a fantasizer, she could
see that he had a certain…something. And she found
it almost as disconcerting as the way his deep brown
eyes were radiating pure unadulterated hatred.

She tried to think of what to say, but her letter had
said it all, so she simply waited for him to break the
silence.

"I'd like to talk about this problem with my
funding," he said at last.

"Ahh . . . yes, I feel badly about that, Mr. Sullivan."

"Sully," he corrected her, leaning forward in his chair. As he did, she noticed at least seventeen muscles ripple beneath the T-shirt.

"I feel pretty badly about it myself," he continued. "So I thought we could discuss whatever concerns you have. Thought there must be some way we could work things out."

He paused, as if giving her a chance to say there was. But she was hardly going to lie to him.

Finally, he pressed on. "I know Eagles Roost is one of the smaller homes in the Foster Alternatives program, but we've got a solid success rate."

"Yes . . . yes, you do. Wait just a minute and I'll find your file." She leaned back, pulled out the file drawer in her desk and dug out the folder, glad she'd come up with a way to escape his gaze—even if it was only a temporary escape. Opening the file, she began leafing through it. Anything to keep from having to meet his eyes again.

"I guess," he said, "it was the trouble with Leroy Korelenko that got you worried about what we're doing up there. But that was an isolated incident, and I should never have taken him in the first place. He was fifteen, and my kids are always younger than that. But his caseworker said there was nowhere else for him to go, so . . . well, I guess that's beside the point. I shouldn't have let her convince me to take him."

"Yes, but that's the only major trouble you've ever had, isn't it," she said, flipping over a few more pages and building up her courage. Once it got as high as she figured it was going to get, she looked at Sully again.

"The problem," she managed to say evenly, "is that even though you've been doing a good job, I'm afraid there's simply no way I can help you at the moment. But if you reapply again next year—"

"Next year?" He leaned forward again—quickly and menacingly this time. Then he slowly rested his forearms on the edge of her desk.

She couldn't help noticing how tanned and strong-looking they were. Then her gaze drifted to that long nasty scratch and she wished again the cat had kept his claws to himself. Finally, she met Sully's gaze once more—and wished she hadn't. The look in his dark eyes had gone beyond hatred. Now it was saying he'd like nothing better than to strangle her.

"Let's stick to *this* year," he said at last. "Because right now I've got five kids at Eagles Roost, and I'll probably be sent another one before we're into August. And...I don't imagine you've ever tried to look after half a dozen kids at once, have you?"

"No, but—"

"No, I didn't think so. Well, I'll tell you, it's no picnic in the park. 'Specially not when every one of the boys who comes into my program has been yanked out of some completely intolerable family situation. They all have a million problems and a level of self-esteem that's down below their ankles. Giving them enough individual attention to do any good is full-time work, so I can hardly go out and get a nine-to-fiver to support them. And I've got to pay my teacher and housemother, too."

"Yes, of course." Lauren retreated to the file again and turned some more pages. "Otis and Grace Plavsic. I see they've been with you since the program began."

"Right. For almost five years. And I can hardly ask them to start working for nothing. So if you can't reconsider things, is there at least enough money floating around to carry us while I find funding somewhere else?"

"I...I really am sorry," she murmured. "But the board's made its decision and—"

"Decisions can be changed," Sully snapped. "If people actually want to change them."

She took a deep breath, trying to think of words that would diffuse his anger. "Mr. Sullivan... Sully...I don't know if Matthew Grimes ever explained this to you, but the decision-making power of the foundation lies with the board, not with the director. I only study the grant applications and report on them."

"Oh? And the board members don't make their decisions on the basis of your reports?"

"Well...basically, yes."

"Then it's obvious you gave my program a lousy review, isn't it."

"The obvious," she said quietly, "isn't always the truth." She was very tempted to tell him exactly what the truth was in this instance. Then he could go and glare at Hunter Clifton instead of at her. But it would hardly be a professional way of handling the situation.

Sully sat looking at Lauren Van Slyke, trying with all his might to keep his mouth shut. But he couldn't stop the next question from slipping out any more than he could keep the sarcasm from his voice. "Don't you think, just in the name of fairness, you should have talked directly to me before you wrote your report on Eagles Roost? Instead of snooping around behind my back?''

She stared at him evenly for a minute, then said, ''I have no idea what you're talking about.''

The sudden arctic chill in her voice almost made him shiver, and he could feel the final remnants of his control slipping away. She was the one who'd done the snooping, so where did she get off playing Ice Princess when he called her on it?

''You're saying,'' he muttered, matching her tone right down to the last icicle, ''that you didn't phone Otis Plavsic nine or ten weeks ago? Didn't ask him all about Eagles Roost?''

''I most certainly did not.''

He sat back in his chair, at a loss for words. He knew how to handle a kid who was lying through his teeth, but what the hell did he do here? He *knew* she'd phoned Otis, because Otis had told him all about their conversation.

''Was there anything else, Mr. Sullivan?''

Looking at her again, he realized those murderous impulses had returned. ''No. No, I guess if the decision can't be changed, then my funding's done as of the end of September. So there's no point taking any more of your time.''

Lauren Van Slyke gave him a cool smile. ''Well, as I said before, please feel free to apply to us again next year.''

''Yeah.'' He shoved himself out of the chair and headed across to the door. When he reached it he looked back. ''If my program's still around next year, I'll keep that in mind. Thanks.''

For nothing, he silently added, closing the door behind himself. And next year be damned. He'd had enough of Ms. Lauren Van Slyke to last his entire lifetime, and then some.

Her mother, in chilly silence, rang up the sale.
Silent anyway. And then she thanked the A and
credit-or, Mrs. Carson. Wait by the cart with the
life and they waited.

CHAPTER TWO

FAMILY MATTERS

LAUREN SAW HER three-thirty appointment out
through the reception area, in case the cat decided to
make a break for freedom while the door was open.
Once it was safely closed again, she turned to Rosalie—who definitely did not look happy.

"The cat's been giving you problems?" she
guessed. At the moment, the little guy was sitting on
the corner of Rosalie's desk, contentedly chewing on
the fronds of her spider plant.

"Well, that depends on what you consider problems," Rosalie muttered. "He's ripped my panty
hose, scratched the hell out of the carpet, tried to
climb the coat tree about a hundred times, and now
he's having my plant for an afternoon snack."

"Ahh," Lauren murmured, making a mental note
to stop on her way to the office in the morning and
pick up panty hose and a new plant. "Maybe I'd better leave early and get him out of your hair."

When Rosalie said that sounded like a fine idea to
her, Lauren started back toward her office to get her
things. Before she reached it, though, the hallway
door opened again and Elliot walked in.

"Well, if it isn't my brother the lawyer," she said,

reversing course and giving him a hug. "What are you doing here?"

"Oh, I just wanted to talk to you about something. But the better question is what's that doing here?" Elliot pointed to the cat.

"It's a long story. Come into my office, though, before he starts your allergies acting up." Glancing at Rosalie, she added, "Just a few more minutes?"

"Sure. But if he starts trying to climb the walls, I'll be knocking on your door."

Smiling, Lauren ushered Elliot into her office and sat down beside him. "So, what's up?"

He shrugged. "There's a little problem I want to let you know about. Roughly seven years ago, I defended a really nasty client named Ken Higgins. He ended up getting a ten-year sentence."

"Not one of your more successful defenses, then."

"I didn't have a prayer. In fact, the guy was lucky he didn't get twenty years instead of ten. Unfortunately, though, he didn't see it that way. He figured I should have pulled a rabbit out of a hat so the judge would let him walk. And when that didn't happen, he said he'd get me once he was out."

A chill settled in Lauren's chest. She adored her big brother, and the fact he was telling her this meant he was awfully worried about it. "Is that common? For lawyers to get those kinds of threats?"

Elliot nodded. "Common enough that, normally, I wouldn't give it much thought. But as I said, this guy's really nasty. And he's written me a few times, telling me how much he's looking forward to seeing me again—letters worded innocently enough that they got past the prison check, but with a clear message to me."

"And he gets out ... ?"

"He got out today. Nobody ever serves their full time these days."

"So what are you doing?" She was trying to stay calm, but she could feel the chill spreading through her entire body.

"I'm being damn careful, and I've hired people to guard the house so that Ursula and the boys will be safe."

"The boys," Lauren murmured, almost to herself. Her nephews were three and five, and the thought of anything happening to them or Ursula ...

"But the reason I'm telling you this," Elliot went on, "is because the guy threatened to get me ... or someone I love. So, just in case, I want you to be really careful for the next little while."

"Oh, Lord," she whispered. "What about Mom and Dad? And Marisa?" she added, thinking that the man her sister lived with was away at the moment. And that Marisa didn't like being alone in her apartment.

"I've already talked to them," Elliot said.

"How did they take it?"

"Well, Mom's pretty upset about it, but she's got nothing on Ursula."

When Elliot anxiously clasped his hands together, Lauren rested her hand on top of his. "You must be worried sick."

"I'm trying not to be. The odds on the guy actually doing anything are low. It's rare for that sort of threat to really lead anywhere."

"How rare?"

"Rare enough that I considered not even telling the rest of the family about it, so you wouldn't worry. But

I decided I had to, no matter how low the risk. So even though the chances of anything happening to you are awfully remote, you keep a sharp eye out, okay? And if anything makes you even the least bit anxious, call the police. Immediately.''

She nodded. ''I will.''

Elliot gave her a forced-looking smile. ''With any luck, the guy will be back behind bars in no time. He's the kind who'll spend most of his life in prison.''

Her thoughts racing, Lauren walked Elliot out and gave him another hug—a long, hard one this time. ''You take care,'' she whispered. ''You take really serious care.''

When the door closed behind him, she looked over at the cat, half wishing he was a stray Doberman rather than a half-grown tom.

''I SWEAR,'' SULLY MUTTERED, ''there should be a law against women like her.'' He paced across the kitchen once more, then turned and looked back over to where Otis and Grace were sitting at the table.

Listening to him rant and rave wasn't part of the job description for either teacher or housemother, but he'd been so steamed when he'd left Manhattan that even the four-hour drive back up to Eagles Roost hadn't completely cooled him down. And filling them in on his visit with Lauren Van Slyke had made him angry all over again.

Maybe she didn't give a damn what happened to his kids, or to all the ones who'd be coming through here in the future—assuming he could keep the program going—but he sure as hell cared. And he cared about what would happen to Grace and Otis, too.

Back when he'd started the program, he'd been damn lucky that Otis had decided to pack in his inner-city teaching job and come to work here. He and Grace were a lot of the reason Eagles Roost was a success. And what did a couple in their late fifties do if the rug was suddenly pulled out from under them?

"How," he said, shaking his head, "could they appoint a complete incompetent as the director of a foundation? Even if she *is* family?"

"Will you take it easy," Otis said quietly. "You're going to give yourself a heart attack."

"Take it easy? Otis, you weren't there. You weren't the one she conscripted to help catch a soaking-wet cat. You aren't the one who's got a ten-inch gash in his arm." He brandished the scratch at them again.

"We really should get that cleaned up," Grace told him. "You don't suppose there's any chance of rabies, do you?"

"It wouldn't surprise me in the least. Hell, it wouldn't surprise me if the woman had rabies, never mind her damn cat. I mean, she's simply not a normal person. Who would think of bringing her cat to the office, let alone bathing it there?"

"Well, it does sound peculiar," Grace admitted. "But maybe she had a reason."

"Right," Sully muttered. "The reason is that she's a total wing nut. I'll bet she's lived her entire life without having a reason for *anything* she does. We're a perfect example of that. She doesn't have a clue what goes on up here, yet she merrily chops our funding."

"I thought she said the decision was the board's, not hers," Otis pointed out.

Sully shot a glare in his direction. "Stop trying to be so damn reasonable. The woman's a liar. She straight out denied having phoned you, and there's no doubt she did, is there?"

Otis shook his head. "I talked to her for a good half hour. And as I said at the time, the more questions she asked, the more it seemed she was trying to unearth problems."

"Exactly. Which tells us how much faith we can put in anything she says."

"Well, it doesn't matter anymore," Grace said, "because we're obviously through dealing with her. But where do we go from here?"

The worried expression on Grace's face made Sully suddenly wish he'd soft-pedaled things. Eagles Roost was her home. And Otis's, too, of course.

"Maybe," Grace murmured to Otis, "we should postpone our vacation for a while. Until we get this sorted out."

"No," Sully said firmly. "It's me who has to sort it out, not you, so you're leaving on Saturday as planned. I'll bet your relatives have a ton of things organized for your visit."

"Well... you're probably right," Otis admitted. "They usually do."

"Exactly. And you both need a break from here. So you'll go and have a good time, and by the time you get back, I'll have other funding lined up."

"Sully...what if that doesn't turn out to be easy?"

He shrugged, trying to look as if that possibility wasn't worrying him at all. "You know the answer as well as I do. If we don't have funding, the authorities will shut us down just as fast as they can find new placements for the kids. But that's not going to happen. It's just a matter of figuring out…" He paused, hearing a noise on the other side of the door.

"Sully?" Billy the Kid called a second later. "Okay if I let Roxy in there? I think she wants a drink or somethin'."

"Yeah, sure," he absently called back.

The door swung open from the lodge's main lounge—which these days served as a family room— and Roxy lumbered in. At a hundred-and-twenty pounds, with a rottweiler mother and a Saint Bernard father, she wasn't a dog who normally moved very fast.

"Is dinner gonna be soon, Mrs. Plavsic?" Billy asked politely.

She nodded. "Half an hour or so. Can you last till then, or would you like an apple?"

"No, I'm okay, thanks."

AFTER BILLY HAD BACKED out of the kitchen and shut the door again, he realized he was shaking. He was almost afraid to believe they hadn't known he'd been standing there listening. Sully was always suspicious about stuff like that.

Turning to the rest of the kids, he whispered, "That was close. I *told* you not to make any noise. They might of caught me."

"So what was they sayin'?" Freckles asked. "What happened in New York?"

Billy nodded his head in the direction of the bedrooms. If they stood here talking, they'd get caught for sure. He started off across the lounge, glancing back to make sure the others were following. They were, of course. He'd been at Eagles Roost the longest, so that kinda made him the leader.

Besides, he was twelve, so he was oldest. Freckles was eleven. And the terrible twins, Tony and Terry, were only ten. And Hoops…well, Hoops was twelve, too, but he never said much unless it was about basketball. So when something was happening, it was Billy the Kid everybody mostly listened to.

And they were *really* listening to him about this, 'cuz if he hadn't been practicing up on his detective stuff they wouldn't know nothing 'bout what was going on. But after he'd snuck into Sully's office the other day and read that letter, he'd told the rest of them that the rich lady wasn't giving the chief eagle any more money to run Eagles Roost.

He led the others into the room he and Hoops shared, and plopped down on his bed. Hoops grabbed his basketball and started slapping it back and forth between his hands, but the rest of them just stood waiting.

"So?" Freckles asked. "What'd they say?"

Billy shrugged. "The chief eagle said he couldn't make her change her mind. She just ain't goin' to give him no more money."

The twins looked at each other, then Tony said, "So what's gonna happen to us?"

"We'll havta go someplace else," Freckles muttered. "That's what'll happen to us."

Terry looked like he was going to start crying, but Tony gave him a sharp jab in the ribs that kept him quiet.

"I don't wanna go no place else," Hoops said.

His dark face almost never showed what he was feeling, but right now Billy could tell Hoops was scared. It made the flip-flopping in his own stomach even worse. He was scared, too, but he couldn't let the rest of them know. Leaders weren't supposed to get scared.

"We don't wanna go no place else, either," Tony said. "We heard about some of 'em other places."

"Okay, don't worry," Billy told them. "We're all gonna stay right here." At least he sure hoped that was what would happen, 'cuz he didn't want to go no place else, either. Not unless he could go back home, and Sully said that wasn't on. Not as long as his mom was still living with *Uncle* Brian—with his big drug deals and his even bigger fists.

"So what are we gonna do, Billy?" Freckles asked.

"Well, see, from what Sully was sayin', I think that lady could give him the money if she really wanted to. But I think when he went to see her he kinda blew up. You know how he does sometimes. So maybe she didn't understand that's just his way. Maybe he made her so mad she wouldn't listen."

"So...?" Tony said.

"So, if she *did* listen...see, Sully said she doesn't have a clue what goes on up here. But if she did, she'd give him the money, right?"

"You sure?" Freckles said.

"Yeah, I'm sure. And I gotta plan, too. But everybody's gotta help with it."

LAUREN CLOSED the Eagles Roost file and set it aside. After yesterday's visit from Jack Sullivan, she'd been strangely curious about him—and had realized she didn't know the history of his program.

When she'd first taken over as director, there'd been so much to learn that she hadn't had time to read all the material in *any* of the files. And the Eagles Roost file had been intimidatingly thick.

But now she'd read every detail, even though that seemed a lot like locking the door after the thief had left. It had kept her mind off the threat to Elliot, though, and had also gone a long way to satisfying her curiosity.

Matthew Grimes had collected a lot of detailed information about Jack Sullivan, undoubtedly because of his criminal record. But from what she'd read it didn't seem that Sully had an innately criminal character. He'd simply had some incredibly bad breaks—a father he'd never known and an alcoholic mother who'd died when he was eighteen were two of the worst. At any rate, she now knew a lot more about Jack Sullivan's life story than she had before.

She glanced at her watch, wondering if she should phone over to Nate's and get something delivered for lunch. Hunter Clifton was so late for their appointment she was starting to wonder if he was coming at all. But she definitely wasn't going to leave the office and risk missing him—which was really pretty ironic when he was her least favorite board member. After Sully's visit, though, she had to talk to Hunter.

She couldn't shake her sense of guilt about that funding being cut off, because as far as she was concerned it should have been continued. So even though Sully was obnoxious as all get out...

And he really *was*. He might look as if he belonged in a dream, but his personality was nightmare city. She could still hear the way he'd snarled at her. And that remark about her snooping behind his back had been absolutely dripping sarcasm—whatever he'd meant by it.

But it was the kids at Eagles Roost who'd be hurt if his program went under. So the least she could do was talk to Hunter about it. Because if she could get him to do an about-face, then convincing the rest of the board members they should at least *try* to find some extra money would be a piece of cake.

As if on cue, there was a knock on her door.

"Who is it?" she called.

"It's your father."

She headed over to unlock the door. With the corporate offices of Van Slyke Enterprises on the top floor of the building, her father was always dropping in. And now that the family was threatened, he'd probably be doing it even more frequently. He and her mother had kept her on the phone for an hour last night, warning her about a thousand and one different things. Then they'd done the same thing to her sister. Marisa had called later, to compare notes.

"Rosalie's not at her desk," her father greeted her when she opened the door.

"No, she usually goes out for lunch with a friend on Fridays."

He nodded. "Well, I'm glad to see you had your door locked. I've put extra security in the building, but there's not much more I can do. What about the idea of your taking some time off, though? Did you give that any more thought?"

"Dad, as far as I'm concerned we finished that discussion last night. Elliot said the chances of anything happening were really remote, remember? So I'll be fine. I'm sure we'll all be fine. Elliot included," she added, praying she was right.

Her father didn't look happy, but changed the subject, saying, "Your mother asked me to stop by and tell you Marisa's invited herself for dinner tonight. So if you'd like to come, too..."

"I'll call Mom later and let her know," she said absently, tucking the idea of dinner into the back of her mind. At the moment, she had something more pressing to think about. How to politely get rid of her father.

As much as she loved him, the last thing she wanted when Hunter got here was an audience. Especially an audience who didn't believe she was capable of doing anything right.

"Well," she said at last, having come up with no better excuse than the truth, "if there's nothing more, Hunter Clifton's coming by to see me any minute, so—"

"Hunter? Oh, well then, I'll just wait and say hello."

She silently groaned as her father sat down across from her and began smoothing his already perfect gray hair.

"You know," he said, "I don't think I told you, but Hunter and I have worked out the most interesting financing on that project in SoHo. He's much more of a risk-taker than most bankers. He's a good man."

"Mmm." She smiled again. Her father didn't actually know Hunter very well. They'd only met about six months ago, when Hunter had volunteered for the board. But Roger Van Slyke had always been one to judge a book by its cover. She clearly recalled him telling her, years ago, that Brandon was a good man, that she'd be a fool not to marry him.

Her failed marriage, though, was a whole other story. Unless her father had any ideas about . . . no, Hunter was married, plus being at least ten years older than she was. And even her father would never think Hunter Clifton was her type.

Roger Van Slyke was just launching into the details of his SoHo financing when Hunter finally appeared—looking, as he always did, like one of the older male models from *GQ*. She suspected he had his hair trimmed weekly and spent at least fifteen minutes a day in a tanning salon.

He and her father greeted each other before Hunter even glanced in her direction.

"I've got your papers all ready," she said when he did. Then she hesitated, reluctant to raise the other issue. But her father clearly wasn't going anywhere, and Hunter was a genius at avoiding phone calls, which left her little choice.

"Hunter," she began, "there's something I'd like to ask you about while you're here."

"Uh-huh?" He pointedly checked his Rolex.

"I had a visit from Jack Sullivan yesterday. The Foster Alternatives program at Eagles Roost," she elaborated at Hunter's blank look.

His expression went from blank to annoyed in the blink of an eye. "I guess he wasn't very happy."

"No. And it started me wondering . . . what would you think about the board reconsidering his application? After all—"

"I think," Hunter interrupted, "that would set an extremely bad precedent. And, frankly, in my opinion Jack Sullivan shouldn't even be licensed to run a program like that, never mind get money from us. Why the hell the Foundation's been funding an ex-con is beyond me."

"An ex-con?" Roger Van Slyke said. "We've been giving money to an ex-con? Hell, that's really ironic, isn't it, considering this problem Elliot has."

Lauren swore to herself. Her father had never really been interested in the details about projects the Foundation funded, and she'd just as soon keep things that way.

"Your son has a problem?" Hunter said.

Roger shook his head. "It's nothing." Then he looked at Lauren again and demanded, "What kind of ex-con? What did he do?"

She shrugged and said, "Nothing much," hoping he'd let it go. The tight set of his mouth, though, said she'd have to tell him what she knew. "He broke into a few apartments," she explained. "But he was only nineteen when he went to prison, only twenty-one when he got out. That was thirteen years ago, and he's been straight since then."

"You mean he hasn't been arrested since then," Hunter said. "I know," he added, turning to her father, "that I haven't even been a board member for a year yet. And I've tried not to criticize what's been done before, but I really felt I had to object to that program."

Roger Van Slyke looked across the desk and pinned Lauren with his gaze. "Did you support it?"

"Well...yes. All the reports Matthew Grimes wrote on it were very positive."

"Lauren, what your predecessor approved is past history. You're the director now."

"I know that, but I understood why Matthew liked the Eagles Roost concept. Jack Sullivan had a rough childhood, just like the kids he takes on. They're all at high risk for messing up their lives, and he tries to ensure they won't, that they'll never end up in jail the way he did. And the program has a lot of things going for it."

"Such as?" her father asked skeptically.

"Well, for starters, the place he owns used to be an isolated fishing lodge, so he's able to take these kids away from the problems in the city and put them in a completely different environment."

"A lodge? How did an ex-con get his hands on something like that?"

"I wonder," Hunter said snidely. "Maybe he broke into a few apartments *after* he served his time. Or maybe he pulled off something even bigger."

Lauren resisted the urge to glare at Hunter and kept her eyes on her father. "Sullivan inherited the property."

"From?"

She shrugged again. When she'd read that, she'd wondered the same thing, but the file hadn't specified.

"Humph . . . inherited it," her father muttered, as if he'd forgotten how he'd gotten all *his* property. Not to mention all his money.

"At any rate," she pressed on, "Jack Sullivan provides a strong male role model that most of the boys have never had and—"

"A strong male role model?" Hunter interrupted. "Lauren, the man's a criminal."

"He *was*, Hunter. Back when he was only a kid himself."

"He's still an ex-con, which is hardly what I'd call a good role model. The idea of him being responsible for a bunch of impressionable boys would have struck me as absurd even if there hadn't been that trouble.''

"What trouble?" Roger demanded.

"Oh, Lauren hasn't mentioned it? Well, it's quite the story. Back in January, one of Sullivan's kids went into the nearest town and robbed a bank.''

"Good God," Roger muttered. "And you thought we should continue funding the man?" He eyed Lauren critically, obviously certain this was yet another of her little errors in judgment.

When he finally looked away, Lauren shot a few daggers at Hunter Clifton. She knew damn well why he'd been so concerned about that *trouble*. The bank Sully's kid had robbed just happened to be a branch of the bank Hunter was a vice president of.

Clearly oblivious to her daggers, Hunter said, "Let me offer you a little advice, Lauren. I know you have the paper qualifications for this job...."

Pausing, he glanced over to where her master's degree hung on the wall. His gaze lingered long enough to let her know he considered it to be from a second-rate school. Or, more likely, a ninth-rate school.

"But you don't have much practical experience," he continued, focusing on her again. "And you've got to keep in mind you're an administrator, not a social worker. And that there isn't enough money in the world to make everyone happy. So you simply have to trust the board's decisions, and not worry about the people we turn down." He concluded his lecture by flashing her a phony smile, then looked at her father. "Had lunch yet, Roger?"

"No, I haven't."

"Then how about that Japanese place down the block? I know sushi is passé, but I still enjoy it."

"Lauren?" Her father glanced at her. "Join us?"

"Thanks, but I've got a lot of work to get through this afternoon," she lied. "So you two go on ahead." *And I hope you, Hunter,* she silently added as they headed for the door, *get a fish bone in your sushi and choke to death.*

CHAPTER THREE

THE VISITATIONS

AFTER HER FATHER and Hunter left, Lauren sat staring at nothing, feeling more like a child who'd been sent to her room than a thirty-year-old woman. Then she glanced at the Eagles Roost file and felt yet another twinge of guilt.

She was at least partly to blame for Sullivan's losing his funding. If she'd written a dynamite report on his program, rather than just a standard recommendation for continued funding, he'd probably have gotten his money again. Regardless of Hunter Clifton's objections.

Her thoughts were briefly interrupted by Rosalie, buzzing to say she was back from lunch. Then Lauren returned to wondering why she just didn't seem able to do anything right—no matter how hard she tried.

Sometimes, she was sure there'd been a mix-up at the hospital, because she was nothing like either Elliot or Marisa. And while neither of her parents had ever come right out and said it, she knew she was a disappointment to them. Especially to her father, who expected so much of people.

She glanced over at the degree Hunter obviously held in such disdain and reminded herself that Hunter was an insufferable snob. Even if Washoe University wasn't Harvard, at least she'd tried to make her father happy by going back to school after her divorce.

And her graduating in business administration *had* pleased him. His being pleased, though, wasn't the same as his actually having faith in her. She knew he'd only pressed her to come and work for the family foundation because he doubted she could make it in the real world.

"Ms. Van Slyke?" Rosalie said over the intercom.

She leaned forward to answer, wondering what the *Ms. Van Slyke* was about. Rosalie only bothered with formality when she wanted to imply that her boss was an important woman. "Yes, Rosalie?"

"Ms. Van Slyke, there are two gentlemen here asking to see you. Two gentlemen without appointments."

The way Rosalie was saying *gentlemen*, Lauren knew her visitors were anything but.

"They say," Rosalie continued, "you won't know their names, but that it's important you talk to them."

There was a brief silence, then Rosalie added, "They say, Ms. Van Slyke, I should tell you they've come all the way from Eagles Roost."

"Well . . . please show them in."

When Lauren rose to greet her visitors, she was taller than either of them—which was unusual. But then, her visitors were generally adults and these two couldn't be more than about twelve.

She sized them up while they nervously introduced themselves as Billy and Hoops, two of Sully's kids. They were dressed in standard adolescent summer uniforms—sleeveless T-shirts, shorts and high-tops without socks.

Billy was a little shorter than five feet and Hoops an inch or two over. But what they lacked in size and eloquence, they made up for in sincerity, launching right into telling her how great Jack Sullivan was and how much they liked being at Eagles Roost. Billy did most of the talking, with Hoops nodding along, his dark face solemn.

Listening, she could feel those twinges of guilt developing into a full-blown case. Maybe Sully was obnoxious, but he'd clearly won both the respect and affection of these kids.

"So," Billy finally concluded, "we thought if we explained to you how things was up there, you'd understand why we don't wanna get shipped off someplace else."

"Yes...I see," she murmured, wishing she could assure them there'd be no problem about their staying right where they were. Instead, she said, "Is Mr. Sullivan aware you've come to see me?"

The two exchanged a guilty glance, and Billy began twisting the baseball cap he'd whipped off his head when Rosalie had ushered them in.

"Sully doesn't exactly know we came," Billy admitted.

"Well how did you get here?"

Hoops cleared his throat. "We hitched."

A funny feeling settled in the pit of her stomach. For all they were trying to act like adults, these were children, and she couldn't help imagining what might have happened if the wrong driver had picked them up.

"You hitched," she said at last. "Does your Mr. Sullivan allow that?"

"No...we're not supposed to," Billy admitted. "We're not supposed to go very far without tellin' him, either. It's just that this was important."

"He mostly always knows where we are," Hoops added quickly. "It ain't easy to put nothing over on Sully."

"Ahh...I see. And if he finds out you came here, what will he do?"

"Well," Billy said, "I guess that depends."

"On?"

"Well...Ms. Van Slyke...see, I know me and Hoops aren't explainin' this too good. So what we was thinkin', was maybe you could come back to Eagles Roost with us?"

"Kinda see how it is up there?" Hoops put in. "For yourself?"

"If you did that," Billy went on, "I don't think Sully'd be so mad about us comin' here. He'd see that we helped."

The boys stood gazing across the wide expanse of her desk, both their expressions pleading for her to go along with their crazy scheme.

"It just don't seem fair," Billy pressed, "to cut Sully off without you even havin' a look."

"And isn't that sorta your job?" Hoops added. "To see what you're getting for your money?"

The question hit Lauren hard. With all there'd been to do during her first months as director, she'd cut any corners she'd felt she could. And not bothering with a personal inspection of Eagles Roost had been one of those corners.

"So?" Billy said. "Are you at least thinkin' 'bout the idea?"

"Yes, I'm thinking about it," she said, although she knew that even considering it meant she was having a lapse of sanity. After all, she'd tried to reason with Hunter and failed. There was really nothing more she could do.

But, looking at the boys, all she could think about was that if she didn't drive them back they'd be hitchhiking again. And this time it could be a psychopath who gave them a lift.

Lord, she desperately didn't want to make one of her little errors in judgment here. And the foundation office *was* pretty quiet on Fridays.

The cat had to be fed, of course. *Her* cat, she might as well start calling him. Even though she hadn't decided on a name, she knew he'd be staying. But Jenny wouldn't mind popping across the hall and checking on him.

So was there really any reason not to take the afternoon off and drive up to Eagles Roost? She could spend an hour or two there and still not be awfully late getting back. Then, if Jack Sullivan did apply for funding next year, she'd be all set to write an accurate, informed recommendation.

"It's real nice up there, Ms. Van Slyke," Billy said. "Kinda like Central Park, but without any joggers or muggers or crazies."

"Yeah, there's a million acres," Hoops added. "And a huge lake and everything."

"Yes. Hidden Lake. I remember reading that in the file." She looked out the window, through the pollution-laden haze that was hanging over Mad Ave. The heat still hadn't broken; the city still smelled of

rotting waste and the seamier side of life. So what
could be wrong with getting some fresh country air
and doing her job at the same time?

HALF ANGRY, HALF WORRIED, Sully stood staring
down the dirt road that led from the clearing to the
edge of his property—and thinking the story about
what Billy and Hoops were doing was awfully vague.
And why hadn't they mentioned yesterday that
someone had offered them a day's work? *If* it was
true.

It seemed awfully suspicious, the way they'd high-
tailed it out of here before he'd even gotten up this
morning. If they didn't show soon, he decided, he'd
have to go looking for them. The only problem would
be where to start.

"Damn," he finally muttered.

When Roxy looked up at the sound of his voice, he
scratched her neck. She enthusiastically began wig-
gling her big behind against his leg, shoving him
backward a couple of inches.

"What?" he asked her. "You think we look too
anxious, standing here?"

She gave him another solid bump, so he turned and
started back across the clearing in the direction of the
lodge, telling himself Billy and Hoops weren't up to
anything they shouldn't be. But ever since Leroy
Korelenko had gotten into trouble, he worried when
any of the boys disappeared. Especially when one of
them was Billy, who got into more trouble than the
rest of his kids combined.

Sully stepped up onto the porch and headed into
the lodge, where Freckles and the twins were glued to
the television. Grace had let them out of kitchen duty

because the Yankees were in Oakland for an afternoon game.

Roxy wandered across the lounge and flopped down beside Terry, her current favorite among the boys. Sully strode over and stopped in front of the television—which started all three kids hollering that he was in their way.

Having gotten their attention, he moved to one side and focused on Freckles. "You're sure Billy and Hoops didn't say anything more than you told me?"

Freckles shook his head. "Alls they said was it was a job clearing brush someplace. And that they'd be back in time for dinner."

"They didn't say who hired them?"

"Nah, I told you, Sully, they didn't say."

"Well the rest of you keep in mind that I like to hear things straight from the horse's mouth, huh? Because I'm not impressed with the way those two handled this. If you've got any reason to go someplace, tell me directly. You all got that?"

The three of them nodded as if the thought of doing anything else would never enter their minds, then got back into the game. He stood watching it with them for a few minutes, but he wasn't really crazy about TV.

He was a book man—had started reading in prison, when he'd been getting the last of his high school credits, and hadn't stopped. When your education was nothing to brag about, you could learn a lot from books. Everything from good grammar to art appreciation.

Once the inning ended, he went into the kitchen where Grace was chopping carrots and had Otis peeling potatoes. They hadn't said anything about the funding since yesterday, but he knew they were still as worried about it as he was, so he wanted to tell them he'd talked to Ben Ludendorf.

North Head's resident lawyer wasn't the brightest light in the legal profession, but at the moment he just might be their salvation—their temporary salvation, at any rate.

"The boys get back?" Otis asked, glancing over.

"Not yet."

"Well, don't worry about them," Grace said. "They'll be along any time now. They may be cutting it close, but they wouldn't miss the last dinner I'll be cooking for them in three weeks. Not that you can't cook, Sully, but..."

He nodded. He could open cans with the best of them, but that hardly put him in Grace's league.

"Besides," she went on, "I told them yesterday I was making roast beef tonight, so those two will be here for sure."

"Yeah, I guess you're right," he said, leaning against the counter. "But the reason I came in was to let you know I had an idea for getting some money."

The couple looked over at him and waited.

"Remember, last fall, some guy had Ben Ludendorf approach me about selling?"

Grace and Otis glanced at each other, then at Sully again. "Sure, I remember," Otis said, "but if you sold..."

"Sully," Grace murmured, "you don't mean you're thinking of just giving up the program...do you?"

"No, that's the last thing I'm thinking of." The relief on their faces almost made him smile. "But that fellow who asked Ben to sound me out wasn't really interested in buying the lodge itself. Ben said he figured it was too old—that he'd want to tear it down and replace it."

"Then why on earth was he interested in buying it?" Grace asked.

"Because he wanted a big chunk of secluded land. And Ben said Eagles Roost was exactly the kind of property he'd been looking for. So I figure, if he's still interested, maybe I can sell him some acreage on the far side of the lake. That would give me more than enough to tide us over until we can get new funding. And with any luck, we'd never even know he was there."

"Sully," Otis said slowly, "last fall was a long time ago. Whoever was interested in this place has probably bought somewhere else by now."

He shrugged. "Maybe. But I figured it couldn't hurt to check. Ben's going to get back to me as soon as he's talked to the guy."

Neither Grace nor Otis looked hopeful, which dampened Sully's mood considerably. He was just about to tell them that if this idea didn't pan out he'd think of something else, when Roxy started barking.

A few seconds later, the screen door slammed. A moment after that, the kitchen door burst open and Freckles was standing there, his lower jaw practically on the floor.

"What's wrong?" Sully demanded.

"Nothing! But, holy moly! You guys gotta come see what Billy and Hoops just got drove home in!"

When Sully reached the front of the lodge, he saw it was a silver Mercedes. A sexy two-door coupe with those dark tinted windows that give the occupants total anonymity.

He stepped out onto the porch with Otis and Grace, relieved to see for himself that there'd really been nothing to worry about. Hoops and Billy were fine— Hoops standing beside the car, Billy leaning back in through the open passenger's door to talk to the driver.

Freckles, with Roxy on his heels, charged down the steps and across the clearing to join the twins. They were standing a couple of yards away from the car, and the way they were staring at it in total awe made Sully smile.

Then he let his gaze detail the Mercedes' sleek lines, thinking that owning it and hiring child labor didn't quite compute. Like most guys who drove minivans, he didn't know exactly what Mercedes-Benz got for its top lines, but he'd guess this baby went for well over a hundred thousand.

"What a beauty, huh?" Otis said.

As Sully nodded, Roxy lumbered over to the car and began curiously sniffing one of the tires, not seeming quite sure what it was. No doubt she'd never smelled such expensive rubber in her life.

Turning his attention to Billy and Hoops again, Sully discovered they were both eyeing him—and saw that they looked nervous as hell. Then he realized they didn't look as if they'd been clearing brush all day.

Nobody wore shorts to clear brush. And nobody looked that clean after hours of physical labor. So if they hadn't been working...

He swore silently, his relief rapidly dissolving into anger. If the car meant they'd been hitching, they'd just had the last ride of their lives, because he'd ground them from here to eternity.

INSIDE THE CAR, Lauren watched uneasily as Sully started down the stairs. When she'd first seen that old porch, the thought had crossed her mind that it looked like a very relaxing spot—complete with big Adirondack chairs and old half-barrels spilling over with flowering plants.

But standing on the porch didn't seem to have made Sully the slightest bit relaxed. He was wearing a glare that could probably kill at forty paces.

She lowered her gaze from it, which left her looking at how his jeans and black T-shirt fit snugly enough to define a whole lot of his lean muscles.

Billy and Hoops had been referring to him as the chief eagle, and he might well be a bird of prey at the moment—one who'd spotted his victim and was closing in for the kill. And since he was heading straight for her car, she knew who was cast in the role of victim.

That thought started her heart beating a nervous tattoo. Now, when she was actually going to have to face him again, she wished she'd given this trip a little more consideration. What had seemed like a good idea in Manhattan was seeming like a really bad idea here in the Adirondacks.

She tried to calm herself by looking completely away from Sully and focusing on the older man and woman following him down from the porch. They had to be Grace and Otis Plavsic, and she was relieved to see that neither of them seemed even slightly threatening.

Otis was about sixty and almost bald, but he gave the impression of being both fit and easy-going. Grace, who was positively tiny, had gray hair curling around a friendly, youthful face. She looked like everybody's favorite aunt.

Sully, though, Lauren thought as her eyes strayed back to him, didn't look like anybody's favorite anything. Not the way he was glaring.

The nearer he got to the car, the more tempted she was to throw it into reverse and get the hell out of here—before he discovered who was behind the wheel. But if she did that, Billy and Hoops would have to do all the explaining, which would hardly be fair.

Taking a deep breath and smoothing the skirt of her dress, she told herself that if she didn't stay long enough to have a tour of the place the boys would be awfully disappointed. Besides, after a four-hour drive it only made sense to finish what she'd started—whether Jack Sullivan liked it or not. It was his kids' feelings she cared about, not his.

Sully took a final glance at the Mercedes' windshield and decided he'd need X-ray vision to see through it, even from close range. Then he looked at Billy and Hoops—fixing them with a stare he'd perfected years ago, in prison.

"So?" he demanded. "What's the deal here? This the fellow you were working for today?"

"Not exactly," Billy mumbled, suddenly fascinated by the toes of his high-tops.

"Then who is he...*exactly?*"

Hoops was wordlessly edging around the back of the car to the driver's side. As he reached out and opened the door, Billy said, "Well...Sully...see, it's not exactly a he."

Hoops gave Sully an extremely anxious grin, then offered his hand to the driver. A delicate white hand took his black one. A pair of shapely ankles appeared beneath the car door.

Sully knew he'd seen those ankles before—and then the rest of Lauren Van Slyke emerged from the Mercedes.

He simply stared at her for a minute, hoping he was hallucinating. He wasn't, though. Honey-colored hair, cornflower blue eyes, luscious mouth, the faint scent of that sinfully sexy perfume wafting toward him—it was definitely her.

She was wearing a pale yellow dress today, when if she had any sense of the appropriate she'd be wearing something the color of storm clouds. Because she was one of the last people on earth he wanted within a hundred miles of Eagles Roost. But here she was, uninvited yet come to pay a call, anyway.

He wasn't sure what had him more furious: the fact his kids had lied about what they were doing, that they'd obviously hitched all the way to Manhattan, that they'd brought *this* woman back with them, or that she'd come.

And why had Billy and Hoops gone to see her in the first place? They knew the Van Slyke Foundation provided their funding, but they didn't know there was any problem. He hadn't said a word about it, except to Grace and Otis.

Before he could figure out what was up, Lauren gave him a deviously innocent smile and extended her hand. "Mr. Sullivan... Sully. It's so nice to see you again."

He shook hands with her, but only because he was always lecturing his kids about manners. He didn't say it was nice to see *her* again, though. He was also always lecturing them about telling the truth.

Turning her smile on Grace and Otis, she said, "You must be Mr. and Mrs. Plavsic. It's a pleasure to meet you. I'm Lauren Van Slyke."

"Well..." Grace said, decidedly nonplussed. "Well...it's a pleasure to meet you, too." She glanced at Sully, raising her eyebrows to ask if he could have been mistaken about Lauren, silently suggesting she seemed like a perfectly lovely young woman.

In the meantime, Lauren had looked over at the other boys and was positively beaming at them. "And you three must be Freckles and Tony and Terry. Billy and Hoops told me all about you while we were driving."

"Hello, Ms. Van Slyke," Freckles stammered.

"Oh, I want all of you to call me Lauren. Billy and Hoops started off calling me Ms. Van Slyke, but I asked them to stop because they were making me feel a hundred years old."

When Grace cleared her throat Sully glanced at her and realized her friendliness was on the verge of taking over. Before he could do anything to stop her, she said to Lauren, "After that long trip, you must be dying for a cold drink, so let's go inside and get you one."

"In a minute." Sully reached for Lauren's arm. "I'd like to speak to you alone," he added, dragging her away from the car.

Since seven curious stares were following them, Sully kept on walking until he was sure he and Lauren were out of the others' range of hearing.

"What are you doing here?" he finally demanded, stopping and letting go of her arm.

For a moment, she simply looked up at him as if he were a few trees short of a forest. Then she said, "I'd have thought that was perfectly obvious. Billy and Hoops showed up at my office, so I drove them home."

"In other words, you rewarded them for breaking the rules."

"I beg your pardon?" She drew herself up to her full-if-not-very-impressive height, and those big blue eyes began flashing warning signals.

He ignored them. He might be glad the boys were safely home, but for all he knew, bringing them here herself was part of some malevolent plan she'd hatched.

When common sense told him he was being paranoid, he ignored that, too. He hadn't forgotten Lauren Van Slyke wasn't a straight shooter, so the smartest thing to do was get rid of her. Fast. And that shouldn't be tough. He'd simply get her so annoyed she'd be happy to leave.

"What I said," he told her, although he knew she'd heard him the first time, "was that by driving Billy and Hoops home you rewarded them for breaking the rules. Hell, I'll bet you even stopped on the way and fed them, didn't you?"

"I hadn't had any lunch," she said defensively. "And I could hardly eat in front of them, so I bought them burgers."

She looked so darned guilty she'd probably bought them fries, shakes, onion rings and pie, too.

"Terrific," he muttered. "So they do something they know damn well they shouldn't and what happens? It gets them a ride in a fancy car and a free lunch."

He eyed her closely for a second, deciding she was getting angrier. That did his heart good. Why should he be the only one with elevated blood pressure?

"Didn't you wonder," he pressed on, "what on earth they were doing in the city on their own? Weren't you suspicious about how they'd gotten there? Didn't it occur to you they'd probably broken some rules?"

"Of course it occurred to me," she said in the Ice Princess voice he'd found so infuriating yesterday. "And I asked what the story was. But what do you think I should have done when they admitted they'd hitchhiked? Told them to hitchhike back?"

"No, you should have called me and let me know they were with you. I'm responsible for them. I'd have handled it from there."

"Oh, really. Well, excuse me for not thinking of doing that, *Mr.* Sullivan. Excuse me a whole bunch for just doing what I thought was best. For spending hours driving in Friday afternoon traffic so that two boys, for whom *you* are responsible, would get home alive and well."

"Now, just a minute here."

"Don't you *just a minute here* me," Lauren snapped. Then she tried to rein in her anger. But she'd done the man a major favor and was he even a little grateful? Hah! Not a chance.

When the boys had been going on about how great their chief eagle was, she'd started wondering if it was possible she'd pegged him wrong. But she hadn't. There wasn't the slightest doubt that he was totally obnoxious. And an ungrateful jerk as well.

She glared up at him, counting to ten, while she wondered how Billy and Hoops could possibly respect him as much as they did. Then she counted to ten again, wondering how Grace and Otis could have worked for him for five years.

"Look," she said when she'd regained at least partial control over her temper. "Billy and Hoops *asked* me to come back up here with them, because they were trying to help you. They'd gotten it into their heads that if they could convince me to have a look at Eagles Roost for myself, I might do something about your funding problem."

The pulse in Sully's temple began to throb. This woman had lied to him yesterday, when she'd denied ever talking to Otis about the program, and he'd just caught her at it again.

"I have trouble seeing how that's true," he told her coldly, "since I haven't told them there's a funding problem."

"Oh?" She gave him such a superior look his blood pressure climbed a few more points. "Well, then Billy and Hoops must be junior mind readers, because they most definitely know. And as I said, they thought if I came up here and looked around it might help things."

"But you knew it wouldn't, so—"

"I knew it wouldn't for *this* year. Maybe it would for next. But that wasn't the main reason I came. I really just wanted to be sure those two didn't end up hitching a ride with some homicidal maniac. So, now that they're here in one piece—or two pieces, as the case may be—why don't I just pass on the looking around and get going." She gave Sully a final angry glare, then turned and began stomping back toward her car.

Fine! he muttered silently. The sooner he saw that damn million-dollar Mercedes on its way, the happier he'd be.

He watched her for a moment. Angry as he was, he couldn't quite force his gaze off the sway of her hips, couldn't quite help thinking what a cute little behind she had. Then other thoughts took over—thoughts about how the boys' trip might have ended if she *hadn't* driven them home.

He resisted for another few seconds. Then, half against his better judgment, he called, "Lauren?" and started after her.

She didn't glance back and she didn't slow down. Her high heels were digging into the dirt with each step, though, so she wasn't exactly doing a five-minute mile. It took him only a few strides to catch up with her.

"Look," he said, swinging around in front of her and blocking her path. "I'm sorry, okay? It was extremely good of you to drive them all this way."

Her eyes were still angry, but there was something else in them, something that made him feel two feet tall. Maybe she wasn't a straight shooter. Maybe she was a bit of a wing nut. And maybe she had thrown his program's future into jeopardy. But she'd gone out of her way to bring his kids home safely, so he really shouldn't have criticized her for it—especially not when there were so many other things he could justly criticize her for.

"All right, Sully," she finally murmured. "Apology accepted."

There wasn't, he noted, even the trace of a smile to say she actually meant that.

"And," she continued, "since I promised Billy and Hoops I'd have a look around, I guess I'd better. But I'll make it brief. It must almost be your dinnertime."

When she started for the car again, he followed along. Grace, Otis and all five boys were still standing right by it, watching and waiting.

Grace smiled at Lauren as she neared them, then glanced at Sully. "Are you done with her? Can I take her inside for that drink now?"

He nodded. "And if you wouldn't mind, you could give her a little tour of the place. I think Otis and I should have a talk with Billy and Hoops," he added. Then he glanced at the twins and Freckles. "You three go on in and catch the end of the ball game, but we'll want to talk to you later."

"Talk to *us*?" Terry said in a squeaky voice. Tony elbowed him, then all of them took off like frightened rabbits. It went a long way to confirming Sully's suspicions that it wasn't only Billy and Hoops who'd known he'd lost the funding. Or who'd been in on the plans for the trip to Manhattan.

He'd deal with the others later, though. Once he had the full story from his hitchhikers.

CHAPTER FOUR

BEAUTY MEETS THE BEASTS

WHEN LAUREN HAD DRIVEN IN, her first glimpse of Eagles Roost Lodge had reminded her of a picture from one of those wall calendars that feature rustic scenes. Her initial impression had been a fleeting one, though, because once the picture had come alive with people she'd focused her attention on them.

But now that she and Grace were heading for the lodge and she could really look around, it was obvious Sully owned a little piece of paradise.

The clearing was surrounded by trees, trees and more trees, growing so densely she couldn't see even a glimpse of Hidden Lake. The air rustling the leaves was fresh smelling and crystal clear, not hazy with pollution, and the birds were chirping and calling.

Nestled at the far end of the clearing, the buildings seemed so perfectly in tune with the setting that they must have been here for ages. The main lodge was a rambling old place constructed of hand-hewn logs—as was the cabin that stood off to the right and the huge garage on the left.

"Do you know the history of the place?" she asked Grace.

"More or less. It was built in the 1920s as the private retreat of a Wall Street tycoon. After he died, it became a commercial fishing lodge. Then Sully had the idea of turning it into a Foster Alternatives home and . . . well, you know the story from that point."

She nodded, although she wished Grace had explained how Sully had come to inherit Eagles Roost. Now that she'd seen for herself what an incredible amount of property there was, she was even more curious about who'd left it to him.

"When we go inside," Grace was saying, "you'll think you've walked through a time warp. The original owner's widow sold it complete with contents, and nothing much has been changed since. I keep telling Sully everything will soon qualify as antique."

Lauren smiled. She might not be able to see what the boys liked so much about Sully, but it wasn't hard to tell why they were fond of Grace.

"That's where Otis and I live." Grace pointed to the log cabin. "Why don't I show you it first," she suggested, abruptly changing course. "It used to be the caretaker's cottage, so it's not very big. But we like having a separate place. As much as I love the boys, I wouldn't want to be under the same roof with them twenty-four hours a day the way Sully is."

"No, it must be demanding."

"*Very* demanding, even with only the five of them. Usually, we have six, which is twice as many as Otis and I raised and twenty times the problems. Sully thrives on always being right there for them, though. I don't know how he does it."

When Grace didn't volunteer anything more, Lauren said, "It's unusual...what he's doing. Living out in the middle of nowhere and devoting his life to other people's children."

"Uh-huh. Sully's an unusual man."

They walked a few more steps, Lauren doing her best not to say another word about Jack Sullivan. She didn't know why she was curious about him, but she didn't like it. A moment later, though, she found herself saying, "Doesn't he get lonely for adult company? Not that you and Otis aren't adults but . . . you know what I mean."

Grace nodded. "Yes, I know what you mean. And he does have friends his own age. But he doesn't spend as much time with them as I think he should. And when it comes to women," she added, giving Lauren a sidelong glance, "he just never gets serious about anyone. Every now and then he'll start seeing someone, but it never lasts long. Most of the time, he might as well be a candidate for the priesthood."

Following Grace into the cabin, Lauren decided that if Sully lived in the city he'd have women pounding on his door twenty-four hours a day. Because regardless of what she thought about his personality, she could hardly deny he was inordinately attractive. So even though he was a little rough around the edges . . .

No, it went far beyond *a little.* Jack Sullivan had more rough edges than a mile-high stack of sandpaper. Still, there was no getting away from the fact he had the kind of animal magnetism that would make a lot of women drool.

Not that it made *her* drool. In fact, it made her downright uneasy. She was a city girl, and her newly acquired cat's animal magnetism was about her limit.

After she and Grace had finished their quick tour of the cabin, they headed over to the main lodge. When they reached the front door, Lauren took a final glance at the great outdoors—deciding Billy and Hoops had misled her completely.

Eagles Roost was nothing at all like Central Park. This was such total wilderness she could easily imagine the bears and cougars and such that must live in those woods.

She quickly followed Grace inside. If she ever had to choose, she'd far rather take her chances with a mugger in Central Park than a bear in the Adirondacks.

"This, obviously," Grace said, gesturing around the large main room, "is the original lounge."

Lauren smiled over at Freckles and the twins—who each had one eye on the baseball game and one eye on her—then looked around. As Grace had told her, the interior of the lodge evoked the same sense of the twenties as the exterior. Only the television was from the wrong decade.

The chairs and couches, big heavy pieces covered in dark green leather, looked as if they'd been made to last forever. Faded oriental carpets covered most of the polished hardwood floor, and a stone fireplace stretched across half the far wall.

A collection of stuffed animal heads peered down from either side of the fireplace—a moose, a brown bear, a deer, and an assortment of others. They all had either very large antlers or very large teeth. A few days of having them watch her and they'd be making regular appearances in her nightmares.

"I know," Grace said as if she were a mind reader. "They're leftovers from the early years, too. And I guess they were okay when this was a fishing lodge, but I could live without them."

"Did you ever suggest they go?"

"No. When Otis and I first arrived, it didn't seem right to start telling Sully I thought he should do some redecorating. He's content to leave things the way they were when he came, and after a while I became oblivious to them. But come and see the kitchen."

It, too, was a huge room, with a table in the center that would easily seat ten or twelve. The enormous old range and ancient refrigerator looked like a matched pair; the modern freezer seemed completely out of place.

Dinner was apparently almost ready, and the smell of cooking was so heavenly Lauren had to consciously resist the urge to lick her lips. She hadn't been thinking about food, but the smell made her realize she was absolutely starving.

She and the boys had stopped for lunch at a roadside diner—one with trucks parked outside, because Billy and Hoops had assured her that meant the food would be good. But her burger had been so greasy she'd eaten only a couple of bites, even though the boys had polished off two each, plus fries and onion rings.

"Just let me check the roast for a second," Grace said, "then I'll show you the rest of the place." She opened the oven door to peer in, which made the smell of food stronger and even more inviting.

"You'll stay for dinner, won't you?" she asked, closing the door again. "It's roast beef with all the trimmings, and you certainly can't drive back to the city without eating."

Lauren hesitated. The offer was very tempting. But she knew taking Grace up on it wouldn't be wise. If she stayed, Sully would undoubtedly glare at her through the entire meal and give her indigestion.

"BUT HE WAS only tryin' to help," Billy pleaded again.

Sully nodded. "I heard you the first twelve times, Billy. I just hope both of you—" he glanced at Hoops "—heard what I was saying, too. I'll come up with the money to keep this place going. That's not your job. Your job is to make sure you never do anything like that again. You ever think of another scheme you figure might even bend the rules, I want you talking to Otis or me before you do anything. Got it?"

"Yeah," they mumbled in unison.

"Good. Otis? You have anything more to say?"

He simply shook his head, so Sully looked at the boys again. "Okay, then I want you to hit your room and figure out what you think is a suitable punishment. After Lauren's gone, I'll come in and discuss it with you."

"Listen, Sully," Otis said as the boys took off for the lodge. "I—"

"Otis?" he interrupted. He already knew he'd come down pretty hard on them. "I was listening to them. I know they just wanted to help. But they could be lying in a ditch someplace."

Otis shook his head. "That's not what I was going to say. There's something wrong here that I haven't had a chance to tell you about and . . ."

As Otis's words trailed off, Sully followed his gaze across the clearing and saw that Grace and Lauren were halfway to the Mercedes. He watched them for a moment. Well, actually, he watched Lauren, thinking it would be easier to keep on hating her if she looked like the old crone he'd originally expected her to be.

Of course, he wasn't having any *real* trouble keeping on hating her. No, it was no trouble at all, he told himself firmly. And the sooner she was gone, the better he'd like it.

Then Grace called, "Sully?" and he glanced at her. "I invited Lauren to stay for dinner, but she says she has to get going. Maybe if you asked her...?"

"Oh, I really can't," Lauren said, looking over toward the men. "I appreciate the invitation, but I don't want to be too late getting back to the city."

"Don't let her leave yet," Otis said quietly.

"Are you kidding?" Sully muttered. "It's getting late. If she stayed for dinner, the next thing we knew Grace would be saying she shouldn't drive all the way back tonight, and invite her to stay till morning."

"But, Sully, I—"

"And I sure don't want her here overnight," he said, starting for the car. "So don't you go pressing her to stay for dinner."

"But, I'm just trying to—"

"I mean it, Otis." There was no way he was risking the possibility of that woman being at Eagles Roost overnight. Maybe she hadn't had any ulterior motives for coming here, but there was still the little matter of her having gone behind his back and calling Otis. And besides that... Hell, he wasn't even clear on all the *besides,* but if she was here when he woke up in the morning he'd probably find her trying to bathe Roxy in the kitchen sink or something.

"Well," Lauren said, extending her hand to Sully when he reached her. "Grace showed me around. So next year, if you apply for funding again, I'll be in a better position to help you out."

He nodded, shook her hand and forced a "Thanks." But there was no way in hell he'd ever ask for her help again.

"I said goodbye to the boys," she went on. "And to Grace. So I guess that just leaves you, Otis. It was nice meeting you. All of you," she added, her glance encompassing the three of them. "I hope things work out."

"They will," Sully assured her curtly.

"Thank you again for bringing Billy and Hoops home," Grace said, shooting Sully a dark glance.

"Yes. Thanks," he muttered.

Lauren gave them a final smile, then climbed into her car. Her dress hiked up a little when she sat down, exposing a few more inches of those gorgeous legs and making Sully's mouth suddenly cotton dry. Then she closed the door and became invisible behind the dark glass.

He exhaled slowly, surprised that he didn't feel like shouting hallelujahs. Another minute or two and the woman would be driving out of his life, which was exactly what he wanted. So why was he thinking he really should have insisted she stay for dinner?

"You weren't very hospitable, Sully," Grace whispered as the engine purred to life.

"She's really very nice," she added when he said nothing.

"Look, Sully," Otis said, "you've got to listen to me before she takes off. That woman—"

"Sully?" Billy the Kid hollered from the porch.

Sully turned as Lauren began backing her car around.

"I told you," he called, "to stay in your room."

"Yeah, but I just thought of somethin'."

"Dammit, Sully," Otis snapped, "in another three seconds it'll be too late."

As Sully looked at him, Lauren gave a short toot on her horn and started down the road, tiny clouds of dust rising behind her wheels.

"Sully, make her wait a minute," Billy yelled, racing down off the porch and starting across the clearing at a dead run.

"I'm telling you, Sully," Otis muttered. "You might be real sorry you didn't listen to me."

"Billy, what's wrong?" Grace asked as he reached them.

"Sully," he said, "I forgot before, but doesn't Joe's garage close at six?"

He nodded.

"Well it's after six, and she's outta gas."

Sully stood staring at Billy, telling himself the boy was joking. He didn't look as if he was, though.

"Really, Sully, she is. When we was comin' home, a warnin' light came on. Way before we even turned off the highway. And a little bell kept dingin'."

"Well why didn't you point out Joe's when you got to North Head? Hell, you had to drive right past it."

"We did point it out. And we told her it was the only gas station around, too. But she asked how far from town to here. And when we said only about five miles she said she still had a gallon or two, so she'd gas up on her way back to the highway. That she didn't want us to be even later gettin' home."

"Sully?" Grace said. "You'll have to go after her."

He nodded, although he hardly needed Grace to point it out. This wasn't New York City, where Lauren could hail a cab if she actually did run out of gas. But that probably hadn't even occurred to her. Hell,

Lauren Van Slyke shouldn't be let loose without a keeper. She was worse than any of his kids. Nobody in her right mind would merrily drive past the only gas station within thirty miles when she was almost out of gas.

"Can I go with you, Sully?" Billy asked.

"No. You can go on back inside," he said, checking his pocket for his car keys.

"Now," Otis muttered, "do you finally have time to listen to what I've been trying to tell you, Sully?"

"Can't it wait until he gets back?" Grace said. "Lauren's going to run out of gas and not know what to do."

"Grace, she's hardly going to have a nervous breakdown if she has to sit in her car for two minutes."

Sully wasn't sure that was true. Lauren Van Slyke didn't strike him as a picture of stability. But even though he doubted she'd remain exactly calm, cool and collected, he stood waiting for Otis to tell him about whatever he figured was so damn important.

"That woman who phoned me," Otis said, "wasn't Lauren Van Slyke."

"What woman?" Sully asked.

Otis gave him an impatient look. "The woman who phoned asking questions about Eagles Roost. If that was Lauren Van Slyke who was just here, then the woman who phoned wasn't her."

"What?"

"I told you, that other woman's voice was all scratchy."

"Well, yeah, I remembered that. But I figured she must have had a sore throat or something."

"Uh-uh. It's not only the voice. The way she talked was different. Which is why I was trying to tell you about it before she left. So you could ask her what the deal is. I mean, why would the other woman have identified herself as Lauren?"

Sully wearily shook his head. "I don't know. Maybe Lauren asked her to."

"That doesn't make any sense," Grace put in.

"No? Well it makes as much sense as driving around in the wilds of upstate New York with almost no gas. Or taking her cat to the office for a bath."

"Oh, she didn't do that at all," Grace told him. "The cat was a stray she'd just picked up outside the building. And she was bathing it because it was filthy. She told me the story while I was showing her around."

"Oh," Sully said. In that case, maybe she wasn't *quite* as flaky as he'd thought. Still, no one would ever suggest her chief virtue was common sense. He'd bet her Mercedes was gasping its last this very minute.

"You know, Sully," Grace continued, "I really think you misread her yesterday. And now that Otis is saying she isn't the one who phoned him . . . Well, I just wonder if there've been funny things going on that we don't know about."

LAUREN DRUMMED her fingers on the steering wheel, trying to drown out the voice in her head. It sounded exactly like her father's, and it was saying she'd just made another of her little errors in judgment. Unfortunately, it was right.

She'd been certain she had enough gas left to make it back to Dead Head—or whatever that little town was called—but it turned out she'd only had enough to get about halfway. Which meant that last night hadn't been the greatest time to forget to charge her cell phone.

She glanced at it again and mentally kicked herself, then stuck it back into her purse. At least the phone being useless didn't count as an error in judgment. She could blame that little problem entirely on the cat.

He hadn't liked the drive home from the office any better than he'd liked his bath, and he'd conveyed his feelings by caterwauling the entire way from Mad Ave. and East Fifty-second up to East Seventy-third—which was an awfully long twenty-one blocks in the five-o'clock traffic even without a cat yowling in your ear. And that was exactly where he'd been yowling, because he'd decided the only safe place to be was wrapped around the back of her neck—like one of those horrible dead-fox-neck furs her great-aunt Dorothy still loved to wear.

At any rate, when she'd finally gotten him up to her apartment he'd dashed around as if possessed, bouncing from one piece of furniture to the next. And she'd been so busy chasing after him, making sure he didn't commit cat suicide by diving headfirst into something hard, that the last thing on her mind had been plugging in the phone.

Putting her thoughts of both the cat and the phone aside for the moment, she tried again to decide which direction she should walk. Despite being certain there were wild animals in those woods, she'd ruled out simply sitting here and hoping help would come along.

She hadn't grown up in New York City without learning it could be fatal to trust a stranger. If someone came along offering to help, the odds on his being a serial killer had to be at least as high as on his being a Good Samaritan.

Besides which, the road between Eagles Roost and Dead Head was just some kind of secondary back road and there hadn't been a single other car along it since she'd left the lodge. So either she walked into town, where she knew there was a gas station, or she walked back to Eagles Roost.

There was no gas there, of course, but there was that roast beef dinner with all the trimmings. Merely recalling how delicious the kitchen had smelled was enough to make her stomach growl.

Then she thought about the thunder-at-midnight look Sully would give her if she turned up at the lodge again, and decided that going on to Dead Head would be the better choice.

Grabbing her purse, she got out of the car, locked it, and started in the direction of town. She'd only gone about a hundred yards, though, before she heard a car coming down the road behind her.

Fervently hoping it was the Good Samaritan and not the serial killer, she stopped and looked back. What she was hearing actually proved to be an old pickup truck covered with more brown rust than black paint.

When it pulled up beside her, her heart began beating faster. The two men in the cab were in their early thirties and muscular, with greasy long hair. Neither was wearing a shirt, and for a moment she couldn't help wondering if they were completely naked—a couple of Adirondack nudists.

They looked, though, more like they might be escapees from the nearest maximum-security prison than residents of a nudist colony. In fact, one of their faces... She wasn't sure, but she thought she might have seen it one night while she was channel surfing—on a segment of "America's Most Wanted."

"Hey, darlin'," the passenger said, leaning his head and bare shoulder far enough out the window that she could smell beer on his breath. "That your Mercedes back there?"

She nodded, telling herself to relax. She didn't necessarily have reason to panic.

"Problem with it, darlin'? Want us to take a look under the hood?"

For an instant, she considered saying she'd intentionally parked it back there and had some good reason for hiking down the road. When she couldn't think of any reason that was plausible, though, she simply managed a smile and said, "Thanks, but I just ran out of gas."

"Oh, so you need a lift to town," the driver said. Then he belched and wiped the back of his hand across his mouth.

"Well... no. Thanks again, but I enjoy walking."

The passenger's gaze drifted down to her feet, then started slowly up her legs. When it finally got all the way up to her face, he smiled.

That made her more nervous yet. In Manhattan, the only time a stranger ever smiled at you was when he wanted something. And she was afraid to even think about what this fellow might want.

"Darlin'," he said, "town's over two miles from here. You won't enjoy walkin' that far in those high heels. So why don't you just slide on in with us? We won't hurt you none, will we, Roy.''

The driver shook his head. ''You got nothing to worry about from me an' Snake.''

Snake? Her heart began beating faster yet. She'd been right about the prison. Surely only criminals were ever called Snake, which meant that getting into that truck with them would go far beyond any *little* error in judgment.

Before she could think of what to say next, she spotted a minivan heading down the road and began praying there was a white knight driving it.

When it pulled up behind the truck, she saw Sully was driving. That certainly dashed her hopes about any white knight, but under the circumstances she was more than happy to settle for him.

Not surprisingly, the first thing he did was glare at her through the windshield—before he even opened his door. But this time she didn't care. As long as he got her away from these men, he could feel free to glare at her all the way to the gas station.

He climbed out of the van and nodded to the two in the truck, saying, ''Hey, Roy. Snake.''

Lord, he knew these felons.

''Hey, Sully,'' they greeted him.

''Let's go,'' he said to Lauren.

''Lady a friend of yours?'' Roy asked him.

''Something like that.''

''We were tryin' to help her out,'' Snake said. ''But I guess she didn't like the looks of us.''

Sully laughed. ''No wonder. You two really need cleaning up at the end of the day. Roy and Snake,'' he added, glancing at Lauren, ''build houses.''

''Or whatever else needs buildin',''' Snake said.

Lauren cleared her throat uncomfortably. Just because Snake and Roy weren't suits, she shouldn't have assumed the worst. They were merely a couple of working men. And Snake probably only smelled like a brewery because they'd stopped for a beer or two after a hot day's work.

"It wasn't that I didn't like your looks," she offered politely. "It was just...well, as I said, I enjoy walking. I live in Manhattan and everyone walks there. And I thought that since this was such a nice summer day... I guess it's closer to evening by now, isn't it. But, either way, I decided I really wouldn't mind the walk to the gas station and—"

"Can we get going?" Sully interrupted. "Grace is holding dinner until we get back."

"I'm not going back," she informed him with a cool glance. As glad as she'd been to see him, the feeling was fading fast. His *can we get going?* had sounded a whole lot more like an order than a question, and she didn't take kindly to being ordered around.

"I'm going to Dead Head," she elaborated. And if he didn't want to drive her, she'd darn well go with Roy and Snake, now that she knew it would be safe.

Roy and Snake, though, had begun to laugh about something.

"North Head," Sully muttered to her. "The town is North Head, not Dead Head."

"Oh. Well, whatever, that's where I'm going. Then as soon as I get some gas I'll be on my way again."

"Lauren, the gas station in North Head closed at six. And I'm not driving thirty miles and back to the next closest one until I've had dinner. So can we *please* go back to the lodge?"

CHAPTER FIVE

BILLY THE KID'S NEW PLAN

DINNER, SULLY THOUGHT, had taken a lot longer than usual—mostly because every time Lauren had finished telling the boys one story, they'd gotten her started on another. They'd barely sat down at the table before Grace had prompted her to tell them about how he'd walked in while she'd been bathing the cat. And she'd made the story sound a hell of a lot funnier than things had seemed at the time.

All in all, she'd turned out to have a surprisingly good sense of humor—when she wasn't busy cutting off his funding, or playing Ice Princess, or doing one of a hundred other things that he didn't find the least bit amusing.

"Hey, you guys," he said as the last of the boys polished off his second serving of Grace's apple crumble. "None of you helped get dinner ready today, so you're all on cleanup detail."

As they began pushing back their chairs, Sully got the coffeepot and filled four mugs for the adults, glad he was finally going to be able to ask Lauren about that woman's phone call. He'd been awfully tempted to raise the subject earlier, in the van, but he'd decided not to say anything without Otis and Grace there. By triple-teaming her they should be able to get at the truth.

"Let's take our coffee into the family room," he suggested. "Give the boys space to clear the table."

Before any of the others rose, though, Lauren said, "You know, I've been thinking I should just phone a garage and have some gas brought to my car. There's no point in one of you having to drive me someplace. And if I called right now—"

"I think you should stop worrying about getting gas tonight," Grace said. "I think you should just stay right here until morning."

Sully looked at Grace, not wanting to believe she'd actually said that. Was he the only one who hadn't forgotten that Lauren Van Slyke was the enemy?

Around him, the kitchen was silent. The boys had begun clearing the dishes, but now they were all standing like statues. Statues with big ears.

"I'm not sure," Otis said, "that leaving an expensive car just sitting out overnight would be a good idea."

Otis was right, of course, but before Sully could voice his agreement Grace was saying, "Oh, don't be silly, Otis. You locked it, didn't you, dear?" she asked Lauren.

"Yes, but—"

"Then it'll be fine. There's hardly any traffic on that road, especially at night."

"Well, even so," Lauren said, "I really don't think I'd better stay."

Sully breathed a quiet sigh of relief and shot Grace a look that told her to let it go.

Ignoring him, she glanced back across the table at Lauren, saying, "By the time you got gas and started for home it would be after dark. And you wouldn't get to the city until the middle of the night." She turned to Sully again. "She can't be driving all that way alone in the dark."

He gritted his teeth, knowing Grace was right. It really wasn't safe for a woman to be driving alone at night. Especially not a woman like Lauren Van Slyke.

Lauren murmured, "No," though. "Thank you, but I really couldn't impose. Besides, the cat's all alone in my apartment."

"You said you left lotsa food down," Billy piped up. "Or maybe you could phone your friend across the hall. The one you phoned from your office after you said you'd come here."

"Well . . . I really shouldn't leave him alone for too long when the apartment's still a strange place."

There was a silence, then Sully heard himself saying, "Most cats don't really need much attention. We've got three here, and you probably haven't even seen them around."

He paused, trying to stop himself before he made things even worse, but for some reason he couldn't. "So," he added, "if you don't get home until tomorrow, the cat will be fine. And Freckles has a room to himself at the moment, so I can use the second bed in there for the night."

He glanced at Freckles. "You wouldn't mind me bunking in there, would you?"

When the boy shook his head, Sully looked at Lauren again. "That means you can use my bedroom."

"Oh, I couldn't put you out of your own room."

He shrugged. "I can hardly have you sharing with Freckles, and there isn't a spare bed in the cottage."

She'd been watching him as he spoke, searching his eyes with her big blue ones as if wanting to be sure he really didn't mind the idea of her staying. And the strange thing was that all of a sudden he didn't.

He wasn't entirely sure why, except that something in her expression made him doubt she was as self-assured as he'd thought. It was something he often saw in his kids, something that said they weren't used to being accepted simply for themselves. And it was a look that always made him feel he wanted to help.

That was ridiculous, though, he realized a second later. Lauren Van Slyke sure as hell didn't need any help from him.

"Well," she murmured at last, "if you're really sure it wouldn't be too much trouble..."

"Good," Grace said. "That's settled, then. Before bedtime, I'll find a nightgown and robe you can borrow. And what size shoes do you wear?"

"Six."

"Perfect. I'll give you some flat shoes and jeans for the morning. I'm sure I've got things that would fit you. But right now, let's do as Sully suggested and take our coffee into the other room."

Sully glanced at the boys and caught them all giving each other looks. They clearly figured they'd just gotten off the hook, so he said, "We'll save the rest of our discussions about Billy and Hoops' trip to Manhattan for tomorrow."

He turned and followed the other adults out of the kitchen, feeling five pairs of eyes burning holes in his back.

THE MINUTE THE DOOR swung closed behind Sully, Billy wheeled around to the others, saying, "I've gotta plan."

"No way," Hoops told him. "We don't even know how bad we're getting punished 'cuz of your last plan."

"But it worked, didn't it? She's here, isn't she?"

"Well . . . yeah."

"Then, listen," Billy said to all of them. "You still wanna make sure we can stay here, don't you?"

They all nodded—even Hoops—just like he knew they would.

"Okay," he went on. "Then we gotta all swear to help. Swear we're gonna do everythin' we can. Hands," he added, holding out his hands.

The others all piled theirs on top of his. Hoops was last, and kinda slow, but he did it, too.

"Okay, then," Billy said. "Here's the plan. If Sully and Lauren got to really likin' each other, then she'd give him the money, right?"

"But he don't like her," Freckles pointed out. "You know that. You was the one listenin' in yesterday. When he told the Playsics she was a wing nut and all that."

"So what?" Billy said. "Just because he doesn't like her now, doesn't mean she can't make him like her."

"What do you know about that kinda stuff?" Freckles said.

"I know lots. I got three older sisters. And girl cousins, too. And all they ever talk about is how to get guys to like 'em. So I know how they do it."

"But why," Tony asked, "would Lauren want Sully to like her?"

Billy looked at Tony like that was a real dumb question while he tried to think of an answer. "'Cuz that's just how girls are," he finally said. "And even if she doesn't want him to like her yet, if we fix things right then she'll start wantin' him to. And when she does, he'll have to."

"Why?" Tony asked.

"'Cuz she's pretty and rich."

"So what?" Tony said.

"So she must know how to make guys like her way better than my sisters or cousins."

THE MORE DETAIL Otis went into about that phone call Sully had alluded to yesterday, the less sense it made to Lauren.

She had no idea why some woman would have phoned here claiming to be her, let alone have asked all about Sully's program. Or, as Otis had put it, tried to *dig up dirt.* But given the way Grace and Sully were watching her as she listened, they were expecting her to shed some light on things.

Unfortunately, she was no Nancy Drew. She almost never figured out how a mystery was going to wrap up before she got to the ending. And as far as this little mystery was concerned, she was afraid she wouldn't be able to shed even the tiniest ray of light.

"You're absolutely certain," she asked Otis once he'd finished his story, "that the woman said she *was* me. She couldn't have said she was calling *for* me?"

"No, she definitely said she was you."

"*Did* someone call on your behalf?" Sully asked.

"No...not that I know of. I mean, I certainly didn't ask anyone to. I'm just wondering if, for some reason, Rosalie..."

"Rosalie?" Grace asked.

"She's my admin assistant, but I can't imagine why she'd have phoned."

"I met Rosalie yesterday," Sully told Otis. "And she's got a Jamaican accent."

"Then it wasn't her."

"You know," Lauren said slowly, "any woman in the world could have called and said she was me. It could have been anybody who wanted information about your program. And maybe she figured that saying she was me would be an easy way to get it."

"But why," Grace asked, "would anyone be curious about what goes on at Eagles Roost? Anyone aside from Lauren and the social services people, I mean."

Before any of them could hazard a guess, the door to the kitchen swung open and the five boys appeared.

When they stopped as a little group and smiled straight at Lauren, she couldn't help thinking something was up. Then the other four looked at Billy, which made her decide there was definitely a plot afoot and that they'd elected him spokesman for whatever was coming.

"The kitchen's all clean, Sully," he announced. "So we were thinkin' it would be nice if we went and helped Mr. and Mrs. Plavsic pack their car. Like now, I mean. Before it's totally dark."

"You're going somewhere?" Lauren asked Grace, the idea making her a little uneasy. When she'd taken them up on the offer to stay the night, she'd certainly assumed the Plavsics would be right there in their cottage.

"Not until morning, dear," Grace said. "But yes, we're leaving for Minnesota. We drive out there almost every July. We're both originally from Minneapolis, and we still have all kinds of family there."

"Did you *ask* the boys if they'd help you pack the car?" Sully said.

He looked, Lauren thought, very suspicious.

"Why…no," Grace told him. She glanced at Otis, gave him a blatantly conspiratorial smile, then looked back at Sully. "But isn't it thoughtful of them to offer? If we pack up tonight, we'll be able to get a really early start."

"Right," he muttered. "And I'll bet they don't have an ulterior motive among the five of them."

When he looked over at the boys again, Lauren's gaze followed his.

Their expressions made her think of cats that had just swallowed canaries, and for half a second she didn't understand what was going on. Then she realized what they were up to and almost started laughing.

If they thought she had the slightest interest in being left alone with their chief eagle, they were out of their young minds. And as for Grace and that smile of hers … well, Grace must be one of those women who can't resist trying to play matchmaker, whether she was looking at a total mismatch or not.

But Lord, even if you believed in the theory of opposites attracting, she and Sully were a lot more than mere opposites. She doubted they could have a single solitary thing in common.

"Don't you guys go getting any funny ideas," Sully said in a decidedly no-nonsense tone. "Lauren is

staying here because driving back to the city this late
wouldn't be a good idea. Period. Got it?''

"What?" Billy said, all wide-eyed innocence.
"What are you talkin' about? I never said a word
about her. Did I?''

He glanced at the other boys, who immediately
began shaking their heads, then he looked back at
Sully. "We just wanted to help the Plavsics, Sully.
Honest.''

"And I think it's very sweet of them," Grace said
quickly. "So why don't we take them up on the offer, Otis?''

Otis shot Sully an amused glance, then pushed
himself out of his chair, saying, "We'll see you both
in the morning before we take off.''

"I won't forget about those clothes, Lauren,"
Grace added as they started for the door. "I'll send
them over when the boys come back.''

Sully sat watching the others trail out of the
lodge—Roxy bringing up the rear—part of him glad
the boys wanted to stay at Eagles Roost badly enough
to try to help him, another part wanting to strangle
them for their ridiculous plotting. Hell, Lauren was
probably having trouble holding back her laughter.

As the screen door banged shut behind the dog, he
turned to her and shrugged. "Sorry about that.''

She smiled. "It's all right. It just surprised me. I
didn't realize boys that age would think along those
lines.''

"Oh, they can be pretty creative thinkers at times.
And even though Otis and I explained things to Billy
and Hoops—explained there was nothing you could
do about the funding, I mean—if kids don't like reality they tend to ignore it. So they probably figured

you could still come up with the money if you decided you really wanted to.''

"And if leaving us alone together led to anything . . ." Lauren smiled again.

Sully eyed her for a few seconds, deciding she must figure the boys' scheme was about as crazy as they came. After all, the idea of a man like him and a woman like her getting together . . .

Besides which, he didn't even like her. Although, he had to admit she wasn't nearly as bad as he'd figured at first. And she hadn't actually gone sneaking around behind his back the way he'd initially thought.

Fleetingly, he wondered again who *had* made that call to Otis. But it was probably going to remain one of life's little mysteries.

"Well," he said at last, for lack of anything better, "I guess I should find some clean sheets for you."

"I'll help make up the bed," she offered. "It's the least I can do when I'm putting you out of your room."

When she stood up and smiled expectantly at him, the sudden stirring in his groin took him by surprise. She might be a damn good-looking woman, with an eye-catching sway to her walk, but she sure as hell hadn't caused him any of *those* kinds of feelings before.

So the fact he was having them now, he told himself, getting up and starting in the direction of the bedrooms, was strictly a result of the circumstances. He hadn't often changed a bed with a woman. And the times he had, it had always been a prelude to sharing it with her.

LAUREN HAD ALREADY SEEN the boys' rooms, which, when Eagles Roost was first built, had been the three guest bedrooms. But Grace hadn't taken her down to the far end of the bedroom wing. She'd merely pointed toward it, referring to it as "Sully's space."

It turned out to be both larger and less Spartan than Lauren had expected—a suite that stretched across the entire end of the lodge, consisting of a large bedroom and private bath, plus an adjoining study that Sully used as his office.

"That's a separate line from the one in the lounge," he told her, gesturing toward the phone on the desk. "After the first couple of times I caught kids listening in on the extension, a private line started seeming like a necessity."

She nodded, but her attention was actually focused on the books that covered one entire wall of the study. Most of them, she could see, were far too recent to have belonged to the original owner.

"Otis keeps telling me," Sully said, "that wall's going to fall down if I buy many more books. But I prefer reading to television."

For a moment that fact surprised her. Then she realized it probably explained why he was so well spoken for someone without the best of formal educations.

By the time her sixty-second tour of his rooms was over, she'd decided that while the tycoon who'd built Eagles Roost might have wanted a rustic retreat he obviously hadn't wanted to do without his creature comforts.

The bedroom furniture consisted of gorgeous old cherry-wood pieces; the lighting in the room was muted. On the far side of the bed there was only a diffuse glow from a small, electrified railway lantern that served as a bedside lamp. Near where she was standing, a brass floor lamp spread a pool of light over a comfortable-looking leather armchair and matching footstool.

While Sully was getting a set of sheets from the dresser, Lauren peeked at the book lying open on the chair. It was a recent courtroom thriller, and seeing it started her worrying about Elliot again.

Reminding herself he'd said the odds on his ex-client actually trying anything were really low, she did her best to force her worry away.

"Here," Sully said, handing her the sheets. "You take care of these while I strip the bed."

The moment he leaned over to begin, she realized that offering to help the boys pack the Plavsics's car would have been a whole lot wiser than offering to help with this. There was something about being in Sully's bedroom with him that made her uncomfortably aware of his masculinity.

Yes...aware was the right word. She wouldn't go as far as to say she was *attracted* to him, but she couldn't deny being very *aware* of him. And aware that her initial impressions of him had been way off base.

He wasn't totally obnoxious, after all. He was simply, as Grace had told her, an unusual man. Which accounted for why he'd required a little getting used to. But it hadn't taken her very long to realize that under his tough-guy exterior was a man who really cared about people.

It was obvious in his dealings with the boys. And seeing that made her feel even worse that she hadn't written a stronger recommendation to support his program.

She put the top sheet and pillowcases down on the bedside table, then looked at him again, telling herself there was no reason in the world to feel uncomfortable about being in here with him. After all, he hadn't shown the slightest interest in her as a woman. In fact, it went far beyond that. The man had hated her from the moment they'd met.

Or, more likely, he'd hated her even before they'd met—from the moment he'd received her letter.

"There we go," he said, tossing the balled-up sheets onto the floor and looking across the bed at her.

His gaze started a fluttering low in her stomach, which made her suspect those deep brown eyes of his would be enough to turn most women to jelly.

Fortunately, she thought, handing him the clean bottom sheet, she was made of sterner stuff.

When he flicked the sheet across the mattress, she reached for her side of it and did her best to keep her eyes off him as she smoothed and tucked.

Her best wasn't very good, though, and it was hampered by the way every move he made focused her attention on a different set of lean muscles. And every fresh focus started her imagining how sinuous those muscles would feel beneath her fingers.

Each time he bent forward, his dark hair fell over his forehead. Each time it did, she was ridiculously tempted to reach over and brush it back.

That disconcerting animal magnetism of his was just too strong to ignore in the confines of the room, and she was glad the width of the bed was between them—although she was extremely conscious that it *was* a bed. His bed.

The thought that she'd be spending the night in his bed only added to her uneasy sense of intimacy.

She picked up the top sheet and partially unfolded it, then handed Sully his edge. When she did, her hand brushed his and the contact sent a hot little streak of... something racing through her.

When an imaginary voice said, "Something?" Lauren silently swore at herself. Her attempt to deny the obvious was downright pathetic, so she might as well stop trying to tell herself she wasn't attracted to Sully—might as well just admit the hot little streak was desire.

Passing him a pillowcase, she let her eyes linger on the muscles in his arms, deciding it was hardly surprising that Jack Sullivan was making her hot and bothered. After all, she'd never before met such a sexy-looking man—her ex-husband definitely included.

And, Lord, it had been such a long, long time since she'd made love that her hormones clearly weren't the least bit concerned about whether she and Sully had anything in common or not. Which meant that it was a good thing her brain was in charge, rather than her hormones.

Sully picked up the blanket and glanced over at Lauren. She didn't notice, though. She looked as if her thoughts were a hundred miles away.

He'd been doing his best to keep his eyes off her, but now he let himself watch the way her breasts rose and fell slightly with each breath, the way she was absently smoothing the pillowcase even though it was already smooth.

She looked so damn appealing it started those stirrings in his groin once more—his body telling him he needed a woman. He continued looking at her until his face felt hot and his breathing was uneven, then ordered himself to stop. His eyes, though, seemed to have developed a mind of their own.

Telling himself he was crazy, he tried to force them from her. There was no point at all in wanting something he couldn't have.

"Lauren?" he finally said. Her name tasted warm on his tongue, and when she looked across the bed he was momentarily lost in the blue of her eyes.

Before he could say anything more, he heard the front door bang shut and the sound of footsteps in the lodge.

"Sully?" Billy the Kid hollered. "Sully, where are you?"

"In my bedroom," he called, feeling a distinct sense of relief that the boys had come back in.

Tough as it was to believe, in mere hours he'd somehow gone from being convinced Lauren was a total wing nut—not to mention a major pain in the ass—to being attracted as hell to her. Which meant the smartest thing he could do was keep from being alone with her again.

"Oh." Billy appeared in the doorway and stopped dead, causing a pileup of the other kids and Roxy behind him. "Oh...you're in your bedroom with *Lauren.*"

One of the twins giggled. Sully couldn't see if it was Tony or Terry, so instead of saying anything he simply glared at the whole bunch of them. That only elicited a second giggle.

Billy, who was doing a poor job of trying to suppress a smirk, looked at Lauren and held out the small suitcase he was carrying. "Mrs. Plavsic said to give you this."

"Thank you, Billy. I'll just put it here on the bed."

Her words produced yet another giggle from the hallway.

Sully glanced at her, decided she was getting flustered, and looked back at the boys. "All right, guys," he said sternly, "that's enough. Lauren can live without that kind of childish behavior, so I think you'd all better head to your rooms and get ready for bed."

"Aww... Sully," Freckles said. "It's not that late. And it's summer vacation."

"Go," he ordered. "Say good-night to us, then go. You can read for a while if you want."

The five of them mumbled "good-nights" and reluctantly trudged off in the direction of their rooms.

"Well, I guess that leaves just you and me," Lauren murmured. Then she slowly licked the inner edge of her bottom lip with the tip of her tongue.

It was, Sully thought, a very nervous-looking gesture. It was also so sexy it practically made him drool.

Terrific, he silently muttered. Not three minutes ago, he'd decided the smartest thing he could do was keep from being alone with her again. So what a brilliant move he'd made by sending the boys to their rooms.

Hell, things were even worse than he'd realized. Being around Lauren Van Slyke was so distracting he couldn't think straight.

CHAPTER SIX

A SLIGHT MISUNDERSTANDING

SENDING THE BOYS TO BED, Sully decided after he and Lauren had been sitting in the lounge for a while, hadn't been a disastrous move after all.

Despite the disconcerting stirrings of arousal he kept having, it was nice being alone with her like this, without any anger or tension between them. She was easy to talk to—easy enough, in fact, that he seemed to have been doing all the talking.

He'd been telling her stories about the various kids who'd stayed at Eagles Roost, and he was absurdly pleased that she seemed so interested.

He mentioned a few more things about his current boys, then said, "It must be your turn. I've told you everything about myself."

She laughed at that. "Sully, you haven't told me a single thing about yourself. I think you'd rather tell me about Roxy's background than your own."

He smiled, but she was right. There wasn't much in his past he wanted to talk about—certainly nothing before the time he arrived at Eagles Roost. "Well, let's see," he said. "Roxy's mother is a rottweiler who belongs to a friend over near Watertown. And her father was an amorous Saint Bernard. Obviously, they didn't produce a litter of lapdogs, and even in the country big puppies aren't too easy to find good homes for.''

"So you took Roxy.''

"Actually, I took Roxy and one of the males. But he got shot by some fool hunter.''

"Deep down, you're really a softie, aren't you,'' Lauren said quietly.

He gazed at her for a moment, suddenly wanting to kiss her. He didn't try to, though. He wasn't any crazier about rejection than the next guy, and he knew damn well that was what he'd get. The upper class might have met the ex-con, but that didn't mean she wanted any advances from him.

"Nobody's ever accused me of being a softie before,'' he finally told her. "And if I am, it's deep, *deep* down. But now it's definitely your turn,'' he added quickly.

"Where should I start?''

"Oh, how about something easy, like where you live.''

"I have a condo on Fifth Avenue, overlooking the park.''

He was just starting to wonder how many millions an apartment overlooking Central Park was worth when she added, "I bought it after my divorce—kind of a fresh start, something that was mine alone.''

"You've been married,'' he said. "I didn't know that.''

She shrugged. "It wasn't much of a marriage. We were just two people who convinced ourselves we were right for each other when we weren't.''

She didn't elaborate on that, so he asked, "And your family?''

"Well, my parents are . . . parents.''

He nodded, but he knew her parents couldn't be anything like his had been—his unknown father and screwed-up mother.

"And I have a sister, Marisa, who's three years older than I am. She's an artist, studied in Paris and the whole bit. My brother, Elliot, is two years older than her. He's a partner in a law firm."

"And?"

"And?" she repeated.

"And the minute you mentioned him you got a strange look in your eyes."

She exhaled slowly. "Elliot's a *criminal* lawyer. And we're all awfully worried about him at the moment. He has an ex-client who's threatened to get him. And the fellow was released from prison yesterday."

"He thinks the threat's for real? Not just so much talk?"

"He says that's probably all it is, but he's pretty upset. The fellow threatened to harm him *or* someone he loved. And he has a wife and two little boys."

And a little sister, Sully thought, wondering if Lauren was in any danger. The thought that she might be started an uneasy feeling creeping up his spine—and made him awfully glad Grace had insisted she shouldn't drive home in the dark.

Lauren wanted to change the subject, because every time she thought about Elliot's situation it made her anxious all over again. But she was hesitant to ask Sully any personal questions when he so obviously didn't like talking about himself.

"Sully?" she finally said, deciding he could always tell her to mind her own business. "Would you mind if I ask you something I've been curious about?''

"Ask away," he said.

"Ever since I read in my file that you inherited this place, I've wondered who left it to you."

He eyed her for a minute, then said, "I'd almost forgotten how much personal information about me Matthew Grimes gathered.''

She simply shrugged, not knowing what to say. The fact that Sully had a prison record hadn't come up in conversation, and she couldn't help wondering if he'd just now realized she knew about it.

"Well," he said at last, "when I first came to Eagles Roost, I was twenty-one years old and straight out of prison. A man named Frank Watson was operating the place as a fishing lodge, and I ended up working for him. I was only going to stay a few months, but...well, Frank was getting too old to run things by himself, and the longer I stayed the more he came to rely on me.''

"So you never left."

"Right. Then, when he died, I discovered he'd left me the place. He was a widower, with no children, and...we'd gotten pretty close over the years.''

"Ahh," she murmured.

"Giving me Eagles Roost," Sully added so quietly he might have been talking to himself, "was the greatest thing anyone ever did for me.''

Lauren's throat suddenly felt tight. He'd said so little, but she could tell how much Frank Watson had meant to him. And how much it meant that Frank had cared about him.

He squared his shoulders, and she knew that was the end of his telling her anything personal. Then he glanced at his watch and said, "I hadn't realized how late it was. I guess we should turn in."

"I guess," she agreed, although she would've been happy to sit here talking for a lot longer. Which was strange, considering that mere hours ago, if anyone had told her she'd end up liking Jack Sullivan, she'd have told them they were crazy.

Of course, if anyone had told her Sully would end up liking her, she'd have told them they were down-right certifiable. But she was almost positive his feelings had done the same about-face hers had. So, in a way, it was really too bad that after she left in the morning they'd probably never see each other again.

"SULLY?" SOMEONE SAID groggily.

He woke up in pitch blackness and an unfamiliar bed.

"Sully?" the someone said again.

Freckles, he realized. He was sleeping in Freckles' room because Lauren Van Slyke was sleeping in his bed.

"Sully, the phone's ringing."

"Damn," he muttered, feeling around for his robe. There was no bedside clock in the room, but it was obviously the middle of the night. So who the hell was calling?

Telling Freckles to go back to sleep, he rolled out of bed and promptly stumbled over Roxy. Finally making it to the hallway, he stood waiting to hear whether he wanted the line in the lounge or the one in his office.

The next ring told him it was the phone in the lounge, so he headed along the dark hall and into the room, momentarily blinding himself when he switched on the lights.

"If you stop ringing before I pick up," he muttered as he neared the phone, "I'll kill you." He grabbed the receiver mid-ring. "Hello."

There was a moment of silence, then an unfamiliar male voice asked, "Is this Jack Sullivan?"

"Yes, it is."

"Mr. Sullivan, this is Roger Van Slyke, Lauren's father. I apologize for bothering you so late, but I understand my daughter drove to Eagles Roost this afternoon."

"Yes. Yes, she did," Sully admitted, wondering what was up and why it couldn't have waited until morning.

"Well she hasn't arrived back at her apartment," Roger Van Slyke went on. "My wife and I have gotten no answer there all evening, and we haven't been able to reach her on her cell phone. So needless to say, we're very worried."

"Yes... Yes, of course." Sully ran his fingers through his hair, trying to wake himself up. "I can see why you would be, sir, but Lauren's fine. She just had a little car trouble, and it got too late for her to drive back tonight, so she decided to stay here."

"I see. She decided to stay there... with you."

Sully suspected he'd just learned who had taught Lauren her Ice Princess tone. Her father's voice hadn't had much warmth in it to begin with, and with that remark it had turned cold enough to freeze Fiji.

"Yes, sir," he said evenly. "She decided to stay here with me and the five boys. And my teacher and housemother," he added, figuring there was no reason to mention that Otis and Grace lived in a separate cottage.

"I see," Roger Van Slyke said again. "Well, I'd like to speak to my daughter, please."

Sully glanced in the direction of the television and checked the VCR's clock. "Sir, it's three o'clock in the morning."

"I'm well aware of the time, Mr. Sullivan. Now, if you wouldn't mind getting Lauren . . . ?"

He hesitated, thinking it made absolutely no sense to wake Lauren. But since the man's son was under a death threat he was probably hyperanxious.

"I'll go get her, sir." Setting the receiver on the end table, he headed back to the hallway. He flicked the light on this time, and its dim glow stretched ahead of him.

When he reached his bedroom door, he quietly tapped on it. There was no response, so he knocked a little louder—then tried calling Lauren's name.

There was still nothing. He hesitantly cracked open the door and called, "Lauren?"

"Sully?" Freckles said from behind him. "Sully, what's going on?"

"The phone call's for Lauren, that's all. You go on back to bed."

As Freckles turned away, Sully decided that if he stood out here calling for much longer he'd wake the rest of the kids. So he pushed the door open a few more inches and started across the room.

The light from the hall was too faint to help him see, but he could easily navigate his own bedroom in the dark, and all he had to do was make it over to the floor lamp.

When he got to where it should have been, though, it wasn't there. He felt the chair...then the stool...but where in blazes was the lamp?

"Lauren?" he said into the darkness. "Lauren?" He inched his way toward the bed, until his leg finally touched the mattress. Then he gingerly reached down to where he was sure Lauren's shoulder would be. But his hand didn't come to rest on her shoulder. It came to rest on the unmistakable shape of a firm, warm, perfect breast.

He couldn't have pulled his hand back any faster if he'd just touched hot coals, but it wasn't fast enough. Lauren came awake screaming.

"Oh, God!" he muttered, frantically trying to think of what to say. Screaming women were not his specialty. "Lauren, stop that," he tried. "There's no reason for it. I was only trying to wake you."

Apparently, she was screaming too loudly to hear him, because she didn't stop. And if she didn't stop within the next few seconds, the kids would all wake up and hear her. Or, worse yet, her screams were so loud they might carry to the phone and her father would hear her.

Quickly, he leaned down over her and covered her mouth with his hand. Just as quickly, she bit him—hard.

"Yeoww!" he hollered, yanking his hand away. An instant later, excruciating pain sent every ounce of air whooshing from his body.

"Oh, God!" he moaned as the pain doubled him over onto the bed. Lauren had kneed him in the groin. And she kneed as hard as she bit.

"What the hell do you think you're doing?" she yelled.

Vaguely, he realized she was trying to pull the sheet around herself and sit up. She couldn't do that, either, though, because he was slumped on top of her.

"Get off me!" she ordered. "Get off me and get the hell out of here!"

He managed to drag himself off her and roll onto the floor, but the only way he'd be able to get out of here at the moment would be to crawl.

"I don't believe this," she hissed down at him through the darkness. "I simply do not believe this. You should be totally ashamed of yourself, you...you barbarian."

Over her words, he could hear Freckles saying, "Sully, what's wrong? Why's Lauren so mad?"

He tried to answer, but hadn't gotten enough of his breath back to manage words.

Then Roxy started trying to lick his face and sit on him at the same time while the rest of the boys came thundering into the room. For some crazy kid reason, one of them had come armed with a flashlight. The beam of light bounced around, finally settling on him.

"Sully?" Billy said. "Why are you on the floor? How come you're all bent over like somebody just kicked you in the...ohh."

"Ohh..." the other boys echoed.

"I...I..." he tried to say.

"There's someone on the lounge phone," Freckles offered. "For Lauren. That's why Sully came to wake her up."

There was a long silence. Then Lauren said, "Really?"

A second later, she switched on the lantern beside the bed and stared down at Sully.

"It's your father," he gasped out. "He wants to be sure you're okay."

ONCE LAUREN REALIZED that Sully hadn't come into the bedroom with rape and pillage on his mind, and that she'd completely overreacted, she tried to apologize and help him up from the floor.

He wasn't interested in either her apology or her help, though. First he groaned, then he glared, then he firmly waved her off. So, guiltily leaving him slumped where he was with Roxy sprawled across his feet, she tugged on her borrowed robe and started for the lounge—even though talking to her father was the last thing she wanted to do. She didn't know how he'd discovered she was at Eagles Roost, but she knew he wouldn't be happy about it.

All five boys came along with her, although she wasn't sure if Sully had waved them away, too, or if they just doubted she'd be able to spot the phone by herself. At any rate, their little parade was about halfway across the lounge when the front door opened and Grace came hurrying in, Otis right behind her. Both were bleary-eyed and wearing nightclothes.

"I saw the lights on and knew someone must be sick," Grace explained, her eyes flickering from one boy to the next. "You're all fine, though, aren't you, so it's Sully. What's wrong with him?"

The boys looked at Lauren. She knew they were dying to tell Grace exactly what Sully was suffering from, but they didn't—which was the first thing she'd had to be glad about in the past five minutes.

"Sully isn't sick," she said, deciding that wasn't a lie, even though he wasn't in the best of health, either.

Then she realized it would be a good idea if somebody made sure he was all right and glanced at Otis. "I think he might like to talk to you for a minute, though. He's in his bedroom.

"Actually," she said, focusing on Grace again, "the lights are on because there's a phone call for me. I'm just sorry it's gotten everybody up."

"It's her father," Freckles said. "Sully told us."

"Well, if the call's for Lauren, it's only polite to let her take it privately. So why don't the rest of us go into the kitchen and I'll make some hot chocolate. It'll help us all get back to sleep."

Lauren shot Grace a grateful glance. Then, as the others started off, she took a deep breath and told herself that no matter what her father said she wouldn't let it upset her.

Picking up the receiver, she took another deep breath for good measure and said, "Hi, Dad."

"Lauren, you took forever getting to the phone. Are you all right?"

"Yes. Why wouldn't I be?"

She could hear him assuring her mother she was fine, then he got back to her. "Why wouldn't you be?" he repeated. "Have you forgotten you could be the target of that lunatic criminal of Elliot's?"

"Of course not," she said, although she really didn't think there was much chance of the lunatic targeting *her*.

"Then didn't it occur to you," her father asked, "that your mother and I would worry when you didn't phone?"

"When I didn't phone?" She was supposed to have phoned?

"About dinner," her father elaborated. "I told you Marisa invited herself, remember?"

Oh, Lord, dinner at her parents with her sister. She'd promised to call her mother and confirm. Then Billy and Hoops had shown up and she'd forgotten all about it.

"Oh, Dad, I'm sorry. I really am. It completely slipped my mind."

"I see," he said stonily. "Well, we had no way of knowing it had completely slipped your mind. So when you didn't phone, we started thinking something might have happened to you and called your apartment. Then we started trying your cell phone, but that didn't get us anywhere, either."

"It's not working. I forgot to charge it."

"She forgot to charge it," her father muttered to her mother. "Well, we had no way of knowing that, either," he continued on to Lauren. "So, eventually, I called Rosalie, to see if anything had happened at the office. And when she told me where you'd gone..."

Lauren grimaced, imagining the third degree he must have given Rosalie to make her tell. She'd never have willingly volunteered the information. She'd seen enough of Roger Van Slyke to know he'd think taking off for Eagles Roost was a harebrained idea.

"When she told me," he was continuing, "that you'd headed off to the middle of nowhere with a couple of that Sullivan man's criminals-in-training, it certainly did nothing to relieve our minds."

"Dad, Sully's kids are *not* criminals-in-training. They're boys from problem home situations. They're not problems themselves."

"No? You must be forgetting about the one who robbed the bank, then, but let's not get into that at the moment."

Lauren began massaging the right side of her neck where she always felt tension first. It was supposed to be mothers who were the experts at making their children feel guilty, but that wasn't the way it worked in her case.

"By the time I finally called information and got this number, your mother and I were sure you were lying in a ditch somewhere," her father went on, "so I called Sullivan to find out what time you'd left—as a prelude to calling the state police. But what do I find out? That you're spending the night under the same roof as that ex-con! What in the name of God possessed you to do that?"

"Dad, I didn't have much choice. I ran out of gas and the gas station was closed. So what should I have done? Slept in the car?"

"You ran out of gas? Oh, so that's the real story. Sullivan said you'd had car trouble, but I should have known the car wasn't to blame."

Lauren began to massage harder, wishing she hadn't mentioned the gas and wondering if Sully had intentionally tried to help her save face.

She took a few more deep breaths, sure that if her father said one more word she'd end up yelling that she was thirty years old, not twelve. Then she heard her mother saying, "Roger, for goodness' sake, give me that phone."

"Darling," she said, coming on the line, "you're absolutely certain you're all right?"

"Positive," Lauren assured her, immediately starting to breathe a little more easily. She adored her mother, and there was never the sort of tension between them that seemed so frequent with her father. "And I really am sorry I forgot to call," she added.

"Don't worry about it, dear. We all forget things sometimes. And don't be upset with your father. He only sounded angry because he's been so worried about you."

"Yes...yes, I know." But, dammit, she also knew he'd only been so worried because he didn't believe she was a competent adult.

"Lauren, phone us when you get home, will you? Just to check in? You'll be coming back first thing in the morning?"

"Yes, first thing in the morning."

"Well, drive safely, darling."

"I will. Night, Mom."

Lauren had barely hung up before Otis came walking out of the bedroom wing. She was almost afraid to ask if Sully was all right, but when she did, the nod she got in response sent relief rushing through her.

"I guess I'm hardly his favorite person, though," she said.

Otis shot her a wry look. "Kneeing a man in the groin isn't exactly the recommended way to his heart."

"No...of course not." And Otis had just confirmed what she'd already been sure of. Sully was back to hating her again—which made her feel worse than she'd have imagined.

"When Grace finishes in the kitchen," Otis said, heading for the front door, "tell her I've gone back to the cottage, huh? If we're going to be driving all day, I'd like to get a little more sleep first."

He'd barely left before the kitchen door opened and Grace was herding the boys off to bed again. Then she brought a mug of hot chocolate over to Lauren, saying, "I thought you might like this."

"Thanks. And Otis asked me to tell you he's gone back to the cottage."

"Well, I'm on my way there, too. But is everything okay? No family emergency or anything?"

"No, it was really just a little mix-up, but my parents worked themselves into a panic."

"Ahh. Well, parents never stop thinking of their children as children, do they." Grace took a couple of tentative steps toward the door, then stopped. "Lauren, I hope you won't think I'm sticking my nose where it doesn't belong, but when we were in the kitchen the boys were telling me about hearing you screaming and finding Sully on the floor."

"Oh," she murmured, feeling like an idiot all over again.

"And Freckles said he heard you call Sully the barber of On," Grace added.

When Lauren looked at her uncertainly, she smiled. "You'll love hearing the way they figured that one out. They decided On must be a place—like Oz. And that the guy in charge there must be a barber, instead of a wizard. They did think it was a strange thing to be calling Sully, though—couldn't really come up with an explanation for that. But after I sounded it out in my head a few times, I decided you actually might have been calling him a barbarian. Was I right?''

Lauren simply nodded, wishing she could erase the entire episode.

"So I assume there was some initial confusion about what he was doing in your room?"

"Initial confusion," she repeated, thinking Grace deserved an award for understatement. "Yes, that would certainly be one way of putting it. I realize now that it was dark and he just touched the wrong place, but at the time I... misjudged his intentions."

"Yes, I can see how you would. I wanted to be sure, though, that you realize those kinds of intentions would never even cross Sully's mind. He's a very special man—honest and trustworthy and... Well, Otis and I love him like a son, so I didn't want you thinking poorly of him when you shouldn't."

"I don't. It was just waking up suddenly, in a strange place, with a man right there. But I guess that only goes to show my father was right. I shouldn't have stayed here."

"Of course you should have. Given the situation, it was the only sensible thing to do."

Lauren managed a weak smile. "That definitely isn't the way my father saw it."

"Well, people don't always see things the same way. But you have to make your own decisions, don't you. Without worrying too much what other people will think. Because it's you who has to live with the results of those decisions, and... Well, that's enough philosophy for tonight, so I'll see you in the morning."

Once Lauren was alone, she sat down on a couch and sipped her hot chocolate—wishing again that she could erase what had happened. She couldn't, though. All she could do was have another try at apologizing to Sully. The only question was when. Should she go and find Sully now, or would it be safer to steer clear until morning?

She'd pretty well decided on the steering clear route when he struck it from her list of options by appearing.

She eyed him uneasily. He was still wearing the navy bathrobe he'd had on earlier. And she, of course, was still wearing Grace's nightgown and robe. Under different circumstances that might have lent the scene a sense of intimacy, but the only sense she had at the moment was that Jack Sullivan was a very unhappy camper.

When he started toward her she was relieved to see he wasn't having difficulty walking. But her relief was short-lived, because the closer he got the more angry he seemed.

Not that she could blame him for being upset. She just wished he didn't look as if he'd rather have found anyone else in the world sitting in his lounge.

Lord, never mind any*one* else. He looked as if he'd have preferred to find a Jurassic Park velociraptor.

He sat down on the end of the couch, leaving a good three feet between them—undoubtedly because he'd decided she represented a deadly threat to his well-being. Or, at the very least to his manhood.

When he opened his mouth to speak, she wouldn't have been surprised if he'd ordered her to get out of the lodge right this minute. She certainly wasn't expecting him to say what he did.

CHAPTER SEVEN

MORE CAR TROUBLE

"BEFORE I GO BACK to bed," Sully said, looking warily at Lauren, "I want the answer to a question. Why the hell did you move the floor lamp?" Damned if he was going to lie awake the rest of the night trying to figure out that little mystery.

She cleared her throat, but instead of saying anything she simply took a sip from the mug she was holding. It drew his attention to her mouth—which even without lipstick was full and luscious-looking.

He forced his eyes from her lips and waited for her answer. Now that the pain had subsided and he'd put things into perspective, he could see why she'd reacted the way she had. Hell, if their roles had been reversed, if he'd woken up to find Lauren with her hand on his privates, what conclusion would he have jumped to?

Of course, he'd have been more inclined to haul her into bed with him than to start screaming, but that was beside the point. The point was that if she'd left the lamp where it belonged, he'd have turned it on and never made his blunder. And why she'd moved it was completely beyond him.

"You did have a reason, didn't you?" he pressed. "It wasn't just some random senseless act, was it?"

"You'll think the reason's crazy," she said.

Now why, he silently asked, *doesn't that surprise me?* "Try me," he said aloud.

She gave a resigned shrug that for some reason he found absurdly touching. With her honey-gold hair still tousled from sleep, no makeup, and wrapped in Grace's long pink robe, she seemed more like a little girl than a grown woman. Except, of course, there were clearly breasts beneath that robe.

He looked away from them and back up at her face, but he'd already begun remembering how warm and firm and perfect her breast had felt beneath his hand. Just the recollection was enough to arouse him.

"I thought it was a man," she murmured.

"Pardon me?"

"The floor lamp. I thought it was a man."

"Oh," he said, managing to stop himself from asking if anything else in the room had taken on human form. But every time he started forgetting what a screwball she was she either said or did something to remind him.

"I must have rolled over just as I was falling asleep," she elaborated, "and when I caught a glimpse of its shape standing there in the dark, I almost screamed."

"Because you thought it was a man."

"Exactly. I mean, I only thought that for a second, but I didn't want it to happen again, in case I did scream and wake somebody. So I moved it back behind the chair, where it was out of my line of vision. But then...well, then I ended up screaming and waking everyone, anyway, didn't I. Sully, I'm awfully sorry about what happened. I truly am. But I'm an incredibly sound sleeper, and I don't think clearly when I first wake up. Especially not if I'm wakened suddenly. So...well, I really am very sorry."

He'd have jumped in and stopped her mid-apology, but she'd taken him by surprise. After all, he should never have just groped at her, so he was at least partly to blame. And he'd been thinking she had to figure he was *entirely* to blame.

When she finished and sat gazing at him with those big blue eyes, something in her expression kept him from saying anything right away.

She looked as if it was incredibly important to her that he really believed she was sorry, and that gave him the strangest feeling. There hadn't been many people in his life who'd ever given a damn about whether he believed what they told him or not. Usually, you had to care about a person before things like that mattered, and the people who'd cared about him had been few and far between.

Which meant he had to be wrong about the look in Lauren Van Slyke's eyes, because why would it matter to her if he believed her?

It wouldn't, he told himself logically. But for some inexplicable reason, he wished it did.

"So?" she said quietly. "Apology accepted?"

"Sure. It was at least half my fault, anyway."

That made her smile, and he couldn't help thinking she was extremely beautiful when she smiled. Then he couldn't help wondering what it would be like to wake up beside a woman who looked as good as she did in the middle of the night.

He knew it was a very dangerous thing to be wondering about, but he couldn't seem to stop.

THE LONGER LAUREN sat on the couch with Sully, the clearer it became that—insane as it seemed—he was thinking of kissing her.

And that idea...well, she certainly didn't intend to let him. It could only be lust that was making him think along those lines, and close encounters of the lusty kind just weren't her style.

She pulled Grace's robe more tightly around her, despite the fact that his gaze was making her very hot. Then, deciding that looking at him really wasn't the best thing to be doing at the moment, she forced her eyes down to the couch—and discovered that the distance between them had shrunk.

She couldn't remember either of them moving, but one of them must have because that space was no longer nearly large enough for comfort. "Well," she murmured, "if we don't go back to bed soon, it'll hardly be worthwhile."

"Right," he agreed.

Neither of them, though, made a move to stand up. Then they both did. At exactly the same instant. Half an instant after that, the top of her head banged the bottom of his chin.

They collided with a solid smacking sound and Sully sat back down. Fast.

"Oh, Lord," she whispered, her fingers flying to his jaw. "Oh, Lord, I've hurt you again."

"No, I'm okay. How about your head?"

"Fine, just fine." Actually, it was a wonder she was still standing, because she was seeing stars. Sully's jaw had felt as hard as granite.

Realizing her fingers were resting against it, she tentatively brushed them across his skin—just to check whether his jaw really *was* as hard as granite.

It was, and the roughness of his dark stubble electrified her fingertips. Then he covered her fingers with his hand and his touch electrified her entire body.

He gazed into her eyes for an eternity of seconds, while the probability of her melting into a pool of desire increased with each second. Her pulse was racing, and she'd just reached the point of wanting to kiss him as much as he seemed to want to kiss her when he draped his arm around her waist and gently pulled her onto his lap.

"Stop," she said shakily. He might have her more than a little aroused, but she hadn't completely lost her self-control. "Look, Sully," she managed to say, "we hardly know each other."

He gave her a lazy smile that sent even more sparks of excitement through her. "That's true," he said softly. "But you seem to have grown on me awfully quickly."

She eyed him uncertainly, remembering Grace had told her he was honest and trustworthy. And he did sound sincere, as if he really wasn't just handing her a line.

Then he smiled a second time, virtually completing her meltdown, and said, "You know, in your own peculiar way, you're one hell of a woman."

She wasn't sure she liked the *peculiar way* part of that remark. But she did like the *hell of a woman* part. And she wanted to kiss him a whole lot more than she wanted to debate semantics, so she trailed her fingers down his neck and leaned a little closer to those sensuous lips of his.

The moment they touched hers, she knew this was going to be the kind of kiss dreams are made of. It started out slow and tantalizing, his mouth barely grazing hers, his tongue moving lightly over her lips.

She smoothed her hands down his back, caressing some of those muscles she hadn't been able to keep her eyes off when they'd been making the bed. They felt every bit as hard and sexy as she'd imagined they would.

Then she forgot all about his muscles because he was doing such incredibly enticing things with his tongue. When he slid it slowly across her lower lip, from one corner to the other, delight tingled her nerve endings. When it moved back across her upper lip with even more exquisite slowness, her body heat broke the 110-degree mark.

He gradually deepened the kiss until it was so arousing she stopped wondering exactly what he'd meant by her *own peculiar way.* So arousing she stopped wondering about anything.

All kinds of unruly sensations danced inside her while she buried her fingers in his long hair and kissed him back—every bit as passionately as he was kissing her. She'd never before been kissed so thoroughly that it made her lips numb, and she wanted to make the best of it.

THE LONGER SULLY KISSED Lauren, the more certain he was that if he were struck dead mid-kiss he'd die a happy man. She felt so soft and warm he wanted to hold her forever.

The smell of that sinfully sexy perfume was wrapping him in a delicious haze, while her kisses were nothing short of incredible. They tasted of hot chocolate and hot passion, and there wasn't the slightest trace of Ice Princess in her when she kissed. There was nothing but pure, desirable woman, and that was making him positively breathless.

He tried reminding himself that they were as mismatched as two people could possibly be. His self refused to listen, though, so he gave up and went on kissing her—until his need got so urgent he had to either stop or do more than just kiss her.

He stopped. It practically killed him, but he did. He might be almost senseless with wanting her, but he hadn't forgotten that knee to the groin and he sure as hell wasn't risking another one. If there was going to be anything more than kissing, she'd have to initiate it.

When she didn't, that practically killed him, too.

LAUREN LAY AWAKE in Sully's bed, alone with her thoughts—every last one of which was about Jack Sullivan. For a woman who'd never been prone to sexual fantasies, she was certainly making up for lost time.

In the darkness of his room, she began wondering, again, why he'd stopped kissing her. Most men would have taken that little session just as far as the woman involved let them. And Lauren hated to admit how far that might have been in her case. She'd never had a one-night stand in her life, but if Sully hadn't stopped things when he had . . .

It was extremely fortunate, she told herself sternly, that he had. Because in the heat of passion she hadn't been thinking in terms of a one-night stand—hadn't been thinking she'd probably never see him again after she went home. To be truthful, she hadn't been thinking. Period. So it was just as well one of them had exercised some self-control.

She drifted in and out of sleep for the rest of the night, dreaming about Sully. They were absolutely scrumptious dreams, but were distinctly marred by the prospect of never seeing him again. It wasn't a prospect she fancied.

A man like Jack Sullivan didn't walk into her life every day. In fact, no man like him had ever walked into it before, so the thought of his walking right back out again wasn't a happy one.

The more she considered that, the more she realized she'd be a fool to let it happen. Not that she imagined there could ever be anything serious between them, but if they enjoyed each other's company, what harm would there be in getting together now and then?

She was assuming he'd want to, of course, but since he thought she was one hell of a woman it seemed like a pretty safe assumption. Which meant all they'd have to do was discuss the logistics.

IT WASN'T 7:00 a.m. before faint sounds drifting into the bedroom told Lauren that other people were up and moving around the lodge. She had a quick shower, then started getting dressed—blessing Grace for thinking to give her clean clothes.

The blue cotton shirt was a perfect fit, but when she pulled on the faded jeans it was obvious that either Grace was even thinner than she looked or the jeans were from still skinnier years.

She finally managed to wiggle her way into them, got them zipped up by sucking in her breath, then slipped on the deck shoes and headed for the kitchen—where she found the kids already at the table and Sully serving bacon and eggs.

He was wearing jeans and a T-shirt again. A jade green one today. His dark hair was still damp from the shower, and it was curling so enticingly at the bottom of his neck that she wanted to run her fingers through it.

The boys all said good-morning to her, but it was Sully's "'Morning" that made her heartbeat accelerate and the blood in her veins feel warmer.

Then he gave her a smile that upped the warmth of her blood to a sizzle.

"You haven't missed saying goodbye to Otis and Grace," he told her. "They'll be in for breakfast in a minute, so have a seat."

As she'd discovered at dinner last night, eating a meal with five boys wasn't a peaceful, well-ordered experience. It was difficult to pay attention to their chatter and think at the same time. Still, all during breakfast, and then while everyone was saying their farewells to the Plavsics, in the back of her mind she was trying to decide on the best way of beginning the conversation with Sully. Should she just come right out and invite him to something in Manhattan? Or should she kind of ease into the topic of seeing him again?

Otis was already in the car when Grace gave her a warm hug and said, "I hope this isn't the last we'll see of you, dear."

Lauren hugged the older woman back, hoping exactly the same thing.

As the Plavsics's car disappeared from sight, Sully turned to the boys. "Okay, I'm going to take Lauren into North Head to get some gas now, so I want you kids to clean up the kitchen while I'm gone. Terry, you supervise today."

"Are you coming back, Lauren?" Billy asked. "After you get the gas?"

Before she could open her mouth, Sully said, "No, she's in a hurry to get home. So you all say goodbye to her now."

Lauren tried to catch his eye. It was only eight-thirty, so there was no reason she couldn't stay for a few more hours. He didn't look her way, though, and the boys had all started talking.

"You should come visit us again sometime," Freckles told her.

The others all said, "Yeah," or nodded in agreement. All the others except Sully, she noted uneasily.

One of the twins—she was pretty sure it was Terry—wanted a goodbye hug. When the other four boys didn't seem quite certain, she just shook hands with them and patted the dog.

Eventually, Sully dragged her away and hustled her into the minivan. While she was rolling down her window to let in some fresh air, he called to the boys that he'd only be about half an hour.

Deciding that ruled out the easing-into-the-topic approach, the minute he put the van into drive she said, "I really *would* like to come back and visit everyone sometime. It's beautiful up here."

"Yeah, it is, isn't it," he agreed, not taking his eyes off the road.

She waited, but he didn't say anything more. That made her decidedly uncertain. Surely he wanted to see her again . . . didn't he?

No subtle way of asking popped into her head, so as they neared the end of his private road, she said, "Do you come into the city very often?"

Instead of answering, he pulled the van to a stop, shifted into park, then finally looked at her. "Lauren, about last night..."

"Yes?" she murmured, her heart beating double time.

"You're a very difficult woman to resist."

"Yes?" she said again. That had sounded promising, but there was nothing promising in the way Sully was staring straight ahead now, instead of meeting her gaze.

"Look," he said after an interminable silence, "I knew at the time I was out of line but...well, as I said, you're very difficult to resist. The thing is, though...Lauren, it's got to be as obvious to you as it is to me that we live in entirely different worlds."

She simply stared at him. He was giving her the brush-off.

"So there's no point," he continued, "in trying to pretend there's any possible way that... We both know better than to even think about it."

His words cut surprisingly deeply. She forced her eyes away from him, telling herself it really didn't matter whether he wanted to see her again or not. She'd only been thinking about some sort of casual relationship, anyway. Deep down, though, she couldn't help wondering if she'd been thinking about something more.

"It's not that I don't like you," he mumbled at the steering wheel. "I wasn't lying about that last night, I really wasn't. It's just that we'd be dumb to figure..."

"Dumb," she repeated woodenly. "Well...we definitely wouldn't want to be dumb."

Sully nodded. "I knew you'd see it that way, too."

"Yes. Certainly. What other way is there to see it?"

When he shoved the van back into drive and they started off once more, her emotions began teeter-tottering between hurt and anger—with a large dollop of humiliation thrown in for good measure.

She'd made a total fool of herself with her *dumb* idea, because Sully didn't like her at all. Telling her he did had been an out-and-out lie.

Just as she was convincing herself that a man like Jack Sullivan wasn't worth wasting another thought on, he muttered, "Dammit to hell," and swerved to a stop on the shoulder.

"What?" she said. "What's wrong?"

"See that sign?" He gestured toward a sign nailed to a huge tree. It read No Trespassing in big red hand-painted letters, and whoever had created it had started off with too much paint on their brush, because the *N* had sloppy tails of red running down from either side.

"Your car," Sully said, "ran out of gas almost exactly at that sign. Which means somebody stole it."

Even though he looked so serious that it started a nervous fluttering in her stomach, she said, "Don't be silly."

She glanced forward along the empty road, then backward. Her car definitely wasn't in sight, but it had to be along here somewhere. Surely most cars were stolen off big city streets, not off back roads in the country. And how could anyone steal a car that was out of gas? Hot-wiring it wouldn't have done any good.

But when she said that to Sully, he shook his head. "All somebody had to do was syphon gas from the car they were driving. Or maybe they just towed yours away.''

"Oh," she murmured, suddenly not so certain he wasn't right. "But couldn't you be wrong about where the car was? I mean, that isn't the only No Trespassing sign along this road, is it?"

"It's the only one with a messed-up letter like that," he muttered. "We'll have to go back to the lodge and call the police."

His words caused the nervous fluttering in her stomach to turn into a horrible sinking feeling. She certainly didn't want to go back to the lodge with him. But he was already wheeling the van around.

After considering the situation for a few seconds, she decided she'd deal with the police later. As soon as they got back to the lodge, she'd arrange to get herself out of there just as quickly as she could. And in the meantime, she wouldn't think one single more thought about Sully. Racking her brain for another subject to concentrate on, she decided her missing Mercedes would be an appropriate one.

She knew the odds were awfully high that she'd never see it again. And they were even higher that her father would have a fit when he learned it had been stolen.

She swore silently to herself, wishing she hadn't decided to think about her car, after all. Because now she was thinking that her father would be certain she'd left it unlocked with the keys in the ignition.

CHAPTER EIGHT

BILLY THE KID RIDES AGAIN

SULLY SURREPTITIOUSLY glanced across the van at Lauren, wondering if he should say anything more before they got back to the lodge or just leave bad enough alone.

He knew he'd hurt her feelings. But when she'd started hinting about seeing each other again he hadn't known what to say, because he'd only be asking for trouble if he went along with the idea.

There was something about her crazy, ditzy ways— not to mention her looks and those million-dollar kisses—that made Lauren Van Slyke a woman some men would fall hard for. And he had a horrible suspicion he was one of those men.

If he started seeing her, it wouldn't be long before he was in deeper than he'd ever been with a woman. Then, after he was, she'd turn around and vanish into the arms of some Manhattan zillionaire. Someone she had a ton of things in common with. So why would he intentionally go looking to get hurt?

There was no way a man with his past could ever have a future that included a woman like her. Which meant the only smart thing to do was exactly what he'd done.

Exhaling slowly, he congratulated himself on the soundness of his reasoning. Then he stole another look at Lauren and knew that even though there was no problem with his reasoning, there was still a problem.

It was sitting in the seat right beside him, looking so desirable that he felt like pitching his damn reasoning out the window.

THE MINUTE LAUREN and Sully walked back into the lodge the kids appeared from the kitchen. When she told them why she was back, their excitement level jumped perceptibly.

"What are you going to do, Sully?" Freckles asked.

"Call the police."

"No, it's all right," she said as he reached for the phone. "It's my car, so I should look after things. But I'll get in touch with the police later. Or maybe my insurance agent can deal with them on Monday. Right now, though, I'd like to make another call if you don't mind."

"To?"

"I'd like to phone for a taxi. Is there one in North Head?"

"Not one you'd want to ride very far in."

"Where do you want to go, Lauren?" Billy asked. "Sully can take you."

She managed a smile for him. "Well, it would be asking a bit much of him to drive me all the way home."

"Home to Manhattan?"

"Yes."

"You could pay a taxi to take you all the way there?" Hoops put in, his eyes wide. "But that takes hours. It would cost a million dollars."

"Well . . . it really wouldn't be *that* much."

"Lauren?" Sully said.

"Yes?" When she glanced at him he was looking angry, which really annoyed her. Why on earth should he be angry at her when she was trying to get out of here just as quickly as possible?

"This is officially the kids' phone," he said. "Let's go use the line in my office."

"It's okay, Sully," Billy quickly told him. "We don't mind Lauren usin' this one."

"Thanks, but I think we'll head down to my office."

Before she could object, he took her by the arm and propelled her out of the lounge.

"What was that all about?" she demanded the second they were out of the boys' hearing.

He didn't utter a word until he'd closed the door of his suite behind them. Then he turned and graced her with one of his highest-voltage glares.

She hadn't hit anyone since grade one, when she'd whacked Alexandra Throckmorton over the head with a sand shovel, but that glare of Sully's made her want to smack him so hard his ears would ring.

Instead, she planted her fists on her hips and glared back at him, snapping, "What's your problem now?"

"You're my problem," he snapped back. "Look, I know that car can't be very important to you. I realize you could go out tomorrow and buy a dozen Mercedes, so reporting its theft doesn't seem very urgent. But I try to teach my kids by example. Teach them things like respect for the law. Teach them the

police are there to help when people run into trouble.
That if some punk steals her car, a law-abiding citizen reports it to the cops immediately. Even if she's
got enough money in her purse to take a damn four-hour taxi ride. Even if she's got some insurance agent
who'd report the theft for her on Monday."

By the time he finished his lecture, Lauren's urge to
smack him had gotten even stronger. Certain that if
she watched him glare at her for even two more seconds it would become overwhelming, she walked over
to the window and stood staring out, his words replaying in her head.

Finally, she decided she had to give him credit—
grudgingly perhaps, but she still had to give it to
him—for thinking about setting an example for the
boys.

"Well?" he said at last.

She turned and looked at him again. "I was perfectly aware," she said coldly, "that something like a
car theft should be reported immediately. However,
since you were so obviously dying to get rid of me, I
thought speeding things along would be a good idea."

"Dammit, Lauren, I wasn't *dying* to get rid of you.
It was just—"

"Nevertheless," she interrupted, "since you're
apparently even more concerned about my setting a
good example, don't you think it would be better if
we went back to the lounge? So the boys can listen
while I phone the police?"

She started across the room again, her anger already beginning to fade a little. Oh, she was hardly
feeling friendly. Not when she was still hurting from
that brush-off.

But she'd get over it in no time. After all, it wasn't as if she'd fallen madly in love with Sully. She'd merely fallen in like with him. And at the moment she was wondering how even that could have happened.

A few seconds later she told herself she was being childish. She'd fallen in like with him for a lot of reasons, even if none of them mattered at this point. And instead of thinking the way a thirteen-year-old would, she should try to stop blaming him for not liking her back.

After all, people couldn't force themselves to like other people.

As she neared the door, he reached to open it. Just as he did, the phone rang in his office.

"Wait a sec," he said. "I've been expecting a call and this could be it."

She stood where she was for a moment, then her curiosity got the better of her so she followed him into the other room.

"Ben," he said after his initial hello, "I thought it might be you."

He listened a minute, then muttered, "Why the hell would he change his mind?

"No," he said after another minute. "No, there's no way I'd ever sell the lodge, itself. So tell him that and see where it gets us, okay?"

"Problems?" she asked as he hung up. Since she'd been blatantly eavesdropping, there was no point pretending she wasn't curious.

He shrugged. "That was a fellow named Ben Ludendorf, a lawyer who lives in North Head. He handles most of the real estate transactions around here, and last year he had some client who wanted to buy Eagles Roost."

"You were thinking of selling?"

"No. They hoped I might be tempted, but I wasn't. The other day, though, I started thinking I might sell some acreage over on the far side of the lake. So I asked Ben to talk to his client and see if he'd be interested."

"Ahh." She felt a strong twinge of guilt. She'd bet that idea was directly related to Sully's losing his funding.

"The weird thing, though," he went on, "is that last year the guy had no interest in the lodge or the cottage—only in the land. In fact, he told Ben that if he bought the place he'd tear down the buildings and put up something modern. Now Ben says there could still be a deal, but not unless it's for everything."

"And that's out of the question."

"Absolutely. A piece of the land would be one thing, but I could never sell the whole place. Frank Watson left it to me because he knew how much I loved it, so selling it would be like betraying him. Which means there's nothing to do but wait and see if Ben's client is really firm on wanting all or nothing."

"You don't know who the client is?"

"No. I asked last year, but Ben said the guy didn't want me to know."

"That's too bad. I mean, my brother the lawyer would kill me for saying this, but I think that when a lawyer's negotiating a deal... Or maybe I should just say that sometimes *any* middleman only adds complications. It's often far better if the two people involved deal with each other directly."

Sully nodded. "That might be true, but there's not much I can do about it. If Ben wouldn't tell me last year who the guy is, he's not going to tell me now."

BILLY THE KID sat crouched under the open office window until he heard Sully and Lauren going through to the bedroom. Then he pushed off and raced for the front of the lodge.

If he ran real fast, he could almost always make it back into the lounge before Sully got there. Not that he spied very often. He knew if he ever got caught Sully'd kill him.

But if he really wanted to be a private eye when he grew up, he had to practice stuff like spying. And today he'd needed to know what was going on, 'cuz his plan didn't seem to be working.

He'd thought it was a real good sign when Lauren came back with Sully, but he'd been wrong. They just didn't seem to be liking each other the way he'd figured it would happen.

Oh, they'd been talking okay just now, but when they'd first got back they'd looked mad as hell at each other. And if they didn't start liking each other before she went home she'd never give Sully the money.

He zipped around the corner of the lodge, worrying some more that he'd been wrong. That Lauren didn't really know how to make guys like her better than his sisters did.

He couldn't figure out why she wouldn't, being pretty and rich and all, but even his sisters knew you didn't make a guy like you by doing stuff like kneeing him.

When he charged up onto the porch and through the front door, the other kids all turned to him, waiting for him to tell them what was happening.

He glanced toward the bedroom wing. There was no sign of Sully and Lauren yet, so they must have stopped in his bedroom to talk some more. Maybe that was good, and he wasn't giving up on his plan till Lauren left and it was too late. But he was thinking they needed a backup one. Just in case.

"So?" Freckles said.

"So," he said, glancing over to check if the coast was still clear, "Sully's got another way to get the money. But he needs help with it. And here's what we gotta do."

SULLY WAS HALF listening to Lauren finish her call to the police and half watching the boys, trying to figure out what they had up their collective sleeve. They were all looking so innocent that something had to be going on.

Whatever it was, he told himself as Lauren hung up, he'd likely find out soon.

"I'm afraid," she said, glancing at him uneasily, "the phone call wasn't enough. They want to send an officer to talk to me because the car's a little pricey."

He nodded, resisting the urge to point out that *incredibly* pricey would be more accurate.

"They said," she went on, looking even more uneasy, "they probably wouldn't be able to get anyone here for a few hours. Between one and two, they said, and it's not even ten yet. So I guess you're stuck with me a little longer."

"That's all right."

Her expression said she didn't believe that for a minute, said she was still convinced he was dying to get rid of her—which made him feel like a real jerk. Especially since she'd stopped being snippy to him. In fact, she'd almost gotten back to acting as if she liked him.

That had him thinking that maybe, if they had some time without the boys around, he'd try to straighten things out with her. Or maybe he wouldn't. He'd have to give the idea some hard thought, because he suspected it could be a dangerous move.

"Lauren?" Billy said. "What if the cops don't get here when they said. What if there's an accident on the highway or somethin' and they're way later? Then you'd have to stay the night again, huh?"

"No, I definitely won't be doing that, Billy."

"Oh." He glanced at Hoops, his look plainly saying, *Over to you, buddy.*

Sully leaned back on the couch and waited. He'd been right. They were up to something, and he was about to find out what.

"Sully?" Hoops said, "'Member yesterday? 'Member you told Billy and me to think about our punishment?"

He nodded.

"Well, we was thinking maybe it could be cleaning out the garage? Getting all the junk out of there and ready to take to the dump?"

"And Freckles and Terry and me should help," Tony jumped in. "'Cuz we knew they went to Manhattan but we didn't tell you."

Sully rubbed his jaw. The hidden agenda was obvious now, and it was the same as last night's. They figured if they all cleared out, leaving him alone with Lauren, he'd end up getting his funding back.

One day soon, he was going to have to sit the five of them down and have a talk about how things worked in the real world. But he was hardly going to do it right now, in front of Lauren.

As far as their suggestion went, though, he'd be crazy to pass on it. That was a four-car garage, and at the moment there was barely room to get his minivan and Otis's Dodge in it at the same time.

"All right," he said, nodding slowly. "That sounds like a fair punishment."

The boys exchanged self-congratulatory glances, then Billy said, "Sully, we're gonna work straight through till we're done, okay?"

"We'll grab some stuff from the kitchen," Freckles put in, "and eat lunch in the garage."

"So it'll be faster," Billy added. "And could you not come out there till we're finished and come get you? 'Cuz that way you'll be real surprised when you see it."

Sully nodded again. He doubted there was any way they'd get the whole job done in one day, but usually it was better to let kids discover for themselves that they'd misestimated something.

As the boys trooped out, Lauren glanced at him, saying, "Do you mind if I make a couple of other calls? Last night, I promised my mother I'd check in when I got home, and I don't want to take any chances on them panicking again."

"Sure. No problem." He pushed himself up off the couch. "I'm going to make coffee. Would you like some?"

She said that coffee sounded good and reached for the phone. Then, before he got to the kitchen door, he could hear her talking to an operator, putting the first call on her card.

Walking into the other room, he exhaled slowly. He knew she was only being thoughtful, but he wasn't so damn poor he couldn't pay for a couple of long distance calls. And her charging them, as if she figured he didn't have two cents, bothered him. He tried telling himself that was a stupid way to feel, but it didn't help.

He reached for the coffee, thinking that a few other things had started bothering him since she'd come here. Things he normally never gave a second thought. Things like not having a university degree and being an ex-con. If it weren't for things like that, just possibly...

He shook his head. They were facts. So the sooner she went back to her world, the better.

When he took the coffee into the lounge she was still on the phone, so he put hers on the table in front of her. Then he sat down across from her and tried not to stare. But she was sitting sideways with her legs curled up beneath her, which made those tight jeans seem even tighter. And that made what he could see of her cute little behind seem impossibly cuter.

She finally hung up and smiled. "That was my friend Jenny, whose apartment is across the hall from mine. She's going to look in again and make sure the cat's still doing okay. But I'm really going to have to decide on a name for him, aren't I. It seems wrong to just keep calling him the cat."

Sully ran his finger down the scratch on his arm. "I think you should call him Killer."

She smiled again. "I think maybe you're right, although it's not exactly a classy name."

"Lauren, at the risk of stating the obvious, he's not exactly a classy cat."

When she laughed, it started a warm feeling inside him. She had the nicest laugh he'd ever heard, so quiet and velvety it reminded him of a cat's purr.

Not Killer's purr, though. From what he'd seen, Killer was a howler, not a purrer.

"And what did your parents have to say?" he asked after a minute.

She shrugged. "My dad went ballistic, because when I was talking about buying that car he told me not to—said it would be a car thief's dream. And obviously, he was right."

"What about your mother?"

"She was mostly worried about how I was going to get home. Suggested I have a limo drive up from the city instead of calling a taxi from around here. She said that at least she'd trust the driver, then. So I did that. He'll be here at three."

Sully nodded, thinking he'd never been inside a limo in his life.

"I'm just lucky," Lauren went on, "that my parents are spending the rest of the weekend in the country with friends. If they were staying home, they'd probably have asked me to check in every hour on the hour until I was safely back in my apartment."

"I guess that thing with your brother has them really upset."

She gave another little shrug. "That's made it worse, but they're always worrying about me. They'll probably still be doing it when I'm old and gray."

He smiled, trying to imagine her as old and gray. The picture that came to him, though, was absolutely crazy. She was old and gray, all right, but she was also sitting in an Adirondack chair on the porch of Eagles Roost—beside an old and gray man who looked suspiciously like him.

Forcing that picture from his mind, he replaced it with a realistic one of her getting out of her limo and walking into her ritzy apartment building. Once he had that in focus, though, he couldn't help noticing how enticingly her hips were swaying as she walked.

WHEN BILLY GOT to where it would be about a five-minute run from Mr. Ludendorf's, he stopped his bike and waved the twins to pull up behind him.

"Okay," he said to Terry when they had, "lie your bike on its side and sit down beside it. And you know what to say when he comes, right? You say you banged your head when you fell, but you're startin' to feel better now. But if he tries to leave too soon, you gotta pretend to be dizzy or somethin'."

"What if he wants to take me to a doctor?"

"Don't let him. Just keep him here for a while. You can do it. And Tony'll come back with him to help you."

"Billy, I really don't wanna do this," Terry whined for about the hundredth time. "Sully's gonna kill us."

"Do you want to stay at Eagles Roost or not?" Billy snapped. Tony wasn't bad for a ten-year-old, but sometimes Terry was a real pain.

"Of course he does," Tony said. "We all do."

"Well we can't unless Sully gets money from someplace. And you guys heard Lauren say she's goin' home today for sure. So it don't look like he'll get it from her."

"But why do Tony and me have to do this?" Terry sniveled. "Why couldn't Freckles and Hoops?"

"I already told you," Billy said. "'Cuz you two are the youngest. And the younger you are, the easier it is to get someone to help you. And 'cuz they're bigger, so they can get more of the garage cleaned and maybe Sully won't know we were gone."

"He's gonna know."

"Maybe not," Billy insisted. "If we just tell him Mr. Ludendorf phoned and left a message and stuff."

"He's gonna know," Terry said again. "And he's gonna be so mad he'll—"

"Oh, stop being such a baby," Tony muttered.

"I'm not a baby. I'm three hours older than you."

"Then act like it. Let's go, Billy."

"We're all countin' on you, Terry," Billy said. "'Member that," he added, pushing off.

He and Tony rode most of the rest of the way to Mr. Ludendorf's house, then they stopped and he stashed his bike behind a bush.

"Okay," he said once it was out of sight, "you know which door is to his office?"

Tony nodded.

"Okay, then give me time to hide by it, then come ridin' up."

"You really think he works on Saturdays?" Tony said. "You really think he'll be in his office?"

Billy shrugged, trying to look cool. "If he's not in there, go to the front door."

"But then how'll you get into his office?"

"Maybe he won't have the door locked. Or maybe through a window. Private eyes always find a way."

"But you're not really a private eye."

He shrugged again. Maybe he wasn't, but he wanted to be one even more than Hoops wanted to play basketball for the Knicks. And he'd watched a million detective shows on TV, so he knew all about how they did stuff.

"I'll get into the office," he said. "Don't worry."

When Tony nodded again, Billy took off running. He'd just gotten himself hidden—around the corner of the house from the office, where he could peek out far enough to see—before Tony came racing into the drive, the wheels of his bike spitting up gravel.

He hopped off and started yelling, "Mr. Ludendorf! Mr. Ludendorf!" while he ran up to the house.

He was reaching out to knock when the office door opened and Mr. Ludendorf was standing there.

Billy swallowed hard. His stomach felt woozy, but at least the plan was working.

"What's the matter?" Mr. Ludendorf asked. "You're one of Sully's kids, aren't you?"

"Yes, sir," Tony told him. "And I need help. My brother fell off his bike just down the road, and I think he's hurt bad."

"Oh, God, I'll just grab my car keys and we—"

"No, it's not far. Just down the road. We can run there in a minute."

"All right, let's go."

Billy held his breath, hoping the lawyer wouldn't take time to lock the door.

He didn't. He just started off after Tony.

The second they were down the drive, Billy hurried along the side of the house and into the office. Shutting the door fast, he looked around. There was a desk with a computer and stuff, a couple of chairs, a photocopy machine humming in the corner, and two filing cabinets against a wall.

He hurried over to them, trying to decide where he should look first. Under *E* for Eagles Roost? Or under *S* for Sullivan?

Pulling open the drawer labeled *D-G*, he started looking through the *E* files. Lauren had said it would be a lot better if Sully could talk to Mr. Ludendorf's client himself, and the guy's name had to be in these files somewhere. A real detective would find it.

CHAPTER NINE

DECISION TIME

THERE WAS OBVIOUSLY something on Sully's mind, and Lauren wished he'd tell her what it was.

Not that she imagined it was anything she'd like, but she didn't like the way he was looking everywhere except at her and not saying a word, either. She'd been doing her best to be pleasant, while he seemed to be doing his best to make her uncomfortable.

Drinking the last sip of her coffee, she decided that if she didn't speak up they'd be sitting in silence until the police arrived. "Sully?" she said. "Is something wrong?"

He looked at her for a moment, then said, "Do you want to take a walk? It's not far to the lake."

"Sure. I really haven't seen anything except the lodge and the cabin."

When they got outside he glanced over at the garage, saying, "It doesn't sound like there's much activity in there, but I guess the kids must be working."

He didn't say anything more, so she simply walked along with him—across the clearing and into the thick woods where the air smelled of fresh earth and pine trees. It was cooler once they were out of the late morning sun, and the quiet...well, for someone used to the relentless clamor of "the city that never sleeps," the quiet was incredible.

There wasn't a corner of Manhattan that was even remotely like Eagles Roost, and she couldn't help wishing there was. Everyone should have a place like these woods to walk in.

Ahead, through the trees, she caught a glimpse of Hidden Lake, and in another minute they'd reached the shore of a sheltered cove. The water was blue crystal, sunlight shimmering diamonds on its surface.

A weathered wooden boathouse and dock reached out into the water, and beyond the cove the lake sprawled like glass in all directions—the far side visible but distant.

"It's beautiful," she murmured. "Absolutely beautiful. Do you still appreciate that after all these years?"

Sully nodded. "It's funny. I grew up on the streets of the Bronx, but now I can't imagine living anywhere except here."

"No, I can see why." She looked out over the water for a few more seconds, then gazed at him and caught him watching her. Her heart fluttered and she wished it wouldn't. Sully would rather she were long gone, so her heart was being incredibly foolish.

"Look," he said, jamming his hands into the pockets of his jeans. "There's something I want to explain to you."

"Yes?" Gazing at him, she realized his eyes weren't saying he'd rather she were long gone. They were saying he'd put his hands in his pockets to keep from touching her. So if the eyes really were the windows of the soul . . .

She told herself she was misreading what she saw, and waited for him to go on.

"Lauren," he said at last, "when I told you it wouldn't be a good idea to see each other after today..."

"Dumb. You said it would be a dumb idea," she reminded him, feeling hurt all over again and wishing he hadn't started in on this a second time. She'd received his message loud and clear the first time.

"Well look, whatever words I used, I gave you the wrong message. I know you thought I was telling you I didn't like you, but that wasn't it. Because I really do," he added with a smile that made her knees weak.

He liked her after all! The little news flash made her so happy it was ridiculous. But ridiculous or not, she was starting to feel bubbly inside.

Then he burst the bubbles by saying, "And it's because I like you that it's not a good idea for us to see each other again."

She simply stood staring at him—and hoping he never decided to enroll in a Logic 101 course because he'd fail for sure.

Finally, she said, "Let me make sure I'm clear on your thinking. If you *didn't* like me, then it *would* be a good idea for us to see each other again?"

"No, of course not." He gave her another smile. This one seemed puzzled, as if he couldn't understand why she was being so dense.

"Look," she admitted, "I'm missing the point here."

"The point is that you and I have nothing at all in common."

She thought about Logic 101 again and decided he wouldn't have to worry about failing. He'd never even manage to get enrolled. He'd be screened out by an interview or an entrance exam or something, because his reasoning was far too linear to deal with the big picture.

Oh, at first glance, it was clear they didn't have the major, obvious things in common. He wasn't looking beyond that, though, wasn't considering that those weren't always the important things.

She and her ex-husband had come from similar backgrounds, had moved in the same circles, et cetera, et cetera. But those similarities had hardly added up to a happy marriage.

Which wasn't to say she had any ideas about marrying Sully. As she'd been thinking earlier, though, it would be nice to have some sort of relationship with him.

Given the fact that she didn't meet many men she liked, when she met one she did it seemed darned silly to just walk away without seeing...

Without seeing what? a voice in her head demanded.

She wasn't really sure. But she knew she didn't care for the thought of just walking away.

Their last go-around had left her very leery, but she finally asked, "Were you only trying to make me feel better, or do you honestly like me?"

He smiled once more. "I've got my faults, but being a liar isn't one of them. As I said last night, you seem to have grown on me."

She took a deep breath, almost afraid to press, then plunged ahead before she lost her nerve. "Sully, you seem to have grown on me, too. So if you like me and I like you... well, then obviously we like each other.

And in my books that's a pretty good thing to have in common."

"Lauren," he said quietly, "I'm an ex-con and you're a wealthy woman."

"I know that," she said just as quietly.

There it was, then, she thought as she waited for Sully's response. The foremost issue, from his perspective, was that he was an ex-con and she was wealthy. And his laying those cards on the table had her mind racing.

Not that she hadn't been aware of both facts from the beginning. Her trust fund provided her with a far larger monthly income than she spent, and the first time she'd looked at the file on Eagles Roost she'd learned Sully had a record. So if she'd been thinking along the same lines as he'd been . . .

But she hadn't. She hadn't attached particular significance to either fact until he'd put them into juxtaposition like that.

Now that he had, though, she couldn't help seeing that maybe he was right. Maybe the idea of ever getting together again really *was* dumb. After all, precisely where had she expected this . . . whatever it was between them . . . to lead?

Nowhere, she silently answered herself. And since she'd never tried to imagine any long-term future for them, why on earth had she thought prolonging the *whatever* would be a good idea?

It was suddenly clear to her that there was no maybe about this. Sully *was* right. So she'd better tell him that she agreed with him.

She glanced at him again, ready to do just that. But the look in his eyes stopped her in her tracks. His gaze was warm and gentle, and something in it seemed to reach inside her and touch her so deeply she didn't say a word. She merely waited, her chest gradually tightening until she could scarcely breathe.

There was an indefinable quality about this man that made her want to simply remove common sense and logic from the equation. Because, although she barely knew him, she felt as if she knew him incredibly well. And that she was somehow connected to him.

She doubted that made much sense, but it was how she felt. And even if her feelings were downright crazy, she needed time to sort them out.

"You're close to your family," Sully said at last.

"Well . . . yes," she admitted, not liking what she suspected he was thinking. She knew she cared too much about her parents' approval. Her father's in particular. Maybe, though, she should be trying harder to change that. Because something Grace said last night had lodged in her mind.

You have to make your own decisions, she'd pointed out, *without worrying too much what other people will think. Because it's you who has to live with the results of those decisions.*

"Let's just say," Sully went on, "we started seeing each other now and then. How would they feel about it? Your lawyer brother and your artist sister? And your mother who'd worry if you took a taxi home, rather than a limo? And your father who . . . hell, I don't even know what your father does."

"He's the president of Van Slyke Enterprises. And the company does a variety of things."

Sully nodded slowly. "Does it do them out of that big building on Madison Avenue? The one your office is in? The one with the Van Slyke name over the main entrance?''

"Sully, I don't understand why you're so concerned that my family has money.''

He shrugged. "How would they react if you told them you were seeing me?''

"I don't know," she lied. She knew exactly how each of them would take an announcement like that.

Marisa was liberal enough to be okay with it—or at least to hold off judgment until after she got to know Sully. Elliot would disapprove, but he'd keep his opinion to himself. Her mother would want to lock her in a rubber room until she came to her senses. And her father would probably go into cardiac arrest on the spot.

"Well, I know how they'd react," Sully said. "They'd think you'd lost your mind.''

She tried to smile, but it was tough when he'd hit her mother's reaction bang on.

"They'd point out," he continued, "that we come from different worlds. Hell, one of them would probably even suggest I'm a fortune hunter.''

Those words stung. Just because she had money it didn't mean a man couldn't be interested in her for herself. And it didn't mean she was too stupid to recognize a fortune hunter, either. Lord, she'd been spotting them at forty paces since she'd been sixteen years old—when one had almost broken her sister's heart.

Sully, though, obviously figured her family had an awfully low opinion of her. And his assuming that hurt far more than she'd have thought it would.

"Dammit, Sully," she finally whispered, her throat tight. "I'd like to think the people who love me believe I've got a little more going for me than my money."

"I'm sure they do," he said softly. "I'm sure they know you've got a hell of a lot more going for you. I'm just trying to be realistic."

She glared at him. He was being so darn negative that she wished she'd never opened her mouth. She could certainly live without his giving her a David Letterman-type list of the top ten reasons he didn't intend to see her again.

"Lauren, don't look at me like that. As I said, I'm just trying to be realistic."

"Fine," she snapped. "And I'm just going back to the lodge. And let's forget this conversation ever took place, okay? Because I've changed my mind. I wouldn't want to see you again if my life depended on it."

She wheeled and started back the way they'd come, tears stinging her eyes. Tears of anger, she told herself, because anger was the *only* emotion she was feeling. After all, how could she possibly feel the slightest bit hurt or upset when she didn't really give a damn about Jack Sullivan?

SULLY STOOD WATCHING Lauren march away, swearing under his breath. Then, telling himself he just might be making the biggest mistake of his life, he started after her.

"Lauren?" he said, catching up as she reached the clearing.

When he put his hand on her arm, she shrugged it off and kept right on walking.

"Dammit, Lauren," he muttered, falling into step, "will you listen?"

She didn't even glance at him, so he said, "I apologize for hurting your feelings. But you know I'm the one who's thinking straight here."

"And you know what you can do with your apology!"

He glared at her—even though she wasn't aware of it because she was refusing to look at him.

That made him swear to himself again. He hated having to apologize. He hated it even more when he apologized and his apology wasn't accepted.

The pulse in his temple had begun to throb, warning him his self-control was on shaky ground, but he did his best to remain reasonable.

"Lauren, all I was trying to point out was that any relationship we got into would have the life expectancy of a mayfly—for a hundred different reasons."

"So what? I hear all your relationships have the life expectancy of a mayfly!"

"What the hell do you know about my relationships?"

"I know Grace told me they never last. And I can see why. I'll bet there isn't a woman in the entire country who could put up with you for long."

"Oh, yeah? Well bet again. There are all kinds of women who could put up with me just fine. But maybe I've never met one I figured would happily put up with half a dozen stray kids as well. And maybe I've never met a woman I *wanted* a long relationship with."

"Well you don't have to worry about not wanting one with me," Lauren snapped. "Because I don't want one with you. I wouldn't even want one that was as short as they come."

"Good," he snapped back, that shaky ground crumbling completely away. "I'm glad we've finally found something we agree on."

They stomped along in silence until Lauren muttered, "I've never been rejected because of my money before. At least that makes you unique."

"Dammit, I wasn't rejecting you. I just—"

"Just what?" she demanded, stopping dead as they reached the porch steps and eyeing him intently.

He stood gazing down at her. Her eyes were flashing, her face was flushed, and she looked as if she'd like to kill him. She also looked so damn beautiful he knew that chasing after her hadn't been the biggest mistake of his life after all. He was about to make the biggest one right now, by opening his mouth and saying something totally crazy.

"Next Saturday," he said.

"What about next Saturday?"

"The boys all play on the local twelve-and-under baseball team. And next Saturday the coaches are taking the team camping. They'll leave in the morning and won't be back until Sunday evening, so I could come into the city."

"Oh," she murmured, both her flush and her murderous expression fading.

She didn't say a damn thing more, though. When he couldn't stand the suspense a second longer, he asked, "Is that a yes, oh, or a no, oh?"

She slowly licked her bottom lip, the same nervous, sexy gesture he recalled from last night. Once again, it almost did him in. He suddenly wanted her to say yes more than he could remember ever wanting anything.

"Ahh . . . it's a yes," she finally murmured. "It's a definite yes."

"Good. Then it's a definite date."

His blood pounding, he was just about to lean forward and kiss her when she said, "There's only one minor thing."

He froze. Something in her voice told him it was actually a major thing. And that he wasn't going to like it at all.

"The gallery that handles my sister's paintings is mounting an exhibit of her recent ones, and the opening is next Saturday evening. There's a champagne reception and we'll have to at least put in an appearance."

Clearing his throat uneasily, he said, "I assume your parents will be there? And your brother?"

Lauren gave him an anxious smile. "I expect there'll be a few uncles, aunts and cousins, as well."

While Sully was still searching for the right words to explain why his going to Marisa Van Slyke's exhibit opening was out of the question, a police cruiser arrived—even though it was only about eleven-thirty. So he and Lauren went into the lounge with the officer and spent the next half hour answering questions about the car theft.

Not much of Sully's attention, though, was really on the subject of Lauren's Mercedes. He was far more concerned with thinking his way through the predicament he'd gotten into.

He'd made the decision to ask her out against his better judgment. But the minute she said yes, he'd felt such an incredible rush that he knew he absolutely had to see her again. He strongly suspected, though, that if he refused to go to the opening their relationship would be toast.

Despite that, there was no conceivable way he intended to meet her family, particularly not en masse, as soon as next Saturday. Which meant he had to come up with an idea for wangling his way out of going to that opening without wangling his way entirely out of Lauren's life.

He still hadn't thought of a plan by the time they walked the officer back to his cruiser. As the car pulled away and he and Lauren turned toward the lodge, Billy the Kid hollered, "Hey, Sully?"

He glanced over and saw that all five boys were sitting on the grass outside the garage.

"We're just takin' a lunch break," Billy yelled, waving an apple at him. "So don't think we've stopped workin'."

"Okay," he called. "But if you get tired, I want you to quit and finish up tomorrow."

BILLY WATCHED SULLY and Lauren walking back to the lodge. He was still shaking inside, but not so bad now. Not now he knew that cop must have just been the one who was coming to talk to Lauren.

When he'd first seen a cruiser drive in, though, he'd been so scared he'd almost started crying like a baby. He'd been sure the cop had come to take him away, even though he didn't think copying a file could be exactly the same as stealing it—'cuz the real file was still right there in Mr. Ludendorf's office.

All he'd put on Sully's desk was the copies, stuck inside the big envelope he'd grabbed. But he was still real, real glad to see that cop leave.

"Billy?" Freckles said. "Whadda you think? Are we gonna get away with it?"

"Uh-huh," he said, nodding firmly.

"But Sully's gonna be real suspicious when he sees all that stuff. So why'd you copy the whole file? You said you was just gonna find out that guy's name. And tell Sully that Mr. Ludendorf phoned to tell him."

Billy nodded again, casually tossing away the rest of his apple. The way his stomach felt, if he ate another bite he'd hurl for sure.

"Right," he said. "That's what I was gonna do. But lots of times private eyes have to change their plans, and that's what happened to me. When I started lookin' at that file, I could tell there was stuff there.... I'm not exactly sure what, but I know there's somethin' real funny about it. And maybe Sully can figure it out."

Terry sniffed hard and swiped at his eyes. Tony gave him a threatening look that said crying would get him smacked.

"But what's gonna happen," Hoops said, "when Sully asks us who dropped that file off?"

"We just gotta all stick to the story," Billy told him. "We just gotta all say we never saw the guy before."

WHEN THE SCREEN DOOR closed behind Sully and Lauren, the warm smile she gave him made him decide to forget about her sister's exhibit until later. Hell, he had an entire week to come up with an avoidance strategy, but no more than three hours before that damn limo would arrive to take her home.

He was just going to suggest making lunch when she said, "Do you think the boys are almost finished out there?"

He shook his head. "It was a big job."

She gave him an even warmer smile, accompanied by an inviting look that said lunch could wait. Before he had time to take her up on the invitation, though, his office phone began to ring.

"Whoever it is," he said, "will call back."

"It might be Ben Ludendorf," she pointed out. "Maybe he's talked to his client again."

Reaching for her hand, Sully started for the bedroom wing. She was right. It might be Ben, so he'd better answer. But she wouldn't be here much longer, and he didn't like the idea of not having her right with him every second she was.

They made it to his office by the fifth ring, and Sully grabbed the receiver. It wasn't Ben, though. It was Joe Perkins, one of the boys' baseball coaches, with instructions about what they should bring along for the camp out the following weekend.

Sully grabbed a pad, made a couple of notes, then got off the line as quickly as he could. When he put down the receiver, his gaze came to rest on a large brown envelope sitting in the center of his desk—a note in childish handwriting clipped to it. He picked up the envelope and read:

Sully,
Some man none of us new brot you this. You weren't in the lodge, so he brot it to the garage and I brot it to your office.

Billy

"Somebody must have come by while we were at the lake," he said, passing Lauren the note. Then he opened the envelope. Inside were a dozen or so photocopied pages.

"What the hell?" he muttered, pulling them out and gazing at the top one.

"What is it?" Lauren asked, moving closer.

"It's a copy of my title to Eagles Roost."

"Did you ask someone for it?"

He shook his head. "And I don't have the slightest idea who'd have brought it. Or why." He turned his attention to another sheet in the little pile.

It was a copy of the first page of a bank book, showing the account number and telling him it was with a bank in Newcomb. He shifted the papers so Lauren could see what he was looking at.

"Newcomb," he told her, "is about thirty miles from North Head."

The next sheet was the bank book's second page, which revealed the account had been opened back in February, with a deposit of ten thousand dollars. That was the only transaction posted.

He moved those sheets to the bottom of the pile and looked at the next one. It, he could tell from the faint outline of torn edges, was a copy of a scrap of paper roughly five inches square. There was a single name written on it—*Leroy*.

"Do you know who Leroy is?" Lauren asked.

"I'm not sure," he said, staring at it and thinking he only knew one Leroy. Then he turned to the next page—a copy of some rough handwritten notes—and decided they'd been written by the same person who'd scribbled the name Leroy.

"Do you recognize the writing?" Lauren said.

"No. And I don't recognize the name Dirk Blackstone, either." Whoever Blackstone was, though, his name was scrawled across the top of the page and underlined several times.

"But look," he added, his gaze drifting downward and his finger moving to where "Eagles Roost" was written. An arrow pointed from that to where his own name and phone number appeared amid a jumble of single words. None of the words meant anything to him except one—*cash*. Ben Ludendorf had said his client was prepared to pay cash.

"Sully? What's this all about?"

"I'm not sure," he muttered again. Then he turned to the final page and was.

CHAPTER TEN

SOLVING PART OF THE MYSTERY

THE FINAL PAGE had been photocopied from a sheet
of Ben Ludendorf's letterhead. It was a handwritten
memo—in the same writing as the rough notes.

"Well, I'll be..." Sully muttered, skimming what
it said.

Memo to File, September 14
Talked to Dirk Blackstone about Jack Sullivan's
negative answer on Eagles Roost. Told Blackstone I'd watch for other property and keep in
touch.

He handed the memo to Lauren. "Ben's a one-man
show. He doesn't even have a secretary, so all this
handwriting has to be his—unless somebody's been
stealing his letterhead, which can't be too likely."

Lauren gazed at the page for a moment, then said,
"Memo to file. Okay, then if the original of this is in
one of his files, does that mean the rest of what we've
got here was copied from the same place?"

"I guess we can't assume that for sure. But it's a
logical conclusion, isn't it."

"I'd say so. But whether everything came from the same file or not, somebody obviously copied all this for you. And if Ben wouldn't tell you Dirk Blackstone's name, then who wanted you to know it?"

He merely shook his head.

"Wanted you to know it badly enough to... Sully, we're standing here looking at stolen goods, aren't we?"

"Well, I guess you could put it that way. But it's a little late to worry now, after we've already looked at everything."

Lauren nodded. "And since we've already looked, we might as well try to figure things out. For starters, we know this Dirk Blackstone is the man who wanted to buy Eagles Roost last fall."

"Who still wants to," Sully corrected her. "But only if he can have it all."

Lauren slowly pushed her hair back from her face, taking Sully's mind off the photocopies for a moment. She looked as sexy as she did puzzled, and it made him consider saving the mystery to worry about later.

Clearly, though, she'd like to get to the bottom of it, because she said, "May I look at all the pages?"

He handed them to her, then watched her flip slowly through them. When she gazed up at him again, her expression was thoughtful.

"Do you have any idea how all these bits are related?" she asked.

"No, but I think they have to be. Somebody's trying to tell me something."

"There are things missing, though," she said, looking through the papers again. "Why isn't there at least a phone number for Blackstone?"

Shaking his head, Sully picked up Billy's note once more. *Some man none of us new brot you this.* Re-reading that started him wondering if the man none of the boys knew could be a figment of Billy's imagination.

The thought was damn unsettling, because even though he hoped to hell it wasn't Billy who'd copied this stuff, he couldn't rule out the possibility.

He didn't know how Billy would have come up with the idea, but his junior Ace Ventura was always getting carried away with crazy schemes. This, though...

Hell, if Billy was responsible for this, he'd gone far beyond kid stunts. Breaking into someone's office was well into the criminal range.

Anxiously rubbing his jaw, he started trying to figure out the best way of getting at the truth—and the best way of handling things if Billy had actually crossed that far over the line. But he'd establish whether the boy had been involved later, after Lauren was gone.

"Even though the kids didn't know the man who brought the envelope," she said, "they'll be able to give you a description."

"Right, they will." Assuming there'd actually been a man.

"And maybe you'll know who he is."

Sully nodded. "But let's not worry about that right now. First, let's try to put together the pieces we've got here." He moved the copy of his title to one side and spread the rest of the photocopies across his desk. Then he stood staring down at them, hoping they'd add up to something that made sense.

When they didn't cooperate, he said, "Okay. Aside from Ben's memo to himself, we've got a bank account in Newcomb, with ten thousand dollars in it, some rough notes that don't seem to say much, and this *Leroy* clue."

"Clue," Lauren repeated. "Then that name does mean something to you?"

"Well, I might be shooting in the dark, but remember that problem I had? That kid who robbed the bank in North Head back in January?"

"Yes, you mentioned it and there were details about it in my file. But...wait, that boy's name was Leroy, wasn't it?"

"Uh-huh. Leroy Korelenko."

"And you think this name Ben jotted down refers to *that* Leroy?"

"I don't think it's something we should rule out, because Leroy's not a common name around here. But Leroy Korelenko is a fifteen-year-old kid from a welfare family, and Dirk Blackstone is someone with enough money to pay cash for Eagles Roost. So it's hard to imagine what the connection could be."

"Well..." Lauren said.

"Well what?"

"Sully, I'm not much of a detective, but I know something you don't."

He waited.

"I shouldn't be telling you this, because what happens at the Foundation board meetings is confidential. But under the circumstances..."

"Yes?" he pressed, his adrenaline starting to pump.

"I'm probably really reaching, but what if when this Blackstone wanted to buy Eagles Roost last year, he wanted it awfully badly? Badly enough that, when you said you wouldn't sell, he decided he'd try to make you.''

"How?"

Lauren slowly shrugged. "It's not very hard to get information about most things. He could easily have learned where your funding came from. And who the Foundation's board members are.''

"And?"

"And so... oh, probably this is absurd, but what if Blackstone tried to force you to sell by manipulating things so you lost your funding?''

"Manipulating what things?" Sully demanded, his adrenaline pumping harder now.

"Well, this is the part I really shouldn't be telling you. If anyone ever finds out I breached confidentiality..."

"No one's going to find out from me.''

She hesitated, then said, "All right. One of our board members is a man named Hunter Clifton. And it was basically because of Hunter that your funding was cut off.''

Hunter Clifton. Sully mentally filed away the name, guiltily recalling all those murderous thoughts he'd had about Lauren—when some guy named Hunter Clifton was actually the cause of his problem.

"You see," she went on, "Hunter is a vice president of a bank, and the bank in North Head is one of its branches. And he was so upset that one of *your* boys had the audacity to rob one of *his* banks, that he convinced the other board members there must be serious problems at Eagles Roost—that you had no control over your kids, so your funding shouldn't be continued.

"At the time, I thought it was merely a coincidence that bank was one of Hunter's, but now..."

"But now," Sully said slowly, "you're wondering if Blackstone set up the robbery, after he learned one of the bank vice presidents sat on your board."

"Exactly. He'd have been hoping that if one of your kids robbed the bank Hunter would have a fit, which is exactly what happened."

"So maybe Blackstone, or Ben Ludendorf on Blackstone's behalf," Sully muttered, anger coiling in his chest, "approached Leroy and paid him to commit the robbery—figuring a fifteen-year-old could never pull off something like that without getting caught."

"And knowing that when he did, it would reflect badly on your program."

Sully stood, trying to decide whether they were actually on to something. "It's a neat little theory," he said at last.

"Yes. That's the problem, though, isn't it. It's pure theory."

She was right, of course. They might be completely off base. Then again, they might not.

He considered things for another minute and finally said, "You know, I can't see how you got the idea you're not much of a detective. I think you might make a good one, because this theory of yours is definitely worth checking out."

"Really?" Lauren murmured, giving him a pleased-looking smile. "Checking out how?"

"Well, I didn't have much chance to talk to Leroy after the police picked him up. I went to see him in his holding cell but he wouldn't say two words. Then, when I got back to the lodge, I had a call from his

caseworker—basically telling me that since Leroy
wouldn't be back here it would be better if I just
steered clear and let her handle things.''

"But you think you should try talking to him
now?"

Sully nodded. "*Something* made him rob that
bank. So I'll pay him a visit next week and try to find
out what. He's in a juvenile facility just north of
Utica, only a couple of hours from here."

When he finished speaking he simply gazed at
Lauren, thinking they didn't have much time before
her limo arrived. So maybe, now that he had a plan
of action, they should forget about this for the moment.

Before he could suggest that, though, she was
picking up the bank book copies and saying, "What
about this ten thousand dollars? Where does it fit
in?"

Reluctantly, Sully forced his mind back to the subject at hand. "The date of that deposit," he said,
staring at it, "is about a month after the robbery took
place."

"Which means what? Payment to Ben Ludendorf
for recruiting Leroy? You know him, Sully. Is he the
type who'd get involved in a scheme like that?"

He shook his head uncertainly. "I don't know him
very well. But if the money's his, why would he have
opened a separate account with it? Over in Newcomb? If it isn't his, though, then whose is it?"

"I could find out," Lauren said.

"Oh?"

"Piece of cake."

He waited for her to explain, thinking of F. Scott
Fitzgerald's line about the rich being different. He

knew how much success he'd have if he walked into a bank and tried to get information about someone else's account.

"My brother the criminal lawyer knows people whose business is finding out just about anything. So all I have to do is get him to put me in touch with one of those people, and we've as good as got the name of who opened that account."

"He'd do that? Put you in touch, I mean?"

"He might not like the idea. But if I say I'll have to find someone on my own if he doesn't help me out, that'll do the trick."

"Then I think you should talk to him, because I really don't know whether Ben's crooked or not. He isn't the sharpest lawyer in the state, but I've never heard he has a reputation for shady dealings."

"I think," Lauren murmured, smiling a little, "the sort of possibility we're talking about goes well beyond shady."

Sully grinned. "I don't always have the greatest way with words."

"Oh, sometimes you do very nicely."

The invitation was back in her eyes, and this time he didn't let the moment pass. He rested his fingers beneath her chin, tilted her face up to a perfect kissing angle, and leaned forward.

Her lips were even softer than he'd recalled, their taste even sweeter. The scent of her perfume was positively intoxicating, and when he drew her into his arms her body heat sent hot chills through him.

He smoothed his hands down her back, drawing her closer yet. The heat of her hips against his made him ache with arousal.

She slid her fingers up his neck and began tangling his hair around them, pulling his lips even closer against hers as she opened them to his kiss. The sweet, moist heat of her mouth started a pounding in his ears; the fullness of her breasts against his chest made him desperate to touch them.

When he did, slowly moving his hands to either side, she gave an erotic little moan and shifted slightly—so there was space between their bodies to let him slip his thumbs across to her nipples. He slowly caressed their hard roundness, making her moan again.

The sound was so full of longing that he felt as if his loins were on fire. The urgent feelings she was evoking made it almost impossible to keep in mind there were five boys outside—five boys who could come charging inside any second.

He wanted to unbutton her shirt and tease those hard nipples with his tongue. Wanted to unzip her jeans and pleasure her until she was senseless with desire. Wanted her to unzip his jeans and feel how incredibly she affected him. Hell, he was so hot and hard he wanted to make love to her on the damn desk.

But he hadn't quite forgotten about the boys, so he couldn't do any of those things. All he could do was keep telling himself he'd be with her again next weekend. When the boys wouldn't be within two hundred miles of them.

As SULLY TURNED off the highway leading to Utica, onto the road that would take them to the Gravesville Juvenile Correctional Institution, he glanced across the van at Billy.

The boy's face was pale, and he seemed almost as frightened as he had when he'd first admitted to photocopying Ben's file.

He caught Sully looking at him and tried to smile. He couldn't pull it off, though, and finally said, "Sully? Maybe I could just wait in the van while you go talk to Leroy, huh? I mean, they probably don't want to bother givin' me a tour and all."

"They don't mind. I told you, when I called they said they'd be glad to show you around."

Billy swallowed hard and turned to stare out the side window. Sully thought he might be crying and hoped he actually was. Sometimes, there was a lot to be said for scaring a kid silly. And letting Billy see the sort of place he could end up in if he kept doing stupid things would scare the devil out of him.

Sully just hoped it would be enough to scare him straight. Billy was basically a good kid, but you didn't have to be bad to end up in jail. Being foolish and unlucky was often reason enough. That was something he knew from experience.

He focused on the road again, still not certain he was handling this situation the best possible way. Under different circumstances, he'd have taken Billy and the twins straight to Ben Ludendorf and made them confess their sins. Then, he and Ben could have worked out a punishment they both felt comfortable with.

But he didn't want Ben knowing that file had been copied just yet—not until he determined if Ben had some sins of his own to confess. So he'd temporarily put the public confession idea on hold and settled for giving all five boys one of his best fire-and-brimstone lectures.

Hopefully, between that, having their privileges suspended, and being assigned extra chores, they'd think long and hard the next time they were tempted to do something they knew was wrong.

Of course, he hadn't suspended *all* their privileges. He was still letting them go camping on the weekend. And even though he'd tried rationalizing to himself that he had to—because it was a team thing—he knew damn well if he didn't have plans to see Lauren he'd have kept them home.

He smiled to himself, realizing she'd slipped into his thoughts yet again. It was only Tuesday, but since she'd left on Saturday he must have thought about her six million times. And picked up the phone to call her six hundred times. Partly because he couldn't help worrying about that threat; partly just because he wanted to hear her voice.

He hadn't called, though. She'd said she'd call him—as soon as she found out who that bank account in Newcomb belonged to. Besides, he didn't want to seem *too* interested in her.

And he wasn't going to let himself start thinking beyond this coming Saturday. Not when, in the back of his mind, he still wondered if he hadn't made a huge mistake by asking her out at all.

"Sully?" Billy said. "How come I gotta do this alone? How come you didn't bring the twins, too?"

"Because you were the mastermind." He'd considered bringing the twins, though. Hell, he'd considered asking the fellow in charge if all five boys could have a tour. But instead, he'd volunteered the other four to help old Zeke Scrouthy around his place for a few hours. That way, someone was keeping an eye on them and Billy didn't have the strength-in-numbers principle working to his advantage.

If all the kids had come along, they'd have done their best to make a joke of things. So it was better that Billy was on his own. He could be counted on to relay every last horrible detail to the others. Hell, knowing Billy, he'd even embellish them.

"That's it up ahead." Sully glanced across the van again, gesturing in the general direction.

"That place with the big fence around it?" Billy's face lost another shade of tan.

"Uh-huh."

"Sully? That fence wire ain't electric, is it?"

"You mean is it electrified. And I don't know." He took another sidelong look at Billy as the gate guard waved them to a stop, thinking he'd be lucky if the kid didn't pass out on him.

"Name, sir?" the guard asked, looking past him at Billy, then checking the empty back of the van.

"Jack Sullivan. I have an appointment with Mr. Carter."

The guard checked his clipboard, then nodded. "You want the center door of the building. Visitors' parking is to the left."

After Sully had parked the van, Billy reluctantly followed him into the building. The depressing old gray stone structure looked as if it had been there a hundred years and would easily survive a hundred more.

Once they were inside, Sully wasn't sure which made the biggest impression on Billy—the locked doors, the security check, the antiseptic, institutional smell, or the uniformed staff. But Billy clearly didn't like any of them.

Neither did Sully. They brought back too many memories he'd spent years trying to bury.

When a guard delivered them to the administrator's office, Billy started looking downright ill.

Howard Carter was a hulk of a man in his early fifties who'd make most marine drill sergeants look like wimps. He'd arranged for one of his staff to give Billy the tour, and as they headed off Sully couldn't help feeling sorry for the kid. He looked as if he were on his way to death row.

Carter checked his watch. "I'll take you along to see Korelenko in a couple of minutes. They're bringing him to an interview room at two."

"Thanks. I appreciate your letting me see him when it's not an official visiting day."

"No problem. The kid isn't exactly Mr. Cooperation, though, so I hope you don't find you've driven all this way for nothing."

Sully nodded. Carter couldn't hope that half as much as he did.

SULLY SAT LOOKING across the little interview table at Leroy, while Leroy looked at the table.

In the five years his program had been operating, he'd never laid a hand on a kid. Right now, though, he'd like to shake Leroy Korelenko until his teeth rattled.

No matter how many different ways he'd put the question, Leroy's answer had been the same. He'd decided to rob the bank because he'd wanted money. End of explanation.

Telling himself that at least Leroy hadn't clammed up entirely, he shoved back his chair and wandered over to the window. He didn't know whether the bars were necessary or for effect, but he sure as hell didn't like the effect they were having on him. He hadn't had a nightmare about being in prison for years, but he wouldn't be surprised if he had one tonight.

He turned back to look at Leroy again. The direct approach hadn't gotten him anywhere, so it was time to see what a little bluffing could do. "Look, Leroy," he said.

The boy continued to stare at the table.

"I know the real story about the robbery. I didn't say so right off, because I wanted to give you a chance to tell me the truth, but—"

"I've been tellin' the truth," Leroy muttered without looking up.

"Oh?" he said quietly. "That's not what Ben Ludendorf told me."

When the boy's gaze flashed to his, Sully silently shouted "Bingo!" There *was* something more to that robbery than Leroy had ever let on. And Ben was somehow involved.

Then shutters closed over the recognition in Leroy's eyes and he said, "Who's Ben Ludenhorse?"

"Give it up, Leroy. Ben and I are friends, but for some reason we never really talked much about that robbery. We got going on it the other night, though, over a few beers. And that's why I showed up here after all these months."

"Whadda you mean, that's why?"

Sully shrugged. "What do you think I mean?"

"How the hell do I know? I don't even know who this Ben guy is."

"No? Well that's really strange, because Ben sure knows who you are."

"Yeah?" A smirk crept across Leroy's face. "Yeah, well I guess that's 'cuz I'm such a popular guy, huh? People know me who I never even hearda."

Sully resisted the urge to wipe that smirk off the boy's face and went for broke. "Ben knows who really planned that bank job, Leroy. He knows all the details. He even knows something about it you don't. Something that's really going to piss you off when you find out."

The smirk vanished. There was a long silence. Eventually Leroy said, "What? What does this guy I never even hearda know about?"

Sully uttered another silent "Bingo."

CHAPTER ELEVEN

CORNERING BEN LUDENDORF IN HIS LAIR

VISITING THE Gravesville Juvenile Correctional Institution took longer than Sully had originally anticipated because, after his session with Leroy, he'd felt obliged to talk with Howard Carter again.

He'd had to tell the man that Leroy had admitted being paid to rob that bank. Carter, of course, would be informing the police. And they, in due course, would pay Leroy a visit.

By that point, maybe Leroy would be ready to admit he knew the name Ben Ludendorf. As Sully had told the boy, the more Leroy cooperated with the police, the better it would be for him.

But since Leroy had stuck to the story that he'd never even heard of Ben Ludendorf, Sully still only had his suspicions that Ben and Dirk Blackstone were behind the crime. He didn't have facts. Nothing he felt he should be talking to the police about personally. He certainly intended to talk to Ben Ludendorf, though. Just as soon as he could.

At any rate, it was late afternoon when Sully and Billy stopped by old Zeke Scrouthy's place to pick up the other boys, and past six before they got back to the lodge.

Once they'd piled out of the van, Sully asked Freckles to feed Roxy, who, given the enthusiasm of her greeting, must have decided she'd been abandoned forever. Then he put Hoops in charge of dinner—even though he knew that would result in peanut butter and jelly sandwiches.

He didn't want to take the time to come up with a better menu. He was too eager to tell Lauren about his visit with Leroy.

Heading down to his office, he glanced over to make sure the window was closed. He doubted Billy would ever dare spy on him again, but there were no certainties with kids.

After dialing Lauren's number, he waited impatiently through three rings before she answered. When she did, her "Hello" started his heart beating faster.

"Hi," he said. "Everything all right there?"

"Sully?"

He could hear her smile when she said his name. It made him wish she were here with him instead of four hours away.

"I was going to phone you later," she said, "because Elliot's contact got back to me this afternoon. That bank account in Newcomb *is* in Ben Ludendorf's name."

"Good. I'd decided it had to be, but it's nice to know for sure."

"You'd decided because..."

"Because I went to see Leroy today."

"Oh...and?"

"You want the long version or the short?"

"Medium."

He laughed. "Well, it took a while, but I finally got the truth out of him. A good part of it, at least."

"How? No, wait, you can tell me all about your wonderful interrogation skills on Saturday. For now, just tell me what you found out."

"Well, we were right about somebody paying him to rob the bank."

"Was it Ben Ludendorf or Dirk Blackstone?"

"Neither of them directly. Not unless one of them was pretending to be some guy named Gus. According to Leroy, this Gus fellow approached him only a couple of days after he arrived at Eagles Roost, offering him twenty thousand dollars to pull off the robbery—plus he'd get to keep whatever he took the bank for. That's an awful lot of money to a fifteen-year-old," he added, not sure if Lauren would realize that.

"Yes, of course," she said.

"So there was no way he even considered passing on the idea."

"He wasn't worried about getting caught?"

"Oh, sure. But he figured if he did, he'd get lenient treatment because he was still a juvenile. So the risk was worth it to him."

"And what happened to the money?"

"Well, the police recovered what he'd taken from the bank. He still had it on him. But they didn't know anything about the twenty thousand, because Leroy's story was that the bank job was entirely his idea."

"So he's got twenty thousand dollars hidden away someplace?"

"Only half of it. The deal Gus made with him was that he'd get paid in two halves. Ten thousand before the robbery, ten after."

"Which explains the bank account," Lauren murmured. "That ten thousand is the second half, right?"

"I think it's got to be. Gus gave Leroy a name and address—the fellow who'd have the second ten thou for him. And Gus said that even if he got caught, even if he got put away, the money would still be waiting for him after he'd done his time. Once he got out, all he'd have to do was go see this person and ask for a package for Leroy."

"And I assume this person was Ben?"

"That's what I assume, too. The kid wouldn't say, but I could tell he knew Ben's name, even though he didn't admit it."

"So Ben is looking after a bank robber's money for him? Sully, he could probably be disbarred for his part in this."

"I know. And I think that's exactly what's going to make him tell me who Dirk Blackstone is. And why he wants Eagles Roost so badly."

LAUREN SAT WITH the phone to her ear, hesitating. She didn't want Sully to feel she was trying to push her way in where she didn't belong, but she really wanted to be there when he talked to Ben Ludendorf.

At last she said, "Sully, you'll go to see Ben, won't you? I mean, you won't just phone him."

"No, I'll go see him."

"Well, when you do, I'd like to go with you."

She used the pause at his end to try to organize her arguments. They were still pretty disorganized, though, when he said, "Any particular reason?"

"A couple, actually." She took a deep breath, wishing they were face-to-face. She found it hard to discuss her feelings under the best of circumstances, let alone via long distance.

"I know you didn't believe this at first," she finally said, "but I've always felt badly about your losing your funding. And now that I've gotten to know the boys, now that I've gotten to know *you,* I feel even worse. So if I can help...

"Sully, if I went with you, then at the very least you'd have a witness to what was said. And if Ben denies knowing anything, we might get further if there were two of us asking questions. You know, the old two-heads-are-better-than-one theory?"

"It's not a bad theory," he said slowly.

But that didn't tell her what he thought about the idea of her going along.

"And if Ben's story is what we figure," she pressed, "it would let me explain to the board members how you were set up. I'm sure that would almost guarantee they'd reinstate your funding next year. Especially if I'd talked with Ben in person. Then I'd be telling them what I heard him say—so they couldn't suspect you might have twisted the facts to suit yourself."

"I guess that makes sense," Sully allowed.

She still didn't think, though, he was entirely convinced he should let her go with him, so she decided she'd better tell him the rest, even though she didn't want to.

"Sully, there's another reason I'd like to be there, but I'm afraid it's very selfish. You see...oh, this is difficult to explain, but my father doesn't think I'm a very competent person. If I could do something, though, something that would show him I am, if I was involved in blowing the whistle on Ben and whoever this Dirk Blackstone is, my father might finally realize I'm not just bungling my way through life. I know that sounds dumb, but—''

''No,'' Sully said. ''No, it doesn't sound dumb. I understand what you mean.''

She exhaled slowly. After seeing how well he understood the way his kids thought, maybe she shouldn't be so surprised that he was as good with adults. But it seemed strange that her own father was always telling her he *couldn't* understand her thinking when a man she'd known for such a short while could.

''The only problem,'' he was saying when she forced her mind back to his words, ''is that we're pushed for time. After I talked to Leroy, I told the administrator what I'd learned. I didn't figure withholding information was a smart idea.''

''No, but if you told him about Ben—''

''I didn't. As far as Ben's concerned, we've got nothing but our suspicions, and I wouldn't make any accusations based solely on them. But when the police talk to Leroy, they'll tell him they know he was paid off—which will probably make *him* tell them about Ben.''

''But why? If he says anything about that ten thousand, he'll never see it.''

''No, but at this stage he probably won't see it anyway. And I pointed out that if he cooperates he might at least get a few months knocked off his time. At any rate, I want to talk to Ben before the police do, so I was going to phone him tonight, see if I could set up a meeting for the morning.''

''Yes. Yes, of course. I'll call Rosalie and tell her I won't be in tomorrow, that she'll have to reschedule my appointments. And I haven't heard a word about my car, but I can order a limo for first thing in the morning. If I get there about ten, would that be okay?"

"Ten would be fine."

Once they'd said their goodbyes, Lauren sat with the cordless in her hand, worrying about the funny tone that had crept into Sully's voice after she'd told him when to expect her. If she'd been able to see his expression she might have known what it meant. Long distance, though...

Deciding she wasn't at all fond of long distance, she carried the phone across the living room and put it back on its base. Unless she remembered to do that, she was forever trying to find the darn thing.

Then Killer appeared from somewhere, meowing that he'd like attention. The little guy was getting friendlier by the day, and when she picked him up he immediately went into his purring-and-kneading mode.

Absently stroking the cat, she wandered over to the windows and stood gazing down at what her father called her "million-dollar view of Central Park." Her thoughts, though, were two hundred miles away.

There was one more reason she'd wanted to go to Ben's with Sully. She'd never have told him, but it was an excuse to see him again and she desperately wanted to. She was missing him like crazy.

Since she'd left the lodge on Saturday, she hadn't been able to stop thinking about him for more than three minutes at a time. Hadn't been able to stop recalling how she tingled all over when he kissed her, or how his touch made her body ache with desire.

He was the only man she'd ever met who made her feel as if she belonged in his arms. And if it weren't for the problem of all those differences between them ...

She'd been spending a lot of time thinking about everything Sully had said, especially about how awfully unlikely it was that any relationship they got into would last. But despite knowing he was right, that feeling of not wanting to just walk away had been getting stronger and stronger.

In fact, she'd been counting the hours until Saturday, thinking there was an eternity of them still to go. Now, though, she no longer had to wait until Saturday. Now she'd be seeing Sully in the morning.

She closed her eyes and continued stroking Killer—and feeling as if she'd just been given a Christmas present in July.

AFTER HE'D HUNG UP from talking with Lauren, Sully sat staring at nothing, letting his thoughts drift. No matter where they drifted, though, they kept returning to her.

Maybe part of her reason for wanting to help him was selfish, but she was honest enough to admit it. He liked that. And it didn't take away from the fact that she *did* want to help—which he liked even better. It made him feel good inside.

So did the prospect of seeing her again, days before he'd expected to. But the idea of her casually taking another damn limo, all the way from New York City... Hell, there were so many reasons he shouldn't let himself fall for the woman, but he kept forgetting about them.

"You just can't keep doing that, Sullivan," he muttered. "It's only going to land you into trouble."

Talking out loud to himself, he discovered, helped him manage to keep those reasons well in mind through the evening and into the next morning. To be more specific, he managed it until the moment Lauren's limo pulled into the clearing.

Once she'd arrived, though, he had trouble thinking about anything except how much he wanted to take her into his arms and kiss her senseless.

Unfortunately, there was no opportunity. With five boys and a limo driver on the scene, he had to make do with one warm, delicious hello kiss when they left the others outside and came into the lodge. Then she went to freshen up before they drove to North Head, leaving him alone in the lounge.

Glancing out the front window, he saw that the driver had raised the limo's hood. All five boys were crowded around him, peering in at the engine, even though only Freckles had shown any previous interest in auto mechanics.

He stood watching them until he heard Lauren's footsteps coming back down the hall. She appeared in the doorway just as he turned from the window.

"Do I look all right?" she asked.

She was wearing a pale gray suit she'd told him was a "power" suit, and a cool, collected expression. Combined, the look clearly said she belonged in the big city.

Not a bad look for visiting a country-bumpkin lawyer. When Ben saw her he wouldn't know what the hell was going on, especially since Sully hadn't mentioned he'd be bringing anyone with him.

"You look sensational," he told her. That made her smile, and her smile made his heart skip a couple of beats.

"Should we take a few minutes to plan our strategy?"

He shook his head. "We don't know what Ben's initial reaction will be, so I think we'll just have to play things by ear. But he assumed I wanted to get together to talk about selling Eagles Roost. And since I didn't tell him any different, we'll have the element of surprise going for us. So why don't I just start the ball rolling and you jump in when you spot an opening you like."

She smiled once more. This one started him thinking about kissing her again, but since it was already well after ten o'clock he simply opened the door— before temptation could get the better of him.

As they stepped out onto the porch and started down the stairs, he began having doubts about his idea of using the limo for their trip to Ben's, began thinking maybe they should take his van, after all.

He forced the thought away, reminding himself why he'd figured using the limo was a good idea in the first place. Limousines weren't exactly commonplace in North Head, so their pulling up at Ben's in one was bound to throw the lawyer off-balance. Then he'd see Lauren and...

And hell, that meant going the whole nine yards was the right approach. They might need every possible advantage, so why not arrive in style? And this certainly was style. The limo that had come for Lauren on Saturday had been a conservative navy town car. This one was a white stretch job that was almost as long as the Van Slyke Building was wide.

Spotting them, the driver quickly shooed the boys away and closed the hood, then hurried to open the back door.

"All right," Sully said, giving the kids his best stern look as Lauren slid inside. "We won't be long, and I don't want any funny business while we're gone. Everyone stays around the lodge."

They all nodded, but they were clearly more interested in peering into the limo than in what he was saying.

Freckles forced his eyes off the car long enough to ask, "How come you won't tell us where you're goin'?"

"I did tell you. At least twelve times. We've got an appointment in town."

"But you didn't tell us what *kind* of appointment," Freckles pressed.

Billy looked as if he was about to put in his two cents worth, then clearly thought better of it. He'd been treading very lightly the past few days.

"I didn't tell you," Sully said, "because it's adult business. Now, remember, you all stay right here until we get back."

He climbed into the limo and reached to close the door. The driver beat him to it, though, so he just leaned back into the seat and casually glanced around, pretending he'd ridden in a hundred different limos.

The navy plush seat they were sitting on faced forward, with at least a mile of leg room. Opposite them, beneath the opaque window that separated them from the driver, were a couple of single seats—on either side of a wood-grained bar fridge. Sitting above that were a miniature television and a stereo system.

The car's ceiling was the bluish-black of a night sky. And when the driver started the engine, damned if little lights didn't begin twinkling above, like dozens of tiny stars. Sully couldn't help looking at Lauren.

She gave him a wry smile. "If I'd had my choice, we wouldn't have the top of the line. I think the stars are overkill. But since I only ordered it last night, I had to take what was available."

Nodding, he looked out at the boys. The dark windows prevented them from seeing in, but they were all waving as the car started off. He watched them through the rear window until the limo reached the curve in the road and they disappeared from sight, then he turned to look at Lauren once more.

She smiled again. This time, he didn't smile back. He just couldn't manage it. Earlier, when he'd seen the limo driving into the clearing, he'd felt absurdly happy. And when they'd gotten into the lodge and she'd kissed him, he'd been floating on air. But riding in the damn limo with her had brought him back to earth with a thud.

Resting his hands on his thighs, he slowly brushed his thumbs across the smooth, worn denim of his jeans. He was jeans and wilderness. Lauren was designer clothes and high society.

He glanced up at those stupid twinkling lights, thinking they were nothing like real stars in the real world—not *his* real world.

Then Lauren said, "Sully? You're awfully quiet. Is anything wrong?"

"No, nothing." He covered her hand with his and sat staring out at the passing scenery.

It seemed as if, no matter how many times he re-minded himself there were insurmountable obstacles standing between them, a few minutes later he'd have forgotten again. His subconscious was being posi-tively subversive, and that was beginning to worry the hell out of him.

WHEN THEY REACHED North Head the driver slid the dividing glass partway open so Sully could give him directions to Ben Ludendorf's. As he was leaning forward doing that, Lauren watched him uneasily.

It wasn't a very long drive from the lodge into town, but it had seemed awfully long with Sully lost in stony silence. She was afraid he was being so quiet because he didn't really want her with him. But if that was it, wouldn't he have said so last night? Jack Sul-livan had never been exactly reluctant to speak his mind.

"It's the white house ahead on the right," he told the driver, bringing her attention back to the mo-ment.

They turned into a long gravel drive and stopped beside a sign that indicated Ben's office was directly ahead of them—down the side of the large house.

Just as their driver was getting out, the office door opened and a man stepped out onto the driveway.

"Ben?" Lauren asked when he stood staring at the limo.

At Sully's nod, she took a closer look. Unlike any other lawyer she'd ever seen during working hours, Ben Ludendorf was wearing a casual shirt and pants rather than a suit. He was average height, around forty, and about thirty pounds overweight—twenty-nine of which were hanging over the front of his belt.

His brown hair was thin, the lenses in his glasses were thick, and his expression was curious.

"So far, so good," Sully murmured. "He doesn't know what the hell's going on." He reached over and squeezed her hand. "Ready?"

She barely had time to nod before the driver opened her door. Sully opened his and they got out of the limo at the same moment.

Ben's expression grew even more curious. "Hey, Sully," he said. Then his gaze shifted to Lauren and remained there.

She smiled at him. He smiled back. By that point, Sully had come around to her side of the limo. He lightly rested his hand on the small of her back and they started forward.

"Ben," Sully said as they reached him, "I'd like you to meet Ms. Lauren Van Slyke."

"The pleasure's all mine." Ben shook her hand, then ushered the two of them into his office. He closed the door and gestured toward the visitors' chairs. When he sat down behind his desk, he focused on Lauren again.

"And you're in real estate?" he guessed.

Sully had told her he'd start the ball rolling, so she glanced at him.

"No," he said to Ben. "Ms. Van Slyke is the director of the Van Slyke Foundation."

"Oh."

Ben looked puzzled. The foundation's name didn't seem to have rung a bell with him.

Instead of explaining why Lauren was there, which Ben obviously wanted to know, Sully said, "Ben, I'd like you to tell me about Dirk Blackstone."

That name clearly did ring a bell. Ben's puzzled expression was replaced by an unsettled one. "How did you find out his name?"

Sully shrugged. "That's not important. What's important is that I have to talk to him, so I need his address and phone number."

"Sorry, Sully, no can do."

"Look, Ben, if you're worried about losing your fee for negotiating a sale, don't be. There's not going to be a fee, because I'm not selling Eagles Roost. What I want to talk to Blackstone about isn't related to that."

"Sorry, but client information is confidential."

"I understand that," Lauren said, sensing that Sully was quickly losing patience. "My brother's a criminal lawyer," she added. "A partner at Douglas, Algeo and Scrymgeour, in Manhattan. Perhaps you know the firm? Their offices are in the World Trade Center."

"Yes, I've heard the name. Good firm, I think I've heard."

She nodded. "My brother's happy there. And as I said, because he's a lawyer I understand how important confidentiality can be. Especially in criminal matters."

Ben cleared his throat and sat up straighter. "Criminal matters? I'm afraid I don't catch your drift."

Sully shot her a sidelong glance that said *good going*.

She did her best not to smile, but his unspoken compliment made her feel inordinately good.

"Her drift," he explained to Ben, "is that we know you're holding ten thousand dollars for the kid who robbed the bank back in January."

"What?" Ben laughed. It was a very forced laugh.

"You've got it sitting in a bank account over in Newcomb," Sully added.

Ben's Adam's apple bobbed up and down, then beads of perspiration appeared on his forehead. "Sully, what's that robbery got to do with you? How about if you just—"

"What it has to do with me," he snapped, "is that Leroy Korelenko was staying at Eagles Roost when he pulled it off. Do you think that did my program's reputation any good?"

"Well, hell, Sully, I guess it didn't. But what's done is done and—"

"Look, Ben, I've got no interest in a debate. All I want is Blackstone's phone number and address."

"I told you, I can't—"

"Dammit, Ben, either you tell me how to get hold of him, or when Ms. Van Slyke and I leave here we go straight to the police."

"Sully, you can't!"

"Don't bet on that, Ben. Ready, Lauren?" He glanced at her and started to push himself up from his chair.

"Wait," Ben said quickly. "Look," he added as Sully slowly sat back down, "I had nothing to do with the damn robbery. And I wish to hell I had nothing to do with the money, either."

"You did, though," Sully said.

"But I didn't know what it was for. Not at first, I mean. I swear I didn't." Ben picked up a pencil and began fidgeting with it. "And by the time I realized . . . well, there wasn't anything I could do about it."

"You could have called the police," Lauren pointed out.

Ben's pencil snapped in half.

"No, really," he said. "It wasn't that simple. The way things would have looked, they'd have figured I'd been involved from the start. But I wasn't. And I didn't *knowingly* do one damn thing wrong."

"Then how," Sully said skeptically, "did you end up with the money?"

Ben shook his head, exhaling slowly. "Sully," he finally said, "here's what happened—the honest to God truth. A couple of days before the bank robbery, I got a call telling me a package was going to be delivered. And that I should put it away in a safe place until someone came asking for it."

"A call from . . . ?" Lauren asked.

He shrugged wearily. "From Dirk Blackstone."

"And the someone who was going to come asking for it?" Sully said. "Was it Leroy?"

Ben nodded. "But at that stage, the name didn't mean a thing to me."

"So the package came," Lauren prompted when he didn't continue.

"So the package came. And I locked it in the bottom drawer of my desk. Then, after the robbery, once the cops had picked up the kid and his name was released . . . That was when I first started worrying I might have been roped into doing something a little dicey. So I opened the package. And when I found there was ten thousand bucks inside, all in used twenties, that's when I got real worried."

"And then?" Sully asked.

"And then? Nothing. I mean, all I did after that was wait, hoping to hell somebody named Leroy would come asking for the package. Hoping to hell the kid in custody was a different Leroy."

"But nobody came," Lauren said.

"No. So after a few weeks I got in touch with Blackstone and told him that. I mean, I didn't tell him I'd opened the package, only that nobody'd come for it. And he told me to hang on to it indefinitely, that sooner or later Leroy would pick it up. That's when I knew for sure what was going on. And I knew nobody'd show until after that kid was released."

"And you knew," Sully said, "that I'd been set up. That Blackstone had paid Leroy to rob the bank to make my program look bad—hoping I'd lose my funding and be forced to sell Eagles Roost."

"No." Ben shook his head. "No, Sully, I didn't know any of that. Honest to God, I've never known a thing about your funding. And I never knew why Blackstone did what he did. All I knew was that I had ten thousand bucks I shouldn't have and didn't want. And I particularly didn't want it sitting in my office. So I took it over to Newcomb, where the tellers wouldn't know me, and stuck it in the bank there."

"Why didn't you send it back to Blackstone?" Lauren said.

"I couldn't."

"Why not?" Sully demanded.

Ben shook his head. "You're not going to like this, but I don't have either an address or a phone number for Dirk Blackstone."

CHAPTER TWELVE

A MODICUM OF SUCCESS

FOR THE FIRST FEW SECONDS after Ben's statement, Sully simply looked stunned. Then he glared darkly at the other man and said, "That's bull."

"No, it's not," Ben said so quickly the words ran together. "Sully, it's the God's honest truth."

Lauren eyed Sully anxiously. She didn't have to be a mind reader to know he was thinking about climbing across the desk and choking North Head's resident lawyer with his bare hands.

Deciding she'd better do something before that could happen, she cleared her throat. When Sully turned his glare in her direction, she gave him a look that said she could handle the situation.

"Ben?" she began.

The man shifted his nervous gaze to her.

"Ben, you just finished telling us you got in touch with Blackstone to tell him no one had picked up the package. So you must have his phone number."

"No, I don't." Ben began rubbing his neck with one hand, as if he figured that would make Sully keep *his* hands off it. "All I've got is a fax number. When I want to talk to him, I send a fax asking him to call. And he gets back to me. Sometimes it takes a few days, but eventually I hear from him."

"That's certainly an unusual arrangement."

Ben shrugged. "Blackstone's an unusual guy. Hell, he's the only client I've ever had that I've never actually met. He just phoned me up one day last year and asked me if I'd talk to Sully about selling Eagles Roost. Then he sent me a money order with a note saying it was to retain my services—which also makes him the only client I've ever had who gave me money I hadn't even asked for."

"Ahh...well, this fax number you've got for him. May I have it, please?"

The lawyer hesitated. Sully leaned forward in his chair, intensifying his industrial-strength glare.

Ben quickly grabbed his Rolodex, flipped through it, then copied a number onto a sheet of paper and handed it to Lauren.

"The area code's 212," she told Sully. "So he's in Manhattan."

She dug through her purse for the number she wanted, too excited to even think about waiting to make the call later, then looked at Ben again. "I left home in a hurry this morning and forgot my cellular, so would you mind if I used your phone for a minute? It's long distance, but I'll charge it."

Ben wordlessly pushed the phone toward her.

"And would you mind terribly," she added, "giving us a couple of minutes of privacy?"

Ben didn't look happy about that, but he shoved back his chair.

"Can I assume," he said to Sully as he rose, "since I've given you that number, you won't be talking to the police?"

"I won't unless they talk to me first," Sully told him. "But I don't think you should count on not

hearing from them. I've got a feeling Leroy Korelenko might decide to give them your name."

When Ben's expression paled from unhappy to
downright stricken, Lauren said, "We believe you,
Ben. I mean, we believe you didn't knowingly do
anything wrong. So if the police come to talk to you,
I'm sure you'll convince them, too."

"Yeah?" he said, looking a little hopeful.

"I think she's right," Sully told him.

"Well I sure as hell hope so." With that, he wheeled
and walked out of the office.

"Do you really think I was right?" Lauren said
after he'd closed the door.

"Uh-huh, Ben will be okay. All the local cops know
him, so even if they aren't completely convinced,
they'll give him the benefit of the doubt."

She thought about that for a moment, then asked,
"Why couldn't he have told them in the beginning?
Why did he say they'd have figured he was in-
volved?"

Sully shrugged. "I doubt that's really why he kept
quiet. If he'd volunteered the story, he'd have been
telling them that Dirk Blackstone was behind the
robbery. And that would have meant losing the only
client he's ever had who gave him money he hadn't
asked for."

"Ahh," Lauren murmured, deciding she hoped the
police gave Ben a bit of a hard time before they gave
him the benefit of any doubt.

When she reached for the phone, Sully said, "Who
are you calling?"

"Chester, the fellow Elliot put me on to. The one
who can find out almost anything. I'll bet if I give
him Dirk Blackstone's fax number he can get us a

phone number and address to go with it. You *would*
like to have them, wouldn't you?''

Sully grinned at her. ''Yeah, I'd like to have them.
Blackstone wants Eagles Roost so badly he forked
over twenty thousand bucks to make me lose my
funding. Even if he *hadn't* succeeded, I'd have
wanted to know what the hell the story is.''

Lauren dialed Chester's number, spoke briefly with
him, then hung up, saying, ''Mission accomplished.
He says he should have something for us in a day or
two.''

Sully gave her another one of his *good going* looks.

Again, she tried not to smile. She wasn't used to a
man acknowledging she had a brain, but it was
something she could grow awfully fond of.

THINGS HAD GONE SO WELL that Lauren felt like
dancing her way down Ben's driveway. Resisting the
urge, she managed to maintain a serious expression
until she and Sully were safely inside the limo. Then
she looked at him and they both began to laugh. They
didn't stop until they were well on their way back to
Eagles Roost.

''I can't believe we actually pulled that off,'' she
said at last. ''He told us everything he knew, and
getting him to do it was so easy I'm thinking about
changing careers.''

Sully grinned at her. ''Didn't I tell you you'd make
a good detective? But what I can't believe is that your
father doesn't figure you're one of the most competent women on earth. You were terrific in there.''

''Oh, Sully, I was hardly terrific.''

''Sure you were, and it's a good thing, too. I got so
mad I stopped thinking straight, so we probably

wouldn't have gotten that fax number at all if you hadn't stayed cool."

She shrugged, trying not to look as if she was incredibly pleased with herself. But the fact she couldn't stop smiling had to be a dead giveaway.

"Yeah," Sully went on, "I really do like your style, Van Slyke. You were smooth as silk."

"Well, Sullivan, I just thought it made sense to try the good-cop-bad-cop routine. And I guess we make a pretty fair team."

"Pretty fair? We make a great team." Sully reached across the space between them to rest his fingers against her cheek.

His touch sparked a flicker of excitement inside her. Then he eased closer, close enough that she could smell the subtle scent of his maleness. It was a combination of the fresh outdoors and an essence that was his alone—an essence that made her feel decidedly aroused.

Gently holding the sides of her face in his hands, he began kissing her. Long, leisurely kisses she wished would go on forever. Kisses that made her think of gentle rain on a sultry summer's day. Kisses that started a sensation like warm whispers inside her.

Eventually he drew away a little, leaving her longing for more. Then he smiled, his dark eyes so full of warmth it took her breath away.

At that moment she knew she was on the verge of falling in love with him. Or maybe she already had.

The realization was half exhilarating, half terrifying, and it started her thoughts racing. Not wanting to just walk away from him had been one thing. Falling in love with him was something else entirely.

It was happening, though, and now she had to decide what to do about it. Either she took a risk or she didn't.

If she did, there was no way of predicting what would happen. If she didn't, she felt certain she'd always wonder *what if?* and she suspected she'd always regret not finding out.

She focused on Sully again, and when she looked into the dark depths of his eyes, it stirred those warm whispers once more.

This time, though, she could make out what they were telling her. They were reassuring her, calming her, reminding her that sometimes people beat incredible odds. Telling her that maybe she and Sully could be two of those people. Telling her that she knew she had to chance finding out whether they were.

Suddenly, she felt better than she had in days.

"Lauren?" Sully said. "What are you thinking about?"

"Oh..." She invented rapidly. "Just that Chester said he'd get back to me in a day or two. Which means I'll have heard from him by Saturday."

"Great. Then we should be able to track down Blackstone and have a talk with him."

She merely nodded, not really wanting Sully to know how much that *we* meant to her. If he was content to let her tag along to the end of this mystery with him, it meant he hadn't merely been teasing her. He really did think she'd been a help with Ben.

Then she recalled his exact words and smiled to herself. He didn't just think she'd been a help. He thought she was terrific.

"We're almost home," he said, glancing out the window, then at her again. "Can you stay for a while, or do you have to head right back?"

"I can stay." She only wished she could stay for a lot longer than a while.

As the limo turned off the road and into Eagles Roost, she remembered about the champagne and moved over to one of the seats beside the fridge.

"I was hoping," she said, pulling out the chilled bottle of Mumm's and handing it to Sully, "we'd feel like celebrating. And these three other bottles," she added, taking them out as well, "are imitation stuff for the boys. The fellow at my deli swore they'd love it."

"Well, we won't have to wait long to find out." He gestured through the window to where all five kids, plus Roxy and two of the three cats, were sitting on the porch. As the limo pulled to a stop, the boys and Roxy charged down the steps.

"So?" Freckles was asking before they even had a chance to get out of the limo. "Did you guys have a good appointment?"

"It was fine," Sully said.

"Is that champagne?" Hoops asked, staring at the bottles they were holding.

"One is," Sully told him. "The others are kids' champagne. Lauren thought we might want to celebrate."

"Celebrate what?" Billy demanded.

When Sully glanced at her, Lauren gave him a little shrug, hoping he didn't think the champagne had been a mistake. She hadn't considered that he might not want to confide in the boys.

"Celebrate," he said, turning back to them, "that our appointment had to do with the funding for Eagles Roost. And that it went pretty well."

"So we got our money back?" Billy said. "Everythin's fine now? We can stay here? For sure?"

"Well, things aren't quite all worked out yet. But they're looking better."

"All right!" Billy hooted. Then the boys began giving each other high fives and grinning like Cheshire cats.

It made Lauren smile. If her board members had known how happy these kids were at Eagles Roost they'd have doubled the program's funding instead of chopping it. But the fact remained that they'd chopped it. She could feel her smile fading, because she knew Sully wasn't out of the woods yet.

The boys obviously figured that things being not quite worked out meant they were *almost* worked out. Which was undoubtedly what he wanted them to think so they'd stop worrying. In reality, though, things weren't worked out at all. Not for the short term, at least.

The long term would be all right. She was certain that once she explained the true story about the bank robbery, the board members would decide to reinstate Sully's funding for the next fiscal year.

As for the short term, though, every last cent of the foundation's money had been allocated to other programs by now. So Sully was definitely going to have to find another source to keep Eagles Roost going for the next year.

He caught her gaze and motioned that they should go inside. The moment he started toward the lodge, the boys all fell into step after him—making him look like a champagne-toting Pied Piper.

She stood, following the six of them with her eyes for a moment, thinking that one way or another she was going to ensure this program didn't run short of money.

LAUREN WAS GLAD she'd thought about bringing the kids' champagne because it proved a hit. By the time the bottles were empty, the boys were all pretending to be tipsy. And even though they were acting incredibly silly, she couldn't help laughing with them.

It was awfully hard to believe that each of these kids had come from an impossible home situation. Or that, as Sully had told her, they'd all arrived here with low self-esteem and a whole lot of other problems. Obviously, their chief eagle was a miracle worker.

She watched him horsing around with them for another minute, then reluctantly glanced at her watch again. The limo driver had an evening booking, so she really couldn't stay much longer.

"Sully?" she said. "I'm afraid I've got to get going."

"You could sleep over again," Billy said quickly. "The Yankees are in Toronto tonight. You could watch with us."

"You must be forgetting," Sully said to him, "there's no TV-watching these days. That," he added to Lauren, "has to do with their caper at Ben's."

"Well," Billy suggested, "how 'bout Monopoly, Lauren? We sometimes play that."

"I'd like to, Billy. I'm sure it would be a lot of fun. But I really do have to get home."

"I'll walk with you to the limo," Terry offered.

"We'll all walk with her," Tony told him.

"No," Sully said firmly. "You'll all stay in the lodge. I want to talk to her alone for a minute."

The boys reverted to their tipsy routines while they were saying goodbye. Then they stood inside the screen door, giggling and calling more drunken-sounding farewells across the clearing to her, until Sully turned and ordered them to knock it off.

"Now, about Saturday," he said, looking back at her. "The kids are getting picked up around ten, so I'll leave as soon as they're gone. That should get me into Manhattan about two or so. And assuming you've got Blackstone's address by then..." He paused, rubbing his jaw.

"Look," he went on at last, "I'd like to simply show up at the guy's place and surprise the hell out of him. But it would be best if I went on my own. As soon as I tell him who I am, he'll know Ben blew his cover. And he sure as hell isn't going to be happy to see me, so—"

"No, Sully, I want to go with you. I really do. Besides, you might need my help. His building's bound to have security, and it's easier for a woman to talk her way around a doorman. And we make a great team, remember? Which means I should definitely be along."

He didn't say a word, merely stood gazing at her, the look in his eyes saying he'd be kissing her if the boys and her driver weren't watching. So where were magic wands when you needed them? She'd dearly love to make everyone else disappear for a few minutes.

"I know you have a good point," he said at last, "but I still don't think—"

"Let's wait until Saturday to decide, all right?"

"Well . . . all right."

"Good. I'll expect you around two, then. And..." Her heart had started pounding, so she paused long enough for a deep, slow breath. Even though she'd already decided to take the risk, that didn't mean it wasn't incredibly scary.

"And?" he said.

"And you'll stay at my place overnight?"

He gazed at her once more, finally saying, "Do you want me to?"

She took another deep breath and nodded. "I don't think it would be wise to drive all the way down and back the same day. And I have lots of room."

"Well . . . I just don't know if my staying in your apartment would be a good idea."

Oh, Lord! She looked away, flushing. After those kisses in the limo, she'd been certain he'd want to spend as long as possible with her. But he still must have a million reservations about the two of them. Or maybe it wasn't merely reservations. Maybe those kisses hadn't been for real.

Before she could come up with another maybe, he said, "I mean, the last time I was in the same room as Killer, he practically took my arm off. But I guess, if you're sure you can control him this time . . ."

When she looked at him again, he was grinning. Her face grew even hotter, and she couldn't decide whether she felt more like kissing him or killing him. How could she not have realized he was teasing?

"Did I ever mention," he said, still grinning, "that you look terrific when you blush?"

"No, I don't believe you ever did," she managed to say almost evenly. "But getting back to Killer, how about if I promise to keep him in my bedroom with me all night? That way," she added with the most innocent smile she could summon up, "he won't be anywhere near you."

Sully's grin vanished so abruptly she could barely keep from laughing. She managed to not even smile, though. She'd just as soon he didn't arrive feeling certain her invitation extended to her bed. Not that she was ruling out the possibility, but she'd have to play it by ear.

"So," she said as they walked the last few yards to the limo, "I'll see you on Saturday."

"Uh-huh. Around two." Sully eyed her closely, trying to figure out if she'd only been joking about the separate bedrooms.

He couldn't tell. And he couldn't ask. Not with her driver standing right there. But if she thought leaving him hanging like this was funny, she had a far more wicked sense of humor than he'd realized.

A glance back toward the lodge told him the kids were still standing at the screen—which precluded a goodbye kiss. So there was nothing he could do but watch her get into the limo.

"Oh, I almost forgot," she said as the driver was reaching to close her door. "You don't have to wear a suit to the exhibit opening unless you'd like to. A lot of Marisa's artist friends would boycott it if they had to wear suits."

"Oh . . . right . . . glad you thought to tell me."

She gave him a smile that made him wish to hell she wasn't leaving. Then the driver closed her door, climbed into the front, and they were on their way.

Sully stood staring after them, thinking about that damn opening again. He'd thought about it a lot since she'd first mentioned it. But despite all his thinking, he hadn't come up with an excuse to get himself out of having to go. And after she'd come all the way up here and helped him with Ben, there was no way he could say he wasn't going. Not even if, by Saturday, he'd thought of the most fantastic excuse in the history of the free world.

No, he was a doomed man. He'd have to meet her parents. And her sister. And her brother. Not to mention the assortment of other relatives.

It was going to be like running a gauntlet, he just knew it was. Or facing an entire panel of Spanish Inquisitioners. Or being caught in sniper fire in the middle of a barren field.

He didn't have a single doubt about how awful it would be. The only thing he didn't know was which Van Slyke would take the first potshot at him.

RATHER THAN 10:00 a.m., it was more like eleven before the boys got away from Eagles Roost. That meant, Sully thought, glancing at his watch, he probably wouldn't make it to Lauren's before three. If the traffic was bad, it would be well after.

He gave her a quick call to say he'd be late, then loaded Roxy into the van. Once he'd dropped her off at old Zeke Scrouthy's, he headed for the Adirondack Northway—which, southbound, would take him practically into Manhattan.

By the time he reached the highway, he'd begun thinking about how he was going to convince Lauren she shouldn't go to see Dirk Blackstone with him. That just wasn't a good idea when Blackstone was a crook.

Oh, he might be a rich crook, with enough money to pay somebody like Leroy Korelenko to do his dirty work, but he was still a crook. And in case he turned out to be trouble, as well, it would be far better if Lauren wasn't along.

If she was bound and determined to go, though, how was he going to stop her? After considering the question for a few miles, he decided the easiest thing would be to take her with him but convince her to wait in the van. At least until he'd had a chance to scope things out.

That problem solved, he forgot about Blackstone and let himself think about the prospect of spending the rest of the weekend with Lauren. The thought of all that time with her was so appealing that every time the odometer clicked over another mile he grew more eager to reach the city. By the time he was heading across the Triborough Bridge toward Manhattan, he could hardly keep a smile off his face.

He'd always been a decisive man, so all the indecision he'd felt about her had bothered the hell out of him. But he'd done some rational thinking after she'd left Eagles Roost on Wednesday, and he'd realized he hadn't been seeing the forest for the trees, that Lauren wasn't her money or her family or any of the other things that had been bothering him. She was simply herself. So he damn well wasn't going to keep dwelling on the fact that she was up to her beautiful blue eyes in money.

He turned down Lexington, drove south a few blocks, then cut over to Fifth Avenue, wondering why that forest-trees thing hadn't occurred to him right off the bat, why he'd let all the other stuff bother him so much he hadn't zoomed right in on what a terrific person she was.

Because she really was. The kids liked her, Grace and Otis liked her, even Roxy liked her. As for him... Hell, he liked her so much he'd begun to wonder if he wasn't well on his way to loving her.

That possibility, he had to admit, was more than a little unnerving, but he was trying not to let it worry him too much. And as for this weekend, he intended to simply enjoy being with her.

The traffic on Fifth Avenue was heavy, but he eventually reached her building—a beautiful old dark brick place just above East Seventy-third—and turned the van over to the parking valet stationed by the front door. Since there was still no trace of Lauren's car, she'd arranged for him to use her space.

When he got to the building's entrance, he stepped aside and waited while a woman with a large black poodle made her way out. The dog had a rhinestone-studded leash and pink bows on its ears—bows that any self-respecting country dog would have torn to shreds rather than be seen wearing in public.

The doorman exchanged pleasantries with the woman, patted the dog, then turned his attention to Sully. He was extremely polite, but it was clear he was the first line of defense against any riffraff who might try to get in.

The second line of defense was lurking inside the lobby—another doorman type, who called up to Lauren's apartment to make sure she was actually expecting company.

"Mr. Sullivan?" he said, hanging up his phone. "Go right on up, sir."

He nodded, then headed over to the elevators and stood absently gazing around while he waited. From the street, the place had clearly said "money"—even if it said it in a subdued way. In the lobby, the word was quietly echoed by marble, wood and expensive furnishings. All in all, Lauren's building was even more impressive than what he'd been imagining, and he'd been imagining something damn impressive.

When one of the elevators finally arrived and carried him smoothly up to the ninth floor, the door opened onto a hallway with walls papered in pale green grass cloth. The dark green carpet felt a foot deep beneath his shoes.

There were only four apartments on the entire floor, two on either side of the elevators, which meant each of them had to be enormous. He was just about to check the numbers for Lauren's when one of the doors opened and there she was.

CHAPTER THIRTEEN

HOT ON DIRK BLACKSTONE'S TRAIL

"HI," LAUREN SAID from her apartment doorway, giving Sully one of her fabulous smiles.

He simply gazed at her. He couldn't figure out how she managed to keep getting more beautiful every time he saw her, but she did. And the skirt of her pale blue dress was short enough to remind him how gorgeous her legs were, as well.

"Are you coming in?" she asked, stepping back to let him past her and into an entrance foyer as big as an oversized bedroom.

Fleetingly, he wondered how clean her creamy marble floor would stay if his kids were running around on it. Then she shut the door and smiled at him again, driving every last thought of the boys from his mind.

"Let's just hang that in here for the moment," she said, taking his garment bag and slipping it into a closet.

When she turned back to him, he draped his arms around her waist, pulled her close and kissed her. Her lips tasted heavenly. The smell of her perfume went straight to his head; the lush softness of her body against his went straight to his groin.

Just as he was thinking they didn't have to be in any hurry to leave for Dirk Blackstone's, she moved her lips a fraction away from his and murmured, "Sully?"

"Mmm?" He kissed her once more.

"Sully?" She whispered against his mouth. "We have to talk for a minute."

Reluctantly, he loosened his arms to let her take a backward step—pleased when she reached for his hand as she did.

"Come into the living room," she said, leading him across the sea of marble. It flowed from the foyer over to the far side of the living room and along into a formal dining room off the far end. Here and there, the marble was covered by lush area rugs the color of toasted almonds.

Not letting go of Lauren's hand, he wandered over to the windows and checked out her view of Central Park, reminding himself again that he wasn't going to think about her money—which was proving a little tough when her apartment made him feel like the proverbial fish out of water.

"Beautiful place," he said, thinking how completely different it was from Eagles Roost.

"Thanks. I really like it. But let's sit for a minute."

He walked over to a couch with her, taking another quick glance around as they sat down. The room, about the size of a football field, was decorated with a combination of antiques and big overstuffed furniture covered in a pale yellow print. Between the boys' snacks and their sneakers, they could really do a number on that fabric.

The only thing in the entire room that didn't look expensive was Killer, who even clean and groomed looked like a streetwise tom. He sat unobtrusively in a wing chair, watching Sully through golden slits of eyes.

Figuring he'd leave renewing acquaintances with the cat for later, Sully focused on the large paintings that hung on one long wall. Like the furniture, they were pale in color, and the four of them were obviously related somehow—all depicting some sort of Medieval theme. They weren't abstract, but were hardly realistic, either.

"Do you like them?" Lauren asked.

"In a way," he said honestly.

"They're my sister's. Part of a series she's just finished called *Dreaming of Lancelot and Guinevere.* Some of the others are in her new exhibit."

He nodded, wishing he'd known to read up on the Knights of the Round Table.

"So," Lauren went on, "I'm afraid there's been a slight hitch in our plans."

For a joyous half second he thought she was going to tell him the exhibit opening had been postponed. Then she said, "Chester ran into a bit of a problem when he tried to check on Blackstone's fax number. He'd expected that matching it up with a home or office would be straightforward, but it wasn't."

"You mean we don't have our friend's address or phone number."

"No, not yet."

That started a sinking feeling in the pit of Sully's stomach. He dearly wanted to know why Blackstone was so eager to buy Eagles Roost, and the sooner he knew, the happier he'd be. But if he couldn't get to the guy this weekend he'd be out of luck until after Grace and Otis were back. The baseball team's camping trip was a once-a-summer event.

He realized Lauren had been speaking and looked at her once more. "Sorry? My mind was wandering."

"I said that Chester still figures he can get what we want, he just ran out of time. In fact, when he called me to explain what had happened, he was at the airport—on his way to some out-of-town job."

"And he gets back when?"

"In a week or so. But he said if we didn't want to wait, we could have a shot at it ourselves."

"Good, then we will."

Lauren smiled. "Now, how did I know that's exactly what you'd say?"

"Because you're clairvoyant?"

She laughed at that.

When she did, it took a major effort not to reach for her. But he knew, if he did, he might forget Blackstone even existed.

"The only thing about doing it ourselves," she said, "is that Chester was worried we'd blow it. And he said if we did, we might make it harder for him."

"So we won't blow it. What do we do?"

"Well, the problem is that the fax number Ben had isn't for a private fax machine. It's the number of a business called Fax Depot, on Forty-second Street— a place that sends and receives faxes for people. Blackstone's one of their customers."

"I'd have thought," Sully muttered, "a guy with twenty thousand bucks to give Leroy Korelenko would have his own fax machine."

"Maybe he does. Maybe he just doesn't want anyone being able to track him down too easily."

Sully shook his head. "This Blackstone is sounding weirder all the time. But if Fax Depot's been receiving his messages, then they've got to know how to get hold of him. So all we have to do is head over there and get our information, right? It must be open on Saturdays."

"It's open seven days a week, twenty-four hours a day. But as Chester put it, companies don't merrily hand out information about their customers."

"No, I guess they generally don't. So we'll have to convince someone to make an exception."

KNOWING THEY'D NEVER FIND a place to park near Fax Depot, Lauren had convinced Sully they should take a taxi rather than his van. If he'd driven, they'd have ended up with a long walk down Forty-second Street—not something she'd relish even on a day that wasn't sweltering. With its hookers, three-card monte games, porno houses and pickpockets, a long stretch of Forty-second Street was positively sleazy.

"Do you have much cash with you?" she asked as the taxi crawled down Fifth Avenue.

"You mean enough to pay for the cab?" Sully said. "Sure, I can handle it."

"No, I mean enough to get us the information."

Sully shook his head. "It's been a long time since I lived in the city. You forget that people here don't do favors unless there's something in it for them."

"Well, they don't. And Chester figured this something would be a minimum of two hundred dollars."

Sully look distinctly annoyed. "We'd better find a bank machine, then," he muttered.

"No, it's okay. I didn't think you were likely to come armed with a stack of fifties, so I got some." She took the bills out of her purse and handed them to him.

"All right," he said slowly. "After we've seen how many of these it takes, I'll write you a check."

"Oh, don't be silly. The money doesn't matter."

"It matters to me."

She hesitated, something in his tone telling her not to argue. "Fine," she said at last. "Fine, you can write me a check later."

"And what about Chester?"

"What about him?"

"I mean, you told him to send his bill to me, didn't you?"

"There's not going to be one. He said he owed Elliot a couple of favors."

"You're sure?"

"Of course I'm sure."

Sully eyed her suspiciously, which she found rather insulting. "I'm positive," she said firmly. "But I don't know what you're so concerned about. It's only money."

"It's only *your* money," he said slowly, making her wish she hadn't let her remark slip out. It obviously didn't take much to hurt his pride.

"Look," he went on, "we'd better get something straight here. I really like you. I wouldn't be with you today if I didn't. But I'm still having trouble with the fact that you're so incredibly rich."

"I was hoping we were past that," she said uneasily.

"I'm doing my best, Lauren, I really am. I've been telling myself I'm just not going to think about your money, but it's damn hard not to when you give me a wad of fifty-dollar bills.''

"I was only trying to help.''

"I know you were.'' He shot her a wry smile, then took her hand. "Look, I know it wouldn't bother a lot of men but it bothers me. So all I can do is keep trying not to let it, and I'll probably be okay with it after a while.''

Or maybe he wouldn't be. With that thought, a tiny chill wrapped itself around her heart. She looked away from him and glanced out of the taxi.

They'd turned onto Forty-second Street, but were still barely moving in the traffic, and she could suddenly imagine Sully opening his door, getting out of the taxi and walking straight out of her life. That wasn't something she wanted to even imagine, let alone see happen.

When she'd left Eagles Roost on Wednesday, she hadn't been certain whether she was on the brink of falling in love with him or already beyond it. When she'd opened her door today and seen him standing in the hall, she'd felt so overjoyed it had left no doubt in her mind.

So as much as she wouldn't want a man to love her only for her money, she didn't want Jack Sullivan not to love her because of it. Not now that she was sure she was in love with him.

SULLY PULLED THE THIRD fifty out of his pocket and slipped it to the manager—a sweaty guy with beady eyes, a pointy nose and a two-day growth of beard. The three features combined to make him resemble a weasel.

Even as he was slipping the bill into his own pocket, he was saying, "Like I told ya, my friend, my job would be on the line if anyone found out."

When Sully looked at Lauren, she gave him an encouraging smile that said she figured he was almost there, so he temporarily dismissed the idea of grabbing the weasel by the shirtfront and explaining a few facts of life to him.

Instead, he glanced around the nearly empty store and said, "It doesn't look to me as if anybody's paying the slightest attention to us."

"Well, I guess a couple more fifties would make it worth the risk."

Trying to ignore the way the pulse in his temple was throbbing, Sully dug out two more bills. They disappeared into the weasel's pocket faster than the eye could see, as if he knew he'd been pressing his luck.

"I'll be back in a sec," he promised, starting for his office.

"If there are many guys like him wandering around this city," Sully muttered to Lauren, "it's no wonder the murder rate's so high."

"At least we're getting what we want," she pointed out.

A minute or two later, when the weasel popped back out of his office, he was clutching a sheet of paper.

"See?" she murmured. "He's got our information right in his hot little hand."

Sully hoped she was right, but the guy seemed to be sweating even harder than he'd been before, which was hardly a promising sign.

He reached them and cleared his throat. "This here's a printout of Blackstone's account for the month," he said, handing over the sheet. "It's the best I can do for ya, my friend."

"What the hell's this?" Sully muttered, staring at it. The phone number space was blank. And all that was printed on the address line was *Deposit account balance: $216.45.*

He passed the page to Lauren, then focused on the weasel again. "Okay, *my friend,* what's your game? Where's the information I paid for?"

The man took a step backward, saying, "Hey, I ain't playin' no game. See, I kinda forgot that Blackstone never filled out our forms."

"What do you mean?" Lauren said.

"I mean the guy said he didn't like leavin' personal information for just anyone to see. So we got no way of reachin' him. He just calls every couple of days and checks if anythin's come for him. If somethin' has, he stops by."

Sully's patience had run out, so he grabbed the front of the weasel's shirt, pulling him closer. "Look," he said into his face, "don't try to sell me a load of crap. I don't know what you're playing at, but if you don't have an address for him, how do you bill him?"

The weasel swallowed hard. "That's what the deposit account's all about. He paid five hundred bucks up front. And every so often he bumps up the balance. So, long as we got more of his money than he's got fax charges, we can live without an address or phone number."

"Why, you little—"

"Sully?" Lauren said, resting her hand on his arm. "Sully, if he doesn't have them he doesn't have them."

"Right. Well if he doesn't have them he doesn't have our two hundred and fifty bucks, either. Hand it over," he ordered, letting go of the weasel's shirt.

"Wait a sec." He quickly stepped back again—far enough that he was completely out of reach this time. "How 'bout we work somethin' else out?"

"Like what?"

"Like next time somethin' comes in for him, I let you know he'll be comin' by?"

"No good," Sully snapped. He couldn't be two places at once, and he had to head back to Eagles Roost tomorrow.

"Could you at least describe him for us?" Lauren asked.

The weasel looked at her, then gave her a sly smile. "Sure I can, lady. Tell you what. I describe him and I only give your boyfriend back half his money. Okay?"

"Okay," she said before Sully could open his mouth.

"Damn," Sully muttered under his breath. He hadn't wanted to leave this creep with a dime of his money, never mind a hundred and twenty-five bucks. And unless Blackstone had two heads or something, what good was a description when there were seven or eight million people in New York City?

The weasel reluctantly dug $125 from his pocket and handed it over, saying "Okay, Blackstone's a white guy. About forty. Average height. Average weight. Good-lookin' guy, I guess. Yeah, I'd have to say he's a good-lookin' guy."

"Good-looking," Lauren said. "You mean movie star calibre?"

"Nah... well, I dunno. Hell, Danny DeVito's a movie star, right? But by good-lookin' I meant like a straight nose, a tan, all his teeth, that kinda thing. And neat. Clothes always pressed. Short hair. Never needs a shave."

"What color hair?" Lauren asked.

"Brown."

"And his eyes."

"Two of 'em. He's got two of 'em. Two ears, too." The weasel started to laugh at his joke, then turned it into a cough when Sully glared at him.

"I dunno," he muttered. "Who looks at a guy's eyes?"

"What else?" Sully demanded. So far, he hadn't heard anything that would distinguish Blackstone from half the fortyish-year-old men in the country.

"What else," the weasel repeated. "I dunno. He dresses good, I guess. A suit if it's day. Sometimes casual stuff at night. But never jeans and sneakers or nothin' like that. It's always expensive stuff."

"What else?" Sully said again.

"That's about it, my friend. There's nothin' real special about him. But, hey, most of the customers I couldn't describe at all. I only know him 'cuz of the fuss he put up about not fillin' out our forms. And 'cuz he smacked a five hundred buck deposit down on the counter like it was milk money."

"Well, thank you," Lauren said. "Perhaps we'll want to do business with you again."

"Anytime. Anytime." He smiled at her, then gave a sidelong glance in Sully's direction. Clearly, if there was an again, he'd be far happier dealing with Lauren alone.

Sully took her arm and they started for the door. "We might," he muttered, "want to do business with that lowlife again?"

"You never know, Sully. At the moment, he's the only link we have to Blackstone." As they walked out onto the street, she glanced at her watch.

"When do we have to be at the gallery?" he asked, knowing why she was checking the time.

"Well, if it's all right with you, I'd like to get there early. The man Marisa lives with had to be in Europe this month, and she likes moral support at this sort of thing."

"The man Marisa lives with?" he said curiously. From what little he knew about Lauren's parents, he couldn't imagine them approving of that arrangement.

She shrugged. "I know what you're thinking, and no, my parents weren't happy about it at first. But they finally rationalized it as a function of Marisa's artistic temperament. At any rate, is it okay if we get to the gallery early?"

"Sure, it doesn't matter to me. But with that guy who threatened your brother wandering around, is it a good idea for so many members of your family to be in the same place at the same time?"

"Well, Elliot thinks if the fellow was actually going to try anything he'd have tried it by now. And I know he's asked a couple of criminologists their opinions, so we're probably all in the clear.

"Sully?" she went on after a moment. "You're awfully disappointed we didn't get much about Blackstone, aren't you?"

"Kind of."

"Only kind of?" she said softly.

"All right, more than kind of. I keep thinking that if he still wants to get his hands on Eagles Roost as badly as ever, how do I know he won't come up with some other bizarre scheme? As far as that goes, how do I know he hasn't got one in the works already?"

"Yes, I see what you mean. If he'd plan a bank robbery, who knows what else he'd do. But we've got about an hour before we should be getting ready for the reception. So when we get back to my apartment, why don't we sit down and try to figure out some other way of finding an address for him?"

"Sure. Good idea." He doubted, though, they'd come up with any brilliant plan. Besides, he could think of other things he'd far rather do once they got back to her apartment. On the other hand, if they only had an hour...

"If we go to the reception early," he said, "can we leave early, too?"

Lauren smiled. "We're there at six-thirty, we're gone by seven-thirty. Then we've got the rest of the night to ourselves. Does that sound all right?"

Sully smiled back at her. It sounded just great.

THE CHALMERS GALLERY, which handled Marisa's work, was down in SoHo. It was *the* district for an art gallery, but not the safest area to leave a car unattended, so Lauren had convinced Sully to take yet another taxi.

She glanced across the back seat at him and smiled, thinking how absolutely gorgeous he looked. He was wearing good pants and a chocolate brown silk shirt—which he'd said had been a birthday gift from Grace and Otis.

It made his eyes look so deliciously dark she practically melted every time her gaze met his. If this reception had been for anyone but her sister, she'd have skipped it in a minute. Then the two of them could have been alone together the entire evening.

As they crossed West Houston Street, leaving the Village behind and entering SoHo, she rested her hand on his and said, "Have you decided about what we were discussing in the apartment? About hiring a private detective?"

"I've been thinking it over," he said slowly. "But with Fax Depot being open twenty-four hours a day, we'd need more than one person. It would probably take three people to keep it under surveillance. And they'd probably want to try tracking him down other ways as well, which would mean even more manpower.

"So I'm just not sure. As much as I'd like to know what Blackstone's story is, until I get some funding firmed up I really don't want to spend any money I don't have to."

It almost killed her not to say she'd pay for a dozen detectives, if that's how many it would take, but she kept quiet. Until Sully got over this thing he had about her money, she intended to be very careful.

Glancing out of the taxi, she saw they'd almost reached their destination—which started her worrying about how things would go once they got there.

Over the past week, she'd grown awfully concerned that inviting Sully to this opening had been one of her infamous little errors in judgment. And at the moment, the butterflies in her stomach were multiplying at a rate that would put rabbits to shame.

Her father was bound to recognize Sully's name when she introduced them, so maybe she should have forewarned him, should have given both him and her mother time to adjust to the idea. It was too late to think about that now, though.

As the taxi jerked to a stop in front of the gallery, she told herself that no matter how upset her father turned out to be he was far too well mannered to say anything really rude.

Once they were out of the taxi she watched Sully paying the driver, thinking he looked as uneasy as she felt. Then he straightened his shoulders, shot her a quick smile and suddenly looked up to taking on the world.

She only hoped he was. Her little corner of it, at least. With a deep breath, she took his arm and they started for the door.

A woman she didn't recognize was standing just inside, checking invitations. Beyond her, in the long, narrow gallery, two dozen or so other early arrivals were sipping champagne—some looking at the paintings, some standing talking.

Her heart hammering nervously, she scanned the room. She spotted Marisa, then her parents, then Elliot and Ursula. They were all busy talking; none of them had noticed her yet.

"Those are my parents, ahead on the right," she murmured to Sully, hoping her voice wasn't betraying her anxiety. "You see? The man who looks like Alan Alda and the woman who looks a little like Angie Dickinson?"

Sully nodded.

"And that's Elliot and his wife, Ursula, standing over beside the bar. The man in the charcoal suit who—"

"Who looks like Harrison Ford?" Sully said wryly.

She smiled. "I'd have said more like Sam Neill. And Marisa's the one in the black dress, over there who—"

"Who looks a lot like you only not quite so beautiful."

"What I was *going* to say, is that Marisa's the one talking to that man with the beard. And that he owns the gallery."

"You mean the guy who looks like Kenny Rogers?" Sully teased.

"You're impossible," she told him, but he was doing a lot to lower her anxiety level. It was still far too high for comfort, though, and then it jumped even higher because she suddenly sensed something was wrong.

Not far behind them a woman had raised her voice. "Sir?" she was saying as Lauren turned and saw it was the woman checking invitations.

"Sir, this is a private reception," she said while Lauren's gaze found the man she was talking to.

"Look, you can't just barge in here and... Oh, my God! He's got a gun!"

"Nobody move!" he yelled.

The entire room froze.

"Don't move a muscle," Sully whispered.

Lauren doubted she could if she tried. She simply stared, numb with fear, at the man holding the gun.

CHAPTER FOURTEEN

SULLY MEETS THE FAMILY

ADRENALINE PUMPING like crazy, Sully sized up the situation.

The pistol was a .380 semiautomatic. Not especially powerful. Nor accurate. But potentially deadly at close range. The guy brandishing it was about thirty—nervous but not strung out. And the way his eyes were roaming the room said he was here with a purpose.

All at once, he found who he was looking for. He pointed the gun at Elliot Van Slyke and shouted, "You! Lawyer man! I told you I'd get you and here I am."

Elliot's face went white. Lauren made a strangled little noise in her throat. Sully's mind began working flat out. The guy wasn't using both hands to aim. That was good. But probably not good enough.

Just as Sully made his move, the shooting started.

The gallery exploded with the shots. People were ducking and screaming. The smell of gunpowder seared the air. And Sully tackled the shooter from behind.

They both went down. Sully heard the gun clatter onto the floor and yelled for someone to get it. The shooter was halfway to his feet, so Sully grabbed his leg and yanked him off-balance. The shooter hit the floor again—Sully on top of him now, his hands around the guy's throat.

"Okay," he snapped, breathing hard. "Make another move and I swear I'll break your goddamn neck. You understand?"

"Yeah," the man whispered hoarsely.

"Good. Somebody call the cops!" he said loudly, still not taking his eyes off the man he had pinned. Then, his thumbs firmly lodged against the guy's windpipe, he glanced up to see who'd gotten the gun.

Lauren had it. She was standing pointing it at them, a stricken look on her face and her hand shaking so badly he hoped to hell the gun didn't have a hair trigger.

"Way to go," he said quietly. "But it's okay now, so why don't you check on your brother."

THE POLICE had arrived following the shooting— immediately ordering everyone to refrain from talking to other witnesses until they'd given an official statement. That meant Lauren hadn't had a chance to say a word to Sully or anyone else.

But at least she'd been told that Elliot would be all right. The ambulance had gotten there shortly after the police, and the paramedics had said neither bullet that hit him had done any critical damage. So while Ursula had gone to the hospital with him, the police had asked the other family members to remain at the gallery for questioning—along with the rest of the witnesses.

At that stage, between the guests who'd arrived before the shooting and the swarm of uniformed police officers and detectives, the gallery had been fairly full. As witnesses had been questioned and left, though, the numbers had dwindled.

Now, Lauren saw, glancing around while her detective made a few final notes in his book, the only other people still being questioned were Sully and her parents. The hero of the piece and the family of the victim were obviously of more interest to the police than anyone else.

The sole other remaining civilians in the gallery were Marisa—who was standing alone by the bar looking shell-shocked—and the gallery's owner. He was in his office on the phone.

"I think that's everything," Lauren's detective said at last. "Thank you for your time."

She nodded, then looked over at Sully again, hoping he was almost done. She desperately needed to wrap her arms around him and assure herself he really was all right. That was the only thing she thought might stop the shaking inside.

He was still deep in conversation with one of the other detectives, though, so she headed over to her sister and gave her a hard hug.

"Some exhibit opening," Marisa said ruefully.

Lauren managed what she hoped looked like a smile. "Well, it's certainly not one anybody's going to forget soon. Especially not Elliot. Has Ursula called from the hospital?"

Marisa nodded. "She said there were only the two hits, and that the one in the arm is just a flesh wound. The one in his side cracked a couple of ribs, but the doctors taped him up and they'll probably release him tonight."

The news sent a rush of relief through Lauren. Even though the paramedics had sounded sure of themselves, she'd been afraid to entirely believe they hadn't missed something. "We were all so lucky," she murmured.

"Thanks to your friend." Marisa glanced in Sully's direction, then back at Lauren. "I'd just spotted you with him before all hell broke loose. Who is he?"

"His name's Jack Sullivan."

"Well his looks are to die for. Where on earth did you meet him?"

"Ahh... he just walked into my office one day."

"Really?" Marisa glanced over at him again. "But who is he? I mean, aside from being a total hunk. And where on earth did he learn to play Rambo?"

Lauren reminded herself Marisa was the most liberal one in the family and said, "I suppose he either learned it growing up on the streets of the Bronx or in prison."

"What?"

Taking a deep breath, she began at the beginning and raced through the entire story.

"Well, well," Marisa murmured when she'd finished. "And just how serious are things between the two of you?"

"Marisa... I think I'm in love with him. No, I'm sure of it."

Marisa gazed at her for a few seconds, then said, "Aren't you worried that it's happened too fast?"

"I'm worried about a whole lot of things, but that isn't one of them. In fact, I doubt I'd be worried if it had happened even faster, because it feels so right."

"Well, I guess there's no set schedule for falling in love," Marisa said. "But what about Mom and Dad? They don't have a clue about him, do they? Mom would have been on the phone to me right away if they did.''

"No, they don't know anything yet.''

"And how much are you going to tell them?''

"As little as possible for the moment. But when I introduce them Dad will recognize Sully's name. And he knows he's an ex-con.''

Marisa laughed quietly. "And here he is with Daddy's little girl. Do you think Dad can take any more tonight? On top of Elliot's getting shot?''

"Oh, Lord,'' Lauren said, glancing past her sister. "I don't know, but we're about to find out.''

The three remaining detectives had magically wrapped up at almost exactly the same time. And at this very moment, Sully, her father and her mother were all heading from various areas of the gallery over to where Marisa and Lauren were standing.

She still wanted to hug Sully so badly she couldn't have stopped herself if she'd tried, and when he reached her she wrapped her arms around him and clung to him tightly—telling herself it didn't matter that her parents were watching.

Her mother would have sized things up in two seconds, anyway. When it came to her daughters and men, she had better radar than the United States military.

"Hey,'' Sully murmured against her ear, "everything's all right, isn't it? They didn't find anything more wrong with your brother, did they?''

She shook her head against the solid warmth of his chest, aware that she'd been right. The shaking inside had almost stopped. "Elliot's going to be fine. And you were wonderful, Sully. Just wonderful.''

He gently patted her back. "You weren't too bad yourself, Van Slyke. You were the one who ended up with the gun."

"That didn't hold a candle to what you did, Sullivan," she whispered as her parents closed in on them.

"This young man is with you, Lauren?" Roger Van Slyke said, obviously surprised.

She nodded, moving out of Sully's embrace and noting how elated her father looked to learn Sully was her date. Unfortunately, she knew his elation wouldn't last.

While Marisa began filling their mother in on Elliot's condition, their father was extending his hand to Sully, saying, "I'm Roger Van Slyke, and I don't have words to thank you enough. You probably saved my son's life."

"Jack Sullivan," Sully said, shaking hands.

Lauren watched her father's expression. It didn't change. He hadn't picked up on the name immediately, but it was only a matter of time.

"I'm Elliot's mother," Susannah Van Slyke said, "and Roger is right. We can't thank you enough."

"I'm glad I was able to help."

Marisa cleared her throat.

"And this," Lauren said, taking the hint, "is my sister, Marisa. Marisa, Jack Sullivan."

Lauren glanced at her father again. This time, the name had clicked. She could almost see the wheels starting to turn.

"Jack Sullivan," he said. "Jack Sullivan. I know your name, don't I?"

"Yes, sir. We spoke on the phone a while back. When you called Eagles Roost, looking for Lauren."

Sully's words were followed by a dead silence. A very long dead silence.

"You run that program, then," Susannah finally said. The brittle smile accompanying her words meant she'd sufficiently recovered from her astonishment to force herself into charming mode. "It must be very rewarding work."

"Most of the time," Sully agreed.

"And you came here tonight with Lauren," Roger said, clearly having difficulty getting his head around that. "You just happened to be in town or...?"

"No," Lauren managed to say evenly. "I invited him to come in for the exhibit opening."

"Oh," Roger said, glancing at Sully again. "And did you find a hotel you're happy with? I understand some of them leave a lot to be desired these days."

Lauren held her breath. She simply wasn't ready to cope with them knowing too much yet. Then she started breathing again when Sully said, "I'm staying with a friend. I grew up in New York City, so I still know a few people here."

"Oh." Roger apparently had no more questions on the tip of his tongue, because he glanced at his wife for help.

"Well," she offered, "since you're with Lauren, why doesn't Roger take all of us out for dinner? I want to phone the hospital and talk to Elliot, but then we could go to... where do you think, Roger? The Rainbow Room? If you called ahead, I'm sure Franklin would ensure there's a good table for us."

"Oh, Mom," Lauren said, "that's a really nice idea. But I'm afraid Sully and I have plans for the evening."

"I don't," Marisa jumped in quickly, before either parent had a chance to ask if Lauren and Sully couldn't change their plans.

Lauren shot her sister a thankful glance.

Marisa nodded almost imperceptibly and went on, "I mean, I did have plans, but since there's not going to be any post-opening party now, I'd love to have dinner with you and Dad."

"Ahh..." Susannah said. "Well, good."

Lauren glanced at her watch, then at her parents. "I'm afraid we're already late, so we'd better get going. Say hi to Elliot and Ursula for me. And tell them I'll call tomorrow." With that, she grabbed Sully's hand and practically ran for the door.

"Thanks," he said as they hit the street and he hailed a taxi. "I don't think I'd have enjoyed dinner with your parents. They were both itching to grill me, weren't they?"

"Only to within an inch of your life."

When they'd climbed into the cab, she added, "But at least you couldn't have met them under better circumstances."

"Oh, sure." Sully grinned at her. "An art gallery that turns into a shooting gallery. Who could ask for anything more?"

She lightly punched his arm. "All right, maybe I didn't exactly mean circumstances. I should have said you couldn't have made a better first impression. That you couldn't possibly have topped saving their son's life."

"Where to?" the driver demanded impatiently. She looked at Sully. "A restaurant? Or would you rather just grab some takeout from my deli and head back to the apartment?"

"What do you think?" he asked, wrapping his arm around her shoulders.

"East Seventy-third and Madison," she told the driver.

Sully smiled, then leaned nearer and nuzzled her neck. The warmth of his breath sent a delicious hot rush racing through her—and made her wish she'd suggested ordering in, rather than wasting time with a stop.

LAUREN CLOSED the apartment door behind them but didn't turn on any lights. Instead, she took the deli bag from Sully and put it on the foyer table, then reached for his hand and led him across the living room to the windows.

Darkness hadn't totally fallen, but the night city had come alive. Directly below them, Fifth Avenue was a string of headlights. On the far side of the street, the park stretched out, shadowy gray, lit only along some of the pathways and the few streets that wound across it.

Beyond the park, the lights of the big old apartment buildings on Central Park West shone warmly in the distance, while toward Midtown the city exploded in brightness—from the hotels along Central Park South down to the theater district.

Lauren glanced at Sully's rugged profile and her heart skipped a beat. She'd always thought this view at twilight was incredibly romantic, but tonight was the first time she'd shared it with a man she loved.

They stood silently gazing out for a few more moments, then Sully draped his arm around her waist and pulled her close. She rested her head against his shoulder and breathed in that combination of the outdoors and his own intoxicating scent.

It filled her with desire. She hadn't made love since her marriage had ended—hadn't met any man who'd appealed to her enough. But if ever there was a right man, it was Sully. And if ever there was a right time, it was now.

She shifted, trying to see his expression. When she could, he smiled such a sexy smile it did wicked things to her insides. Then he took her face in his hands and kissed her the way she'd been dreaming about since the very first time—a kiss so deep and hard and sizzling it made her lips numb. Lord, she desperately wanted this man.

A demanding "meow" derailed her train of thought, then Killer was wrapping himself around her ankles, loudly informing her he was positively starving to death.

"I can see why cats need nine lives," Sully muttered.

"We could try ignoring him," she suggested. "Or I could feed him. Then he'd leave us alone for a while."

Sully gently kissed her throat and began working his way south. "Leave us alone for how long?" he murmured as he kissed.

"Mmm . . . if I give him his favorite, probably long enough for us to make it to the bedroom."

Sully stopped kissing and grinned at her. "Make it to the bedroom *and* close the door on him?"

Without another word Lauren scooped Killer up, certain she was about to break the world's record for speed in opening a can of cat food.

That didn't prove to be the case, though, because Sully followed her into the kitchen and—as she stuck the can under the opener—wrapped his arms around her from behind. He cupped her breasts and began grazing her nipples with his thumbs.

That was so delightfully distracting the cutting wheel went around the can three or four times before she realized it had done its job. When she did, she hastily spooned some of the food into Killer's bowl and put it down on his mat.

"Quick," Sully whispered, taking her hand. "We've probably got only a minute before he realizes we've outsmarted him."

Laughing, she led him along the dark hallway and into her moonlit bedroom. He closed the door, murmured, "Alone at last," and folded her into his arms.

This time, his lips more teased than kissed. But his hands...oh, his hands were moving possessively over her body in a way that started a slow heat between her legs. It gradually flowed through her body, making her want him so intensely she felt weak-kneed with desire.

He found the zipper on her dress and slid it down. Then he eased her dress off her shoulders and over her hips. When it dropped to the floor and she stepped out of it, he stood gazing at her in the moonlight.

"You know," he finally murmured, "you're an incredibly beautiful woman."

His words made her smile, but she needed much more than words. Her fingers trembling, she reached to unbutton his shirt. When she had it undone, she snaked her fingers through his chest hair, smoothing her palms across the hard muscles of his chest. Touching him sent a sweet surge through her body.

"Oh, Lauren," he groaned, shrugging out of his shirt and reaching into his pants pocket. Tossing a condom packet onto the bedside table, he quickly unzipped his pants and kicked them off.

His arousal was obvious, and seeing it only made her want him more. She stepped closer to him and caressed him through his briefs. Feeling how large and hard he was made the wanting an almost frantic need, so she edged closer yet, pressing herself against him.

Groaning again, he nuzzled her neck and began fondling her breasts. Then he eased her onto the bed and made short work of removing their remaining clothes.

He kissed her deeply, stealing the breath from her lungs. She could feel the kisses everywhere, reaching right through her and making the wanting worse.

His hardness pressing against her stomach fueled her need, and when she reached down to touch him once more he slid his hand between her legs, sending a jolt of electricity through her.

Then he began stroking her, turning the slow heat into a burning ache, sending rushes of excitement coursing through her veins—waves of liquid fire that grew stronger and stronger, until she was drowning in their hot rhythm, until she was making tiny noises in the back of her throat, until she could scarcely breathe...until she came over and over again, with a shattering feeling so exquisite it was almost unbearable.

Then, very gradually, her body grew still. She was left, though, with such a warm, indescribable glow that she lay in Sully's arms wishing time would stand still forever with the two of them right where they were.

"Oh, Sully," she whispered when she was finally able. "Oh, Sully." She wanted to tell him how incredible it had been, but she couldn't manage anything more because he started caressing her nipples, sending aftershocks through her that had her gasping for breath again.

Then he stopped touching her and lay kissing her throat for a minute. Just as she realized he'd been putting on the condom, he covered her body with his and slid inside her. He felt large and hard and wonderful.

When he began moving, each thrust sent another shock wave through her. And when he came, collapsing over her, she felt more incredibly marvelous than she'd felt in her entire life.

She lay drifting in a sensuous haze, loving the solid feel of his body on hers, until he finally shifted to one side and gently brushed her sweat-dampened hair away from her face.

"You okay?" he murmured.

She smiled against his chest. "I'm so far beyond okay I can't describe it." She traced his arm with her fingers, not able to keep from touching him. "Oh, Sully," she murmured at last. "How am I ever going to get enough of you?"

Sully exhaled slowly. Lauren's words had so eerily voiced his own thoughts that it was downright spooky. How was he ever going to get enough of her?

He didn't know exactly how to express the way he felt, but it was as if he'd just discovered a part of him that had been missing his entire life. And he knew it

wasn't only her hot passion that had him feeling that
way. The passion was merely a bonus.

The important thing was the sense that Lauren was
meant for him. That she had to be, because no other
woman had ever made him feel the way she did.

Yes, she was meant for him. But how could he
possibly make her his?

SULLY WAS STILL AWAKE when Sunday morning came
creeping into Lauren's bedroom, splashing sunshine
over the deli debris stacked on her dresser.

Around midnight, they'd remembered about the
food and eaten dinner in bed. After that, they'd
watched a terrible late-night comedy that had seemed
hilarious because he was watching it with Lauren in
his arms.

Then, after they'd made love again, she'd fallen
asleep. But he hadn't wanted to waste a minute while
he was with her, while he had her to touch and kiss
and hold through the night.

He'd save his sleeping until tonight, when he'd be
back at Eagles Roost, alone in his own bed—which
just might be, he reflected, the most unappealing
prospect he'd faced in years.

A loud "meow" announced that Killer had finally
decided to venture into the bedroom. Even though
Lauren had left the door open for him after the movie
had ended, this was the first time he'd appeared.

Standing just inside the doorway, he eyed Sully
suspiciously for a minute, then turned and stalked off,
his tail sticking stiffly up into the air. Obviously, Sully
didn't meet with his approval.

Sully could care less. As long as he met with Lauren's approval, the rest of the world's—human *and* animal—didn't much matter to him. He lay there lightly stroking her honey-gold hair until she stirred. Then he kissed her throat.

"Mmm," she murmured, snuggling even closer. "Mmm, do you think I could have a wake-up call like this every morning?"

Didn't he wish. "It would be an awfully long drive to make every morning," he pointed out, "so maybe I should just stay right here."

She propped herself up on one elbow and gazed at him. "You can stay," she said quietly, "as long as you want."

He felt his groin tightening and slowly brushed his hand across her breast. Her nipple was hard; she made a little moaning sound when he touched it. "I wish I *could* stay," he murmured. "God, but I wish I could stay."

"You can come again," she said, stroking his arm.

Her touch started his blood running hot.

"Not until after Grace and Otis are home."

She nodded slowly. "Sully, in the meantime, what about Blackstone?"

"What about him?"

"Well, I had a weird dream during the night."

"I knew we shouldn't have eaten all that food so late," he teased.

Smiling, she shook her head. "It wasn't that. I think it was because of what you said yesterday— about Blackstone maybe coming up with some other bizarre scheme to get his hands on Eagles Roost."

"Is that what he was doing in your dream?" he asked, wishing she hadn't reminded him about the guy.

"I can't remember that he actually did anything. No, that's not quite true. He was laughing. I could see you and the boys all walking away from the lodge, looking incredibly sad. And there was a man standing on the porch and laughing. A man with no face. And I was so frightened, Sully.

"I don't want you to lose the lodge," she went on after a moment. "And I don't want anything to happen to your program."

"That makes two of us." He put his arm around her and pulled her close again.

"No, listen to me," she said, straightening up and looking at him once more. "I know you have a problem with the idea of taking anything from me, but I need you to listen to what I'm going to say. And then we won't ever talk about it again unless you want to, okay?"

"Okay," he said slowly.

"Sully, if by any chance you can't come up with funding for next year. Or if something else happens with Blackstone and you're in danger of losing the lodge, I'd be more than happy to lend you enough money to see you through."

"Lauren, I—"

She pressed her fingers to his lips and shook her head. "Please, Sully? Let's just leave it at that."

He looked at her for a minute, then finally nodded. Talking about it would only spoil some of their remaining time together.

"I guess," he said, forcing a smile, "if we're not going to talk..." Drawing her close once more, he kissed her. But even the sweetness of her kiss didn't entirely take his mind off what she'd said.

He knew that if it ever came down to a choice between swallowing his pride or seeing his program destroyed, he'd swallow his pride. He hoped to hell, though, that he never found himself in a position where his only option was having to ask Lauren to bail him out.

But if he couldn't handle the thought of that, could there be even a possibility that he and Lauren might somehow...

He drew back a little and gazed into those beautiful blue eyes of hers, daring to let himself finish the thought. Could there be even a possibility that he and Lauren might somehow end up married? A possibility that he could handle being the poor husband of a wealthy wife? Or that she'd have the slightest interest in living at Eagles Roost, rather than in this fancy apartment?

"Mmm," she murmured, leaning closer and kissing him again. Then she slipped her hands beneath the sheet and started to drive him crazy with her touch.

He kissed his way down to her breasts, all rational thoughts beginning to fade. The final one to dissolve was that if only she was as poor as a church mouse, he'd ask her to marry him right this minute.

CHAPTER FIFTEEN

THE BOYS COME TO TOWN

LAUREN SAT CROSS-LEGGED on the bed, her robe tucked under her and Killer purring in her lap, while Sully began putting his things into his garment bag. She hated to see him leave, but since he had no choice she was doing her best not to act depressed about it.

"You know," she said, watching the muscles in his arms and thinking how perfect it felt when he wrapped those arms around her, "you're a terrible influence on me. As much as I like to sleep in, I don't remember ever staying in bed until almost two in the afternoon before."

He grinned at her. "If the boys weren't supposed to be getting back around seven, we could have hung in there even longer."

When he muttered something about his other shoe and started searching under the bed, she sat absently tracing the pattern on the sheet—still trying to decide if she should raise the subject of Dirk Blackstone again.

That dream about Sully losing the lodge wouldn't stop bothering her. And even though she didn't believe she had mystical powers of prediction, why take chances with anything that smacked of intuition or the prophetic? No, she really thought they'd better get to the bottom of the Blackstone mystery. And as soon as possible. She just couldn't help worrying that the man might try some other crazy scheme to get his hands on Eagles Roost.

But since last night, Sully hadn't said a word about her idea of hiring a private detective. She assumed that meant he'd decided against it, and if they didn't do that...

"Sully?" she said, inspiration hitting as he stood up and triumphantly waved his shoe at her.

"Uh-huh?" He sat down beside her to put it on.

"Sully, what if you and I played detective at Fax Depot?"

He gave her a curious glance.

"What if we sent a fax to Dirk Blackstone, to lure him there, then kept an eye on the place until he came to pick it up?"

"Twenty-four hours a day?"

She shook her head. "I was thinking more like from about eight in the morning until nine at night. I mean, from the manager's description, I doubt Blackstone's the type of guy who'd be wandering around Forty-second Street in the middle of the night."

"No, probably not, but—"

"And the foundation office isn't very busy in the summer. So what if I took next Friday off? Or even Thursday and Friday. If we sent the fax Wednesday evening, that would give us four days until Sunday and—"

"Lauren, you know I can't get into the city again until Grace and Otis are back. It's one thing to farm out Roxy, but I can't farm out five boys."

"Well...what if you brought them along?"

He grinned at her. "Joke, right?"

"No, I'm serious. I've got four bedrooms. One for you, two for them—it would work. So why not?"

"Well, let's see," he said, still smiling. "Just for starters, boys are noisy, messy and put their feet all over the furniture. Your place would never be the same."

"Oh, Sully, we're talking five young boys, not five wild animals."

"Sometimes, there isn't a lot of difference. Besides, who'd be keeping them from getting into trouble while we were out playing detective? I wouldn't leave them on their own in this city for a minute, let alone for hours."

"Then maybe they could help. I mean, I know they couldn't stand around for twelve or thirteen hours a day, but I think we'd have to cover the place in two shifts, anyway. So they could help keep an eye out for part of the time. Sully, they've been trying to help all along. Think what a boost it would be to their self-esteem if they actually could."

"Well, that's a good point, but it doesn't—"

"Or what about this? Elliot and Ursula live on Long Island. They've got two kids of their own, a huge pool and a tennis court. And I'm sure they'd take the boys for a day or two."

"Lauren, you can't just go asking people to—"

"They're not people. They're my brother and sister-in-law. And don't forget you saved his life. If he'd saved yours, how happy would you be for the chance to do him a favor?"

"No, look, I know you're trying to help, but what would happen if Blackstone showed up on your shift? I mean, I could just walk up to him, introduce myself and ask him what the hell the story is. But what would you do?"

"I could do the same thing."

"No, what if he's dangerous? It's just—"

"We'd be in the middle of Fax Depot. And there are always cops on Forty-second Street. But I could call you right away and you'd get there in no time. Sully, we'd find out what we want to know."

"No, it's too crazy and too dangerous."

"We'd have four days together," she pointed out.

He looked at her for a long moment. "Well," he said at last, "maybe I was being a little hasty. Maybe if you were only there in the early part of the day."

"I could take the first shift."

"And if you promised not to approach him on your own."

"I guess," she said, deciding *I guess* didn't exactly constitute a promise. If she was there and Blackstone started to walk away, she certainly wouldn't let him.

"Well...then maybe the idea's not *entirely* crazy."

"SULLY? IT'S REAL crowded back here," Terry complained from the van's rear seat.

"It'll be okay as soon as we drop Roxy off," Sully told him. "Then we'll move all your stuff into the back."

"And then we'll be on our way," Freckles said excitedly. "Sully, tell us again what we're gonna do there?"

"He already told us a hundred times," Tony grumbled.

"Yeah, but I like to hear."

"Okay," Sully said. "This is the last time, though. Tomorrow you're all going to help Lauren and me. And on Friday, too, if we still need—"

"To stake out the place," Billy put in. "We'll be real detectives."

"Uh-huh, real detectives." Sully smiled to himself. Lauren had been right. The boys were absolutely thrilled that he was turning to them for help.

He hadn't told them all the details, but he'd explained that Blackstone was responsible for Eagles Roost losing its funding, and that he and Lauren had unsuccessfully tried to track the guy down last weekend.

"Then we get to go to Yankee Stadium," Terry was saying.

"Is that for *sure,* Sully?" Freckles asked.

"Yes, it's for sure. I told you, when Lauren's brother phoned he said he had six tickets for the Friday night game."

Sully thought back to that conversation as he turned onto the road that led to old Zeke Scrouthy's place. It had been the first time he'd talked to Elliot since the shooting. Actually, it had been the first time he'd *ever* talked to Elliot. And the man had fallen all over himself being grateful—and saying that he and Ursula would be happy to take the boys for all *four* days if Sully wanted.

"And after the game he's going to take us back to his house," Billy said.

"Right. So you can spend Saturday in his pool."

"With his two little kids," Tony said.

"Yes. And they're younger than any of you, so don't be rough with them. And don't forget Mr. Van Slyke has two cracked ribs, so absolutely no horsing around with him. And you're going to do everything he and his wife tell you, without a word of talking back.''

"We've got it," Billy said. "We're on our best behavior for the next four days. And we don't put our feet on nobody's furniture, and we don't eat nothin' except when we're in a kitchen."

"Or at the ballpark," Terry said.

"Or by the pool," Freckles added.

Sully turned into Zeke's drive, hoping to hell the kids would remember at least half the rules.

"Sully?" Billy said. "Will we be able to ride in Lauren's car? Did she get it back yet?"

"Uh-uh. And her insurance company says that since it's been missing this long she'll probably never see it again. I think they're going to settle the claim pretty soon."

When he pulled up in front of Zeke's house, one of the neighbors, Alma Merlinski, was sitting on the porch.

She rose when he popped the tailgate, then hurried toward the van as he climbed out.

"What's up?" he asked, glancing around for Zeke.

"Oh, Sully, I phoned but you'd already left. When I came over a while back with some fresh-baked muffins, Zeke looked just dreadful. And he admitted he'd been having chest pains, so I insisted on calling the doctor. And, well, Doc Morely thinks he'll probably be fine, but he took him off to the hospital for observation, just in case."

Sully looked back to where Roxy was sitting drooling in the rear of the van, wondering what the hell he was going to do with her now.

"Zeke didn't want to go," Alma was explaining. "He kept saying you were counting on him to take the dog. But better safe than sorry, right?"

Sully nodded. Then before he could sound Alma out on the idea of dog-sitting, she added, "I'd take her for you myself, but my kids have allergies. There must be somebody, though."

"Yeah . . . there must be." He glanced anxiously at his watch. They were already running late, and now he was going to have to waste time calling around. There weren't many people he'd feel comfortable trying to foist a 125-pound dog on, though.

"Or how about a kennel?" Alma suggested.

"Yeah, I guess I could try calling that one near Newcomb. It's the only one that's anywhere near here, isn't it."

"Sully?" Billy said through the open window of the van. "Why can't we just take her with us. She's no trouble."

"Maybe not at the lodge, Billy, but Lauren's apartment isn't the same thing."

"So what are we gonna do, then?"

"I'll phone that kennel," he said, even though he didn't like the idea of sticking Roxy in a pen.

"The door's unlocked," Alma told him. "And I've got to get going, okay? You can lock up when you leave."

"Sure." He headed up the porch steps and into Zeke's house to make his call.

The kennel, when he finally got the number and called, proved to be fully booked. July, the woman pointed out as if he were an idiot, was the height of the vacation season. Reservations had to be made well in advance.

He hung up and tried a couple of his other neighbors, but didn't get any answers.

Finally, he dialed Lauren's office and explained the situation to her. "So it looks like we're done for the moment," he concluded. "I'll try to line up something tonight, and if I can manage it we'll be able to drive down tomorrow."

"That would give us one less day, though," she said. "And the manager of Fax Depot told us Blackstone calls every couple of days. Four days means he'd be almost sure to check in. But with only three, our odds would be lower. Sully, surely there's got to be a kennel some place around New York that has a vacancy. How about if you just come ahead while I work on lining up something?"

He cleared his throat uneasily. "If you can't find anything, you're going to end up with me and the five boys, plus Roxy."

There was a long pause at her end. Then she said, "Well, you've got the three cats at the lodge, so we know Roxy won't bother Killer. Which means that even if the worst comes to the worst... But there's not going to be any problem. So I'll see you at the apartment in a few hours."

Sully said goodbye and hung up, the phrase *there's not going to be any problem* echoing in his head. Then, as he locked the house and started back to the van, it was replaced by a different phrase: *famous last words.*

IT WAS A DAMN GOOD THING, Sully thought as they rode up in the elevator, that the doorman had remembered him. Otherwise, they'd probably still be standing out on Fifth Avenue, because the man had

clearly been unhappy about letting the five boys and
Roxy into the building.

And the inside man—the concierge, Lauren said
they called him—hadn't been any happier. When he'd
phoned up to her apartment, he'd asked her three
different ways if she was *sure* she was expecting six
guests and a huge dog.

"All right," Sully said when the elevator began to
slow at nine, "remember you're all on your best behavior."

"We'll remember," Billy promised.

The door opened and the kids tumbled out into the
hall—each carrying his sports bag full of clothes.
Sully, his garment bag slung over one shoulder and
Roxy's leash looped around his other hand, followed
them out. "It's the door along there," he said, nodding toward Lauren's apartment.

"I'll knock." Billy hurried down and gave a couple of loud bangs with the brass knocker.

"Well, look who's here," Lauren said, opening the
door and smiling at the boys. Then, as they were saying hello, she glanced over their heads and gave Sully
a smile meant only for him. It started that warm feeling he always got when he first saw her.

"You come right on in," she told the kids, backing out of their way.

"Wow, what a neat place!" Freckles said as the
boys spread themselves out over the foyer.

"Not too loud," Sully reminded him, closing the
door. "Did you find a kennel?" he asked Lauren. He
didn't like the way Roxy had already begun to excitedly sniff the marble floor, her tail twitching.

When Lauren nodded, he felt decidedly relieved.

"I even found one that promised me an oversize run," she said. "It's in Brooklyn, but they have a pickup service. So I told them I'd call back once you were actually here, and they could come then. In the meantime, I put a blanket down in the laundry room, so why don't I take her there and give her some water?"

She took the leash from Sully, adding, "You and the boys figure out how you want to divide up the sleeping space and—"

A loud hiss stopped her midsentence.

When Sully's glance flashed in the direction of the sound, he saw Killer standing just inside the living room. He'd puffed himself up to twice his normal size and his hissing was directed straight at Roxy.

Sully grabbed for the leash but was a split second too late. Roxy had already charged away at full bark, skittering madly across the marble and almost jerking Lauren off her feet before the leash whipped out of her hand.

"Catch her!" Billy hollered.

His words were barely out before all five boys were racing into the living room after Roxy.

"Oh, my," Lauren whispered.

"Dammit to hell!" Sully swore, taking off. He reached the doorway just in time to see Hoops collide with an end table and send the lamp on it crashing to the floor.

"Stop!" he shouted. "Everyone! No one takes another step!"

The boys all skidded to stops and turned back to look at him. Killer streaked around the end of a couch, then tore up onto the back of a wing chair.

Still barking furiously, Roxy launched herself into the air, tipping the chair over onto its back and sending Killer fleeing for his life toward the dining room.

"Roxy, no!" Sully yelled as the dog hit the floor and began scrambling to her feet.

Either she didn't hear him over her barking or she was having too much fun to pay attention. Whichever, she ran on the spot for a moment, her feet flying madly while she did her best to get traction on the marble. Then she succeeded and headed after Killer once more.

She tried to negotiate a turn just as she hit an area rug, and the rug went zooming across the floor with her aboard.

"Wow," Billy whispered loudly. "Looks like she's on a flyin' carpet."

As the rug slowed down, she leapt off and skittered into the dining room, slamming against the far wall on her way. Then there was another crash—a loud, shattering, very ominous-sounding one that said something major had hit the dining room floor.

Sully knew it had to be the five-foot-high Chinese vase that stood in one corner. That *used to* stand in one corner, he corrected himself unhappily. He'd just begun praying it hadn't been authentic Ming dynasty or anything like that when Killer streaked back into sight and tore through the living room again, Roxy still in hot pursuit.

"This is like a greyhound race," Freckles cried, "only with a cat 'stead of a rabbit."

The other boys snickered.

"Yeah," Billy said, "an' only one dog 'stead of a pack. But just think if there was six or eight of them in here, huh?"

Sully shot a death-ray look in the boys' direction, then took off after Roxy again. By the time he caught up with her, she was wedged head-and-shoulders under Lauren's bed, her hind legs straining like crazy while she tried to drag her front end back out.

Killer was sitting dead center on the bed, his tail switching angrily back and forth. His yellow slit-eyed glare said he'd never forgive Sully for bringing a monster dog into the apartment. Not in any of his nine lifetimes.

Ignoring the cat, Sully reached under the bed and got a firm hold on Roxy's collar. Then, by shoving her down flat to the floor with his other hand, he managed to get her unstuck.

"Sit," he ordered once she'd backed out, his hand still firmly grasping her collar.

She sat, but her eyes strayed to Killer and she began to drool.

"Don't you ever," he said menacingly, "do anything like that again."

"Does she understand English?"

He glanced over to where Lauren was standing in the doorway, feeling like the houseguest from hell and trying to think of the right words to say. But he'd bet even Miss Manners would be hard pressed to come up with an appropriate apology if her dog had just trashed somebody's home.

"I'm sorry," he said lamely. "I guess she figures the lodge cats are *her* cats, whereas Killer..."

"Yes, well," Lauren murmured, "at least we won't have to worry about her not getting enough exercise in the kennel. She probably got enough in the last few minutes to do her for days."

"Lauren, I—"

"I was only joking, Sully," she interrupted. "It was one of the funniest things I've ever seen," she added. Then she started to laugh.

That was when he was absolutely certain it was more than simply her passion that had him wanting to spend the rest of his life with her.

BY FRIDAY AFTERNOON, with the Forty-second Street pavement so hot beneath her feet she could feel it through her shoes, Lauren was wishing she'd never suggested the idea of playing detective.

On Wednesday evening, only a couple of hours after Sully and the boys had arrived, she'd sent their fax—ostensibly from Ben Ludendorf—to Blackstone, care of Fax Depot.

So far, though, their lure hadn't worked. And by now she was almost convinced she should simply have hired a real detective agency without telling Sully. Then, once she'd had an address and phone number for Blackstone...

Well, that was where the plan would have run into trouble, and why she'd decided against it in the first place. Sully would have figured out exactly how she'd gotten her information. And given his attitude toward her money, he'd have been angry.

So here she was, standing on Forty-second Street for the second day in a row, roasting half to death while she tried to keep one eye on the five boys and the other on Fax Depot—where the manager, for a suitable potential reward, was inside keeping an eye out for Blackstone.

She glanced at her watch, thinking Sully should be along soon to relieve her. Elliot was picking the boys up from her apartment in a couple of hours, and after that, she thought, smiling to herself, she and Sully would have the evening and all of Saturday alone together.

The thought improved her mood immeasurably. Then she spotted Sully striding down the street and it improved even more. The boys spotted him, as well, and converged on him.

"Still no luck, Sully," Billy told him. "So maybe we shouldn't go stay at Lauren's brother's tonight. Maybe we should come back to the apartment after the game and tomorrow we could—"

"Then we'd miss out on swimmin' in Mr. Van Slyke's pool," Terry whined.

"You boys have helped enough," Sully said. "You really have, so you deserve a day's fun."

"Hey, *this* has been fun," Freckles said. "I never knew there was so many crazies in the world as I been seein' on this street."

"Yeah, well, it wouldn't be fun to be one," Sully told him. Then he glanced at Lauren. "You and the boys had better grab a cab now, so they'll all be ready when Elliot gets there. I'll see you about nine-thirty or ten. No later."

She nodded. "Want to meet me at a restaurant? Or should I just pick up some things at my deli?"

He grinned at her, then whispered, "What do you think?"

WHEN THE CLOCK RADIO came on, the announcer was in the midst of telling his listeners that it was a quarter to seven on another sunny Saturday morning in the city.

Lauren snuggled her naked body closer to Sully's and buried her face against his chest. Since the boys had spent last night at Elliot and Ursula's, she and Sully had been able to share her bed—which meant they hadn't done a lot of sleeping. And now she really, really didn't feel like getting up and heading downtown.

Especially not when they could have stayed cuddled up here all day if it weren't for Dirk Blackstone. She was hating that man more all the time.

"Want me to take your shift?" Sully murmured against her hair.

"Lord, no," she said. "What would I do for fun if I couldn't hang around Forty-second Street?"

After giving him one long, lingering kiss, she forced herself out of bed. He'd absolutely refused to let either her or the boys keep watch in the evening, so they'd been doing the early part of the days, Sully the later. He'd still been getting up first thing in the morning, though, and the hours were beginning to show.

"I could at least come with you," he mumbled as she started for the shower.

"No, you're dead tired."

He gave her a weary grin. "And whose fault is that? Who kept me awake half the night?"

She laughed, thinking she loved the way he looked when his face was dark with stubble. "You stay where you are," she told him, then headed for the shower.

By the time she'd finished in the bathroom, Sully was fast asleep again. She dressed quietly, had a quick breakfast and took a taxi down to Fax Depot. With only Saturday morning traffic to contend with, she was there before eight.

Today, she decided, since she didn't have five rambunctious boys in tow, there was no reason to stand out on the street. No reason not to wait inside where it was air-conditioned. She paid the driver, then went in and nodded surreptitiously to the manager.

She'd only been waiting a few minutes before she happened to glance toward the door and saw a familiar face. It wasn't a familiar face she liked, though. It was the face of her least-favorite board member, so she turned her back and began reading the instructions on a self-serve photocopier. The last thing she wanted was Hunter Clifton spotting her and feeling he should come over for a chat.

By the time she was halfway through the instructions, she'd begun to wonder what on earth Hunter was doing in Fax Depot. She knew he had a fax machine at home because he'd sent faxes to her office from it. And his bank probably had a hundred of them. So why would he be using a commercial service?

She turned around, thinking that maybe it hadn't really been him. But there he was, talking to the clerk behind the counter. Glancing at the manager, she noticed he seemed to have developed a twitch in his right eye.

Lord, he looked as if he was coming down with something. But if he went home sick, who'd point out Blackstone to her?

Her hopes of trapping Blackstone rapidly fading, she turned toward the photocopy machine again.

A minute later, the manager was at her side, hissing, "That's him! That guy just picking up the fax."

"What?" She turned around quickly, but Hunter Clifton was still the only customer at the counter.

"Lady," he muttered. "You said I pointed out Dirk Blackstone, I got two hundred bucks. So how 'bout handin' it over before he takes off, huh?"

"Oh, Lord," she whispered. Dirk Blackstone was Hunter Clifton. Which meant that Hunter had been behind Sully's losing his funding.

Considerably shaken, she turned her back on the counter once more, digging in her purse and deciding there was absolutely no conceivable reason to rush over and confront Hunter.

She handed the manager two hundreds, then took her cell phone out of her purse. The second Hunter was safely gone, she'd call the apartment and tell Sully she knew who Blackstone was and that she was on her way home. Once she got there, they could think through everything they knew and see how much sense they could make of it before Hunter even realized they were onto him.

After all, she knew where Hunter worked and where he lived. Which meant they could pay him a visit whenever they liked.

CHAPTER SIXTEEN

SURPRISE VISITS ARE THE ORDER OF THE DAY

"NO, NO, WALTER." Roger Van Slyke waved off the concierge as he picked up the house phone to call Lauren's apartment. "Don't phone up. We want to surprise her."

"But Mr. Van Slyke, I just came on duty. For all I know, she's not even home."

"My daughter? Up and out this early on a Saturday? That would be highly uncharacteristic, Walter. I'm sure she's in."

"Honestly, Roger," Susannah whispered when they started for the elevators, "you're being absurd. What do you think she'd do if she had two minutes' advance warning? Crawl down the side of the building to avoid her own parents?"

"I don't want her having time to think about what she's going to say. I want an honest discussion about what the hell she figures she's playing at with that man. And since she doesn't think very well on her feet, the best way of getting honesty is to take her by surprise."

"This whole trip here is absurd," Susannah muttered. "I just don't understand why you think you can run her life. You'd never dream of trying something like this with either Elliot or Marisa.''

"Elliot and Marisa have good heads on their shoulders, even if I don't always like what they do.''

They got into the elevator and Roger pushed the button for nine.

"Roger," Susannah pressed, "the idea of coming over here like this, first thing in the morning—"

"If we came later, Sullivan might have already arrived from... Where did Ursula say he was staying?''

"She said she thought it was the same friend he stayed with last weekend. And I gathered that's why she and Elliot ended up taking those boys for a couple of nights—because the friend didn't have room or something. Ursula was very vague about the details. But the point I was making is that the idea of your coming over here like this—"

"You came with me," Roger pointed out.

"Only to ensure you don't say anything *totally* out of line.''

"Me? You think *I'm* being out of line? Susannah, Jack Sullivan is an ex-con who's spending his life looking after misfit kids. He has no education, no money, no prospects, and he lives in some old fishing lodge in the middle of the Adirondacks. Now, do you expect me to believe you think he's suitable for Lauren?''

"I never said he was suitable. All I said was that he seemed like a decent man. And he did save Elliot's life.''

"Fine. He's a decent man and a hero as well. I'm not arguing that, but it doesn't make him suitable for

Lauren. And the fact that he's come into town again, for the second weekend in a row..."

"I'm sorry I ever told you he was here," Susannah snapped. "In fact, I'm sorry Ursula told *me*. If she hadn't, I wouldn't have started worrying and we'd both be home right now, enjoying coffee and croissants instead of about to upset Lauren. Roger, she's an adult, and whether you like it or not—"

"Whether I like it or not, her judgment isn't what it should be. So somebody has to talk to her before she does something ridiculous—like actually getting involved with that man. And if it isn't us, who's it going to be?"

The elevator arrived at the ninth floor and they started in the direction of Lauren's door.

"I think you're making a very big mistake," Susannah muttered as Roger reached for the knocker.

WHEN THE KNOCKING WOKE Sully, it took him a few seconds to orientate himself. Then a few more for it to register that nobody had called up from downstairs, so it had to be one of Lauren's neighbors at the door. Or Lauren herself.

She hadn't been able to find her spare keys, so she'd left him hers in case he wanted to go out. But what on earth would she be doing back?

Unless she'd phoned to tell him she'd spotted Blackstone and he hadn't heard the phone. That was a possibility. She'd turned off the ringer on the bedroom extension last night.

He leapt out of bed and grabbed his robe, hoping to hell he hadn't blown their shot at Blackstone by sleeping in, then strode quickly down the hall.

On his way past the room Lauren used as her office he glanced in. Sure enough, the light on her answering machine was flashing. Swearing to himself, he headed over to it and pressed the play button—just as the knocking started again.

"Sully?" Lauren's voice said on the machine. "Sully, I guess you're in the shower or something, but I know who Blackstone is and I'm on my way home. See you shortly."

"The time of the call…" a mechanical voice started to tell him. He didn't wait to hear, just raced the rest of the way to the door and threw it open.

As he did, a feeling of utter horror seized him. It wasn't Lauren. It was her parents. And he was wearing nothing but a bathrobe—which he was absolutely certain they wouldn't consider appropriate attire for a man in their daughter's apartment. No dictionary, he thought fleetingly, could possibly define *awkward* better than this scene.

While he stood in the doorway desperately wishing he was a thousand miles away, the Van Slykes stood in the hall staring at him—Susannah's eyes filled with surprise, Roger's with what looked like homicidal impulses.

Susannah recovered first, assuming that murmuring "Oh, my" counted as recovering. She quickly followed up with, "We just stopped by to see Lauren, Mr. Sullivan."

"It's Sully," he reminded her. He doubted she could care less, but he was awfully hard-pressed to decide what he should be saying.

"And Lauren isn't here at the moment," he ventured, "but she'll be back soon. So if you'd like to come in and wait, I'll just go along to the *guest* bedroom and put on some clothes."

Before any of them moved, though, one of the elevator doors slid open and Lauren stepped out. "Mom, Dad," she said, starting down the hall, "Walter told me you'd just come up. What are you doing here at this time of day?"

Sully had to give her credit. In the few minutes it had taken to get from the lobby to the ninth floor, she'd done a great job of composing herself.

"We thought we'd stop by and take you out for breakfast," Roger was saying. "We didn't know you had company," he added icily.

"Oh, yes, I do. But that's obvious, isn't it. You remember Sully, of course, so...would you like to come in for coffee?"

It was apparent that what they'd really like was an explanation of exactly what Jack Sullivan was doing here, but they silently filed past him and followed Lauren into the living room.

Shutting the door, he uneasily trailed after them. As badly as he'd like to head for the bedroom and throw on some clothes, Lauren might need his help.

When her parents sat down, she shot him a smile that looked only a little tense. "Why don't you go and get dressed while I make the coffee?"

He nodded. They were her parents, so it made sense to follow her lead. He turned and started away. Then, as he disappeared from their line of vision, he heard Roger say, "Just a minute, Lauren, don't head off. Let's talk before you worry about any coffee."

Sully hesitated, thinking he shouldn't let her face this alone. But she'd told him to go...

Deciding he could get dressed and be back to the living room in thirty seconds flat, he raced the rest of the way down the hall.

"ALL HE'S TRYING TO SAY," Lauren's mother told her in a far more reasonable tone than her father had been using, "is that it wouldn't be wise to become involved with Jack Sullivan."

Lauren nodded. Her mother *always* seemed to be smoothing things over for her father. This morning, though, he'd just gone too far. She couldn't remember ever out-and-out yelling at him in her entire life, but right now she was about a hairbreadth away.

"Dad," she said as reasonably as she could, "I still take your advice about a lot of things. Even though I'm thirty years old, I still do. But, as I recall, you were all in favor of my becoming involved with Brandon. That eldest Stockton boy has brains, you used to tell me, and he's from such a good family. Why don't you go out with him? you'd say. And then, after I'd been going with him for a while, you started telling me that marrying him would be the smartest thing I could ever do."

"I don't remember any of that."

"Well I do. I remember it perfectly. And marrying him certainly *wasn't* the smartest thing. So at this stage of the game ... Look, I'm sorry you don't like the idea of my seeing Jack Sullivan, but I'd really rather you didn't try to give me advice when it comes to my love life."

"Dammit, Lauren, you're a Van Slyke."

"So what?" she snapped.

"So Jack Sullivan is probably a fortune hunter, that's what!"

She felt as if her father had slapped her face. She took a deep breath, then quietly said, "He told me you'd say that. And I told him you thought I had more going for me than just the Van Slyke money. But I see I was wrong."

"Lauren," her mother said quickly, "your father didn't mean to imply that Sully is *only* after your money. All he was trying to say, was—"

"Mom?" she interrupted. "Mom, I'm right here in the room. I've heard everything he's been trying to say. But the bottom line is that I'm a grown woman, so who I fall in love with really isn't anyone's business but my own."

"Oh, Lauren, you and Jack Sullivan can't have anything at all in common, so even letting yourself think about falling in love with him is only asking for heartache."

"Mom, I'm already beyond thinking about it, all right? Which means there's really no point to this discussion. So rather than make Sully uncomfortable, I think it would be best if you and Dad left."

"I think," her father muttered angrily, "Jack Sullivan should be the one leaving."

"Don't make me choose," Lauren said. "Don't make me choose, because you wouldn't like the result."

SULLY QUIETLY MADE his way back down the hallway to Lauren's bedroom and sank onto the bed, his emotions reeling. He'd never been one to eavesdrop, but when he'd neared the end of the hall and tuned into that conversation he'd realized it wasn't something he should go barging into the middle of.

He shouldn't have stood listening, though. Hell, that was something Billy would have done. On the other hand, if he hadn't listened he wouldn't have heard Lauren tell her parents she loved him.

He mentally repeated that part of the conversation, afraid he might have misunderstood. Her mother had said she shouldn't even think about letting herself fall in love with him. And she'd said, "Mom, I'm already beyond thinking about it, all right?"

His heart hammering, he told himself there was no misconstruing that. She was in love with him. Just as he was in love with her. But where did they go from here?

He heard the front door open, then close. A minute later, Lauren appeared in the bedroom doorway.

"They're gone," she said, wandering across the room and sitting down on the bed beside him.

"Uh-huh, I heard them leave." He took her hand, no more sure what to say to her than he'd been of what to say to them.

"I'm sorry they came here like that," she murmured.

Leaning closer, he gently kissed the side of her face. "I'm sorry my being here caused you grief."

"Your being here hasn't cause me any grief, Sully. I love having you here. It was my father who caused the grief."

They sat in silence for a few moments. Then he said, "I overheard part of your conversation."

The way her face turned pink made him smile.

"Do I want to know which part?" she asked.

"I don't know. But there's something I want to tell you."

She gazed at him expectantly.

"I..." He hesitated. He loved her so unbelievably much the words should be easy to say. Instead, they were incredibly difficult. He suspected that was because he'd never said them before. Oh, maybe he had, long ago. Maybe as a child he'd said them to his mother. But if he had, he didn't remember.

"You what?" Lauren said softly.

It was only by closing his eyes that he could make them come out, and even then his "I love you" was a mere whisper.

When he opened his eyes, there were tears trickling down Lauren's cheeks. "What?" he said, wiping them away.

"I didn't know if you'd ever say that. I love you, too, but I thought you were so worried about all the differences that you might never..." She shrugged and gave him a tiny smile, then wrapped her arms around his neck and kissed him.

He could taste her tears and feel her love, and it made him wish the rest of the world didn't exist—at least, not any part of it that didn't think they belonged together.

"Lauren," he finally murmured, "what are we going to do about this?"

"I don't know." She gazed into his eyes and slowly slid her fingers down his jaw. "Sully, all I know is that I've never felt about anyone the way I feel about you. Never felt anything even remotely close."

He eased her down onto the bed, kissing her hair, her eyes, then her lips again. "All right," he finally said, cuddling her to him. "The question is this. How do we end up together? I mean, you *would* like that, wouldn't you?"

"I'd like that very, very much."

He smiled. How could he not smile when the woman he loved loved him. But even though that made all those differences fade in significance, none of them had entirely vanished. And even if some of them might not be nearly as important as he'd once believed, there was still one obstacle that seemed insurmountable.

The likelihood of Lauren deciding she wanted to spend the rest of her life at Eagles Roost was about as low as of his deciding he wanted to spend the rest of his life in the city.

"All right," he said once more. "The problem is, if a dolphin and a meadowlark fall in love, where do they make a home?"

She laughed at that. "Which am I? The dolphin or the meadowlark?"

"I don't know. Whichever you'd like to be. Either way, how do we work things out?"

"Why don't we mull it over for a while," she murmured, trailing her fingers down his chest.

Somewhere in the back of his mind, there was something he'd urgently wanted to talk to her about. He tried to remember what it was, but couldn't. Then she kissed him and he decided it could wait.

An hour later, lying contentedly in Sully's arms, Lauren suddenly realized that the shock of finding her parents here had temporarily driven everything else from her mind. And then, when she and Sully had begun to... Well, making love with Jack Sullivan was almost enough to make her forget her own name.

"Sully?" she said, sitting up and pulling the sheet around her.

"Mmm." He leaned closer and began nibbling on her bare shoulder.

"Sully, listen. I can't believe this, but I forgot all about the reason I came home."

He looked at her blankly for a moment, then said, "Hell, I did, too. But you saw Dirk Blackstone picking up the fax."

"No, not exactly. I mean, Dirk Blackstone isn't his real name. It was Hunter Clifton I saw. My board member. The vice president of the bank—"

"That Leroy robbed a branch of," Sully said, finishing her sentence. "But if our mystery man is actually one of your board members, what the hell does that add up to?"

She shook her head. "I'm not certain, but I did try to make sense of it on the way home. And I think it might be significant that Hunter's fairly new to the board. He only joined it a few months before I became director—only volunteered back around the end of last year."

"Volunteered? That's how it works?"

"Quite often. Sometimes people are invited to join, but often someone simply expresses an interest in being involved. But the point is, you said it was last fall that Ben approached you about selling. So, after you told told him you weren't interested, Hunter could have nosed around about your program, discovered the Van Slyke Foundation funded it, and volunteered."

"So he paid Leroy to rob the bank and got himself on the board, as well. Which meant he was in a perfect position to make a big deal about the robbery *he'd* set up in the first place."

"Right. A big enough deal that it persuaded the others to go along with cutting off your funding."

"Son of a bitch," Sully muttered. "All the pieces fall into place so neatly that's got to be it. But we're still missing something. Why does Hunter Clifton want Eagles Roost so badly?"

"I don't know. But since it's Saturday, you'll be glad to hear that my list of board members includes their home addresses."

HUNTER CLIFTON and his wife lived on Long Island some forty or fifty miles from Manhattan. Their two-story house was large and formal—built of red brick and trimmed with white shutters. The four- or five-acre property it sat on was manicured to within an inch of its life.

Lauren's first thought was that the house and grounds projected exactly the image Hunter Clifton strove to project personally. She knew he had two children, but there were no bicycles in sight, no toys lying on the lawn, no hoop for kids to play basketball on the driveway. Everything looked picture perfect—and absolutely sterile.

"If his taste runs to something as antiseptic as this," Sully muttered, pulling the van to a stop on the drive, "why on earth would he be interested in a wilderness lodge?"

Lauren shrugged. "A change of scenery?"

"Are you kidding? It would be more like complete culture shock."

"Well, I guess we're about to find out why he's interested. Assuming he's home," she added, glancing at the three closed garage doors.

"You know, maybe we should reconsider this plan," Sully said as she reached for her door handle. "Maybe you should wait in the van until I see—"

"No," she interrupted, shooting him a determined look. "In the first place, regardless of what Hunter Clifton's game is, I'm certain he's not dangerous. If I thought there was even a chance of that, we'd have called the police instead of coming here. And in the second place," she added, opening her door, "we already decided that since I know Hunter I'll start the ball rolling this time and you'll be the one to jump in."

Sully muttered something she didn't catch, then came around the van. They started for the house, her stomach feeling a little unsettled. They were basically going to play things by ear again, but Hunter Clifton was a whole lot more intelligent than Ben Ludendorf, which meant this round probably wouldn't be half as easy.

She rang the bell and waited, not even glancing at Sully in case she looked as anxious as she felt. After a few moments, the door opened and a woman stood eyeing them curiously. She was a blonde in her late thirties—extremely attractive, perfectly made-up, and wearing a white cotton sweater and white pants that positively gleamed. All in all, she looked like the ideal wife for Hunter.

"Mrs. Clifton?" Lauren said.

"Yes?"

"Mrs. Clifton, I'm terribly sorry to bother you, but I'm Lauren Van Slyke, director of the Van Slyke Foundation, and something urgent has come up that I have to speak with your husband about."

"Lauren Van Slyke?"

Lauren nodded. "And this is Jack Sullivan."

The woman's gaze flickered to Sully for a millisec-
ond, then she looked at Lauren again and smiled
warmly. "Do come in. Hunter isn't here at the moment, but he's only dropping the children off at
friends', so he shouldn't be long. And I'm so pleased
to have the chance to meet you," she added, usher-
ing them into a large, wainscotted foyer.

"Hunter has often mentioned your name. And
your father's as well. He's so excited about that
project in SoHo they've been putting together. In
fact, just the other day I was suggesting we invite your
parents to dinner. And you, too, of course. I'm sure
we all have a great deal in common. Hunter comes
from an old New York family, you know. Not as
prominent as yours, by any means, but an old established family."

"Ahh," Lauren said. Hunter's wife was obviously
very impressed by the Van Slyke name, which certainly couldn't do any harm. "I wonder, Mrs. Clifton, if—"

"Oh, please," she said with another warm smile.
"It's Christina."

"Christina, then." Lauren matched her smile.
"Christina, Hunter has an office in the house, doesn't
he?"

"Oh, yes, he's an absolute workaholic."

Lauren hesitated, then decided it had to be worth
trying a shot in the dark. After all, there was nothing
to lose. "Well, Christina, Hunter set up a special file
on one of the programs the foundation funds, a program called Eagles Roost. And there are a couple of

things in it that I need to check. So if I could look at it while we're waiting, it would save time."

"You think he'd have it here? At the house?"

"Well, it's not bank business, so he might."

"Yes, that's true. And it certainly wouldn't hurt to have a look for it, so let's go and do that. This way," she added, starting up the stairs.

As they headed after her, Sully gave Lauren a grin and a thumbs-up. She hoped he wasn't actually counting on anything coming of this, though. Just because Hunter struck her as obsessive enough to keep files on all his personal dealings, that certainly didn't guarantee he did. Especially personal dealings that had wandered way over onto the wrong side of the law.

"This is Hunter's office," Christina said as they reached a door at the back end of the upstairs hall. She felt along the top of the doorframe and located a key.

"Hunter keeps the room locked so the children don't go in," she explained, unlocking the door. "Now," she added, leading the way in, "let me just look through these files on his desk.

"No, nothing there," she murmured after a minute. "Let's try the filing cabinet."

Lauren held her breath while Christina rummaged through that, then exhaled slowly when the woman turned back to them, shaking her head.

"There's one more place," she said, heading across the room. Pulling a book from a shelf, she flipped it open and took a small key from between two of its pages.

"For some silly reason," she said, walking back over to the desk, "Hunter keeps the drawers in his desk locked. But I happened to discover this spare key one day while I was . . . cleaning."

Lauren couldn't resist glancing at Sully. She'd bet dollars to doughnuts that Christina Clifton hadn't done a minute's housework in her entire married life.

"If we find what we want in here," she was saying as she unlocked the drawers, "I'll just tell Hunter his desk wasn't locked—that he must have been in a hurry and forgotten or something. Now, Eagles Roost, Eagles Roost. Yes, here we are."

Christina pulled out the file folder and handed it to Lauren—who did her utmost to seem only mildly pleased rather than overjoyed.

"Could we just sit in here and look through it for what I need?" she asked.

"Well, Hunter's a little funny about his office, but I'm sure he wouldn't mind *your* being in here. So, sure. You look through the file while I go down to the kitchen and put on some coffee, all right?"

"Sounds great," Sully told her.

"I didn't get to jump in," he whispered as soon as Christina left. "In fact, I felt like the invisible man."

"Don't worry about it. We got what we wanted. Now, let's hope there's something in here that makes sense." She flipped the file open and started leafing through the papers inside.

"What's in it?" Sully demanded, peering over her shoulder.

"Rough notes that would take me forever to read. Hunter's handwriting is atrocious. And a whole lot of faxes from Ben Ludendorf. And . . . oh, this might be something. Look,'' she said, taking out a long white envelope.

It was embossed with the name and address of a Manhattan law firm. And the writing on the front read, *To be given to my grandson, Hunter Clifton, after my death.* The signature beneath the instruction read Earl Clifton.

CHAPTER SEVENTEEN

THE MYSTERY IS SOLVED

HER FINGERS TREMBLING, Lauren slid the letter out of the envelope. "It's dated five years ago," she said. "But that doesn't tell us how long Hunter's had it. Doesn't tell us when his grandfather died, I mean."

"Let's not worry about that," Sully said. "Just read it."

She nodded and began.

Dear Hunter,
Even as a child, you had larceny in your soul.

"And he certainly didn't outgrow it," Sully muttered.

She smiled, then continued.

I do not mean that as a criticism—although it is certainly why I disapproved of your going into banking. I always considered that far too conservative a career choice, given your predilection for straying from the straight and narrow.

The reason you've received this letter, however, has nothing to do with your career choice. You are the only one of my grandchildren whom I am certain will try to act on what I am about to tell you. That is why it is you I chose to tell.

You see, Hunter, I always hated being unable to take advantage of a golden opportunity. And that is precisely what happened when my old friend, Warren Russell, died in his plane crash so many years ago.

"Warren Russell?" Sully said.

Lauren glanced up from the letter. "You know the name?"

"You bet I do. Warren Russell was the Wall Street tycoon who built Eagles Roost. It was when his widow put it on the market that Frank Watson bought it."

Lauren nodded. Frank Watson's name, she knew. He was the man who'd left the lodge to Sully.

"Go on," he said, "keep reading."

I'm sure you remember the stories I used to tell you about Warren's lodge in the Adirondacks. Those were great times he and I had up at Eagles Roost, and I know something about the place that nobody else ever did—not even his wife. That is what makes me certain the treasure in the cellar must still be there, that no one has removed it since Warren's death.

"Treasure in the cellar?" Sully said. "Lauren, you're reading too slowly! Let me." He grabbed the letter and picked up where she'd left off.

I know I told you, Hunter, that Warren was a truly eccentric fellow. I also told you how unbelievably wealthy he was. What I perhaps never mentioned is that after Wall Street crashed in 1929, Warren developed a fear that he would somehow lose all his money.

This fear drove him to begin buying valuable objects and squirreling them away in various places. He used to refer to the things as his "special insurance policies," but the only one I ever knew about specifically was the one hidden at Eagles Roost. It is a van Gogh painting and is sealed in the cellar wall behind the sixth stair from the top.

"A van Gogh?" Lauren murmured. "A *real* van Gogh?"

"That couldn't be, could it?" Sully said. "I mean, he's so famous, wouldn't all his paintings be accounted for?"

"No, I don't think that's true. I remember Marisa once telling me he was incredibly prolific, but only sold one painting during his entire lifetime. Most of the rest ended up stored in his brother's attic. But there could easily be some unaccounted for."

"But . . . oh, hell, we shouldn't be getting ahead of ourselves here. Maybe there's nothing sealed in that wall at all, let alone a van Gogh. Maybe eccentric old Warren just told Hunter's grandfather there was." Sully turned to the next page of the letter and continued.

Warren bought the painting in Paris one year, and when he brought it back to New York he had it safely crated and encased by some art expert. Then I helped him seal it in the wall at Eagles Roost.

"Sully? If Hunter's grandfather helped, this must really have happened. I mean, they must have sealed *some* painting away."

"I guess." He went back to reading.

I was the only one who ever knew it was there, aside from Warren himself, and I'm sure Warren would have said something if he'd ever moved it to a different hiding place. So, after his death, I tried to buy Eagles Roost—numerous times. First from Warren's widow, but Hettie and I had never had any use for each other, so just to spite me she sold it to someone else—a man named Frank Watson. And no matter how many times I tried to convince Watson to sell, he refused. Finally, I got too old and gave up.

But, Hunter, I can only assume that painting is still there. Nobody knows about it except you now, and there's no need to involve anyone else if you find a way of getting to it. It's so well protected that you could practically dynamite the wall without damaging the painting.

At any rate, I expect you'll do what you can to take advantage of the opportunity. Look on it as my special legacy to you.

Your loving grandfather,
Earl Clifton

Sully looked at Lauren as he finished reading. "Unbelievable," he said. "If this is true, it's absolutely unbelievable."

Before either of them could say another word, they heard footsteps thundering up the stairs.

A MAN WHO was practically breathing fire burst into the room—stopping dead when he saw Sully holding the letter.

"Oh, there you are, Hunter," Lauren said, smiling so sweetly Sully could barely keep from laughing. "I'd like you to meet Jack Sullivan. You probably recognize his name. He owns Eagles Roost."

"What the hell do you two think you're doing?" Hunter hissed. "You can't come sneaking into my house and paw through my private papers! I'm calling the cops!"

"Calm down, buddy," Sully snapped. "We were invited into your house. And we didn't paw through a damn thing. All we did was read what was in this file your wife gave us."

"Sully?" Lauren said. "I don't think calling the cops is such a bad idea. I'm sure they'd love to hear how Hunter hired a fifteen-year-old kid to pull a bank job for him."

"I did no such thing!"

"Okay," Sully said, "you hired some guy named Gus to hire a fifteen-year-old kid to pull a bank job for you. I think they'll see that in pretty much the same light."

Hunter shoved the door closed, rubbed his palms against his thighs, then cleared his throat. "I'll tell you what," he said to Sully. "Christina only gave you that file because Lauren lied to her about it. And if Lauren's father knew what she'd done, he'd be extremely angry. Especially if any bad press about the foundation resulted from its director's . . . poor judgment, shall we call it?"

"Are you trying to intimidate us?" Sully said, taking a menacing step toward Hunter.

"No! No, not at all. I'm merely trying to say there's no point in taking a chance that Roger will find out and be upset with Lauren."

"Oh, you don't have to be concerned about that," Lauren said, giving Hunter another sweet smile. "I'm used to my father being upset with me."

Hunter stared at her for a few seconds, then apparently decided to ignore her remark. "What I'm getting at," he persisted, "is that the three of us should just keep quiet about this. Why don't you hand over that letter, Jack, and we'll forget all about it."

"I don't think so," Sully said, starting to enjoy himself.

"All right," Hunter said slowly. "All right, I can see there's no point trying to play either of you for a fool. But how does this strike you?" he went on, still aiming his remarks at Sully. "What if we get that painting out of the wall? I know people who handle fine art deals on the quiet, and we can sell it privately, through one of them—then split the money. Half for you, half for me."

Sully grinned, *really* enjoying himself now. "I guess I must be missing something here. I own Eagles Roost. And it's my cellar that painting is sealed up in. So why would I want to split any money I got for it with you?"

"Because all I have to do is open my mouth and neither of us will get a red cent. Warren Russell's widow didn't intentionally include that van Gogh when she sold. She couldn't have, because she didn't know it was there. So, legally, it's still part of Russell's estate. Any judge would find in favor of the heirs, which is why we'd have to unload the painting on the quiet."

Sully could feel his grin fading. Sometime in the past few minutes, he'd realized that if that painting really was at Eagles Roost, and really was a van Gogh, he'd be a rich man. Rich enough he wouldn't have to worry about being the poor husband of a wealthy wife. But if what Hunter was saying was true, if he didn't really own the painting, then Lady Luck hadn't wandered into his corner, after all.

When he glanced at Lauren she wasn't smiling any longer, either. "Do you think he's right?" he asked her.

"I don't know. But Elliot will be able to find out."

"I'm right," Hunter said. "Don't you think I looked into it? The only sensible thing to do is unload the painting and split the money. Trust me on this."

Sully wouldn't trust Hunter Clifton as far as he could throw him. But he wanted the answers to a couple of questions before he told the guy what he could do with his *partners* suggestion, so he said, "I've been wondering about something, Hunter."

"What?"

"Last year, you told Ben Ludendorf you weren't interested in the lodge itself. Only the property. Why did you say that?"

Hunter shrugged. "Just to throw you off. I didn't want you starting to wonder why somebody'd be interested in a rundown old lodge. Now, about the painting, I—"

"One other thing," Sully interrupted.

"What?" Hunter said more impatiently this time.

"About three months ago, a woman phoned the teacher who works for me. She claimed to be Lauren, and asked a lot of questions about my program. You know anything about that?"

Hunter shifted his weight from one foot to the other.

"Hunter, I don't like playing 'Let's Make a Deal' with somebody who keeps secrets from me."

The man shrugged once more. "All right, the woman was Leroy Korelenko's caseworker. Those people at Social Services don't earn much, you know, so it wasn't hard to convince her to find a promising kid she could send to Eagles Roost."

"You mean a promising bank robber," Lauren said.

"I suppose you could put it that way," Hunter agreed, focusing on her. "Anyhow, when Leroy's case was assigned to the woman, she called and convinced Sullivan to take the boy on. Then, when I wanted some information about the program, she helped me out again."

"By wanting information," Lauren said, recalling how Otis had put it, "you mean you were hoping to dig up dirt. Find out things that would convince the other board members Sully's program wasn't any good."

"Something like that," Hunter muttered.

Sully shoved his hands in his pockets, resisting the urge to deck the guy.

"So?" Hunter said, looking at him again. "What do you think? Partners?"

Sully exhaled slowly. He was hardly knowledgeable about art prices, but a van Gogh had to be worth a few million. And the idea of having money behind him was very, very appealing. It would mean he'd never again have to worry about funding for his program. And, at least in the money area, things would be a little more equal between him and Lauren.

When he looked at her she was watching him, her expression saying she was certain what his decision would be. He gave her a rueful smile, knowing that if he teamed up with Hunter he'd lose not only *her* respect but every shred of his self-respect. Tempting as the thought of having money was, Hunter's shady proposition went against every principle he'd tried to live by since the day he'd walked out of prison.

"No, Hunter," he said at last. "Not partners. If you're wrong, if the painting is legally mine, I'd be crazy to share the proceeds with you. And if it turns out it's not legally mine, then I guess I'll just be out of luck."

"But you wouldn't even know it existed if it weren't for that letter! So I should be getting—"

"Hunter? The only thing you'll be getting is charged by the cops—for paying Leroy to rob that bank."

Sully glanced at Lauren and smiled again. She was digging into her purse, and he knew exactly why. She was getting her cell phone out to call the police.

WHEN LAUREN LOOKED back from where Sully's van and Marisa's car were idling at the curb, Frederick the doorman was clearly very relieved. He was so obviously glad to see Sully and his kids were leaving, that he must have been worried her guests would burn the building down.

"All right," she said, turning to the boys. "We're all set? Nobody's forgotten anything?"

When they gave her a chorus of "nos," Sully said, "Okay, let's move it, then. We've got a cellar wall waiting for us at Eagles Roost."

"You sure Hoops and me havta ride in the van?" Billy asked him. "When the other guys get to ride with Marisa?"

"Who got to make the trip in Lauren's Mercedes a while back?"

"Me and Hoops, but—"

"Exactly," Sully said.

The kennel people had dropped Roxy off earlier, and she was already sitting in the back of the mini-van. While Billy and Hoops reluctantly climbed into it, Tony, Terry and Freckles scrambled into Marisa's Jaguar.

"You're positive," Marisa murmured to Lauren, "that Sully doesn't mind my coming along?"

Lauren shook her head. "If there's really a painting in that wall, he'll be dying to know if it's a genuine van Gogh. Besides, if it's for real, I knew you'd want to be one of the first to see it."

"You knew I'd *want* to be? How about I'd kill to be? But you told him I won't know for sure if it's authentic. That I'll only be able to give him my opinion."

"Your *expert* opinion."

Marisa smiled. "Even if there doesn't turn out to be any painting, I'm glad you invited me to come. I want a chance to get to know Sully, because the way you two look at each other..."

"What? What about it?"

Marisa laughed. "I don't know how you're going to work everything out, but the way you look at each other makes me think Mom and Dad are going to have some adjusting to do."

"You think they can?" Lauren asked quietly.

"What choice do they have?"

"Oh, Dad might decide to disown me."

"Don't be melodramatic, little sister. He loves you too much to even consider it."

"That's not the way it usually looks from my side of the fence."

Marisa eyed her for a moment, then shook her head. "Lauren, there's absolutely no doubt about how much he loves you. I know the way he acts, it's a little hard to tell sometimes, but... Why do *you* think he's never accepted the fact that you're all grown-up?"

"Because he doesn't believe I can do anything right."

"No, that isn't really it. That's only what he tells himself. The truth is, if he admits his baby is an adult, he might have to admit he's getting older. And he just, oh, you know Dad. The problem lies with him, not with you, so you really have to try to not let it bother you."

"Well, thanks for your analysis, Ms. Freud," Lauren teased.

"Anytime."

Marisa turned and started for her Jaguar, while Lauren climbed into the van beside Sully.

"What was your sister talking about?" he asked.

She glanced back at Billy and Hoops. They were both busily making a fuss over Roxy, so she quietly said, "Marisa was giving me a pep talk. Telling me that even though it doesn't always seem like it, my father loves me."

Sully smiled at her. "Of course he does. Nobody in the world could help loving you."

She leaned back against the seat, so warm and happy inside that the feeling lasted the entire way to Eagles Roost.

SULLY HADN'T ENTIRELY let himself believe the story about the painting until they examined the cellar wall. But knowing where to check, they discovered a section behind the sixth step from the top that looked as if it had once been tampered with—as if part of the wall might have been drilled out and the surface resealed.

The area was about three feet across and close to a foot high. According to Marisa, the height was necessary because the painting would be stretched flat inside a wooden crate—with space above and below the canvas so that nothing was touching it.

Actually seeing the wall had made Sully decide there just had to be something hidden there. And now, as he chipped away at the plaster and lath with a hammer and chisel, his heart was pounding.

"Do you have enough room to work?" Lauren asked.

He nodded, even though she, Marisa and all five boys were tightly packed into the space under the stairs with him. Nobody wanted to miss a second of the excitement. He only wished everyone wasn't *quite* as excited.

He'd explained to the boys that even if they did unearth a valuable painting he wouldn't get to keep it if it legally belonged to Warren Russell's estate.

But they'd apparently decided to ignore that possibility. As far as they were concerned, whatever was in the wall was bound to be the Eagles Roost program's salvation.

He chipped away a few more chunks of plaster, then a larger one cracked free. When he pulled it off, he could see an inch or two of smooth metal.

The collective intake of breath told him the others had seen it, too.

"Is that it?" Freckles whispered. "Is that the painting?"

"No," Marisa said, "that would be an outside case of metal, which means they were being very careful. If art is stored in wooden crates alone, sometimes mice or rats get in and chew the canvas."

Sully began chipping faster, then told himself to calm down—reminding himself again that regardless of what the painting was worth it might not be his. Trying to keep that in mind, he continued working until the last inch of plaster broke free and the entire width of the metal case was exposed.

"Slide it out," Lauren whispered.

There was barely room to slip his fingers between the sides of the opening and the edges of the case, but he managed it. Then he wiggled the case forward until enough of it was protruding from the wall that he could grab the end and pull it forward.

When he got it out, it proved to be a little more than three feet long and a little less than three feet wide. It weighed a fair bit, because of the metal, but wasn't too heavy to manage.

"Let's take it upstairs where the light's better," Marisa suggested excitedly. "Open it up there."

He nodded, even though he was dying to open it right this second. The boys dashed up the stairs and into the kitchen, the three adults on their heels.

Sully laid the case flat on the kitchen table, then stood staring at it—suddenly afraid to open it. What if it *was* a van Gogh? But what if it did turn out that he had no claim to it?

"If you use a knife to slit that sealer," Marisa finally said, "I think you should be able to ease the cover off."

Billy raced over to the counter and returned with a knife.

Sully took it from him, carefully slit the seal all the way around, then tried to lift the metal top from the case. It was tight, but he gradually worked it free. Then he took out the wooden crate that was inside and used a screwdriver to pry the lid.

His heart pounding again, he lifted the lid and revealed the painting inside.

"Oh, Lord," Lauren whispered.

"Oh, Lord," Marisa echoed.

"Is it good?" Billy demanded. "Is it famous? If we get to keep it are we going to be rich?"

Nobody responded for a minute. Finally Marisa said, "We won't know if it's authentic until it's been examined by experts, and that process takes weeks. But...oh, I forgot. Boys, I brought some cases of pop and bags of chips and things for you. They're in my trunk. Here," she added, handing Freckles her keys. "How about everyone going out and helping to bring them in."

As they raced away, Sully shot Marisa a grateful smile for giving him a few minutes without their questions. Then he went back to staring at the painting. It was a portrait of a man, painted predominantly in blues and yellows. And even though he was no art expert, if someone had asked him to guess the artist, his first guess would have been Vincent van Gogh.

"What do you think?" Lauren asked, turning to her sister.

Sully looked at Marisa as well.

"I think it's either a first-rate imitation...or the real thing."

"The real thing," he repeated, trying not to let himself feel too elated. But hell, even if it didn't turn out to be his, having discovered a previously un-known van Gogh would be pretty amazing. And if it did turn out that he owned it...

"And the real thing," he said at last, "would be worth a couple of million dollars or so, wouldn't it?"

Marisa smiled. "You're a bit low. A van Gogh not unlike this one, a portrait of Dr. Gachet, sold five or six years ago for over eighty-two million."

MARISA HAD GONE outside saying she wanted the boys to give her a tour of the great outdoors. Lauren knew, though, she'd actually wanted to give her and Sully some time alone together.

She watched him staring at the painting for a few moments, then said, "What are you thinking about?"

He smiled at her. "Something I shouldn't be. Grace is always warning the boys not to count their chick-ens before they've hatched. But I was thinking about what would happen if this turns out to be authentic. And if it turns out to belong to me, not Warren Rus-sell's estate."

"What would happen?"

Sully wrapped his arms around her and pulled her close. "The first thing that would happen is I'd ask you to marry me."

Her heart began beating faster than a hummingbird's wings. "Sully?" she murmured. "Why don't you ask me, anyway?"

He kissed the top of her head. "Because we're a dolphin and a meadowlark, remember? Because we haven't had time, yet, to figure out how things could work with you in New York most of the time and me here. Because—"

"Because you're still worried that I have money and you don't?"

Drawing back a few inches, he looked at her, his expression serious. "Yeah, that too."

"It's an awfully outdated attitude, you know," she said quietly.

"I know. But knowing that doesn't magically make it go away. I'm still working on adjusting my thinking, though. And with luck, I'll turn out to be the owner of an extremely valuable painting—which would make my outdated attitude irrelevant."

She nodded. But they could hardly count on the painting being either genuine or Sully's. So what if he ended up deciding he couldn't live with her having money? That possibility terrified her, because if she couldn't have him . . . Oh, it was too horrible to even think about.

"Sully?" she asked again. "Would you still love me if I suddenly had no money?"

"Of course. It's you I love, not your damn money. Hell, if that's what I was after, your being rich wouldn't bother me, would it?"

"No, it wouldn't. Because, as you said, it's me you love. The same way it's you I love, not *your* money."

He grinned at her. "I don't have any."

"That's my point. I love you now, but I'll still love you if that painting is authentic and you get to keep it and you suddenly have ninety million dollars."

"That's not the same thing at all."

"Yes. It is. Sully, let's get married before we know anything more about the painting."

"Lauren, that's crazy. It—"

"No, it's not. What if you're suddenly so rich you can have your pick of any woman in the world?"

"I'd pick you."

"Then pick me now. Because I'm the same woman I'll be a month from now or a year from now, and you're the same man. Regardless of anybody's money."

"But there's still everything else to worry about. You can't want to live here at Eagles Roost and—"

"Why can't I want to live here? I love it here. And this is the electronic age, so I could do an awful lot of the foundation work without being anywhere near the Van Slyke Building."

"You're really serious, aren't you," Sully murmured.

She nodded, desperately afraid she was pushing harder than she should, but just as afraid that if she didn't, this was going to be the end, instead of the beginning of the rest of their lives.

"You'd be giving up a lot, leaving the city," he said.

Her heart skipped three beats. He was saying she'd be giving up things, not that the idea was out of the question.

"I'd be gaining more," she whispered. "I'd be gaining you, and that would be worth whatever I had to give up."

"You love me that much?"

"I love you more than that much, Sully. I love you more than I knew it was possible to love someone."

When he slowly smiled, she felt bubbly inside. When he leaned closer to kiss her, though, she pressed her fingers to his lips.

She might be insanely in love, but that didn't make her *completely* insane. And it was hardly realistic to think she could change her entire life-style with the snap of her fingers.

"Sully? This isn't a one-way deal. *Some* of my work is still going to have to be done in the city, and I'd definitely end up staying there overnight now and then. Plus, I know I'm going to need the occasional culture fix. And visits with my family. And time with my friends. So I'd keep my apartment. And as for the lodge... Sully, all those dead animal heads on the wall in the lounge have *got* to go."

He smiled again. "I take it that isn't negotiable?"

"Absolutely not."

"Well, I guess if I was getting you, I could live without them. Is that everything, though?"

"Just about. We'd have to train Roxy not to chase Killer."

"I think we could manage that."

"All right. Then the only other thing is that I'd want you to promise you'd spend at least the odd weekend in Manhattan with me."

"How odd?" he teased.

Her heart began to sing, and she finally decided it was safe to let herself smile back at him. "Should I assume you're willing to go halfway on this, then?" she murmured.

His kiss said he most definitely was.

EPILOGUE

THE BEGINNING OF THE REST OF THEIR LIVES

GLANCING AROUND the Van Slykes's penthouse apartment, Lauren's arm linked through his, Sully was having trouble suppressing a grin. Despite her mother's protestations that it was impossible to plan a wedding in less than a year, Lauren had gotten everything done within the space of five weeks. But even without taking that into consideration, he knew this couldn't possibly be a typical Van Slyke wedding.

In the first place, Lauren wasn't wearing a traditional white gown. Since she'd been married before, she'd chosen a gorgeous dress that was pale yellow—because he'd once mentioned that he loved her in yellow.

In the second place, even though her mother had told her a hundred times that the bride and groom weren't supposed to see each other before the ceremony, Lauren had said she wasn't going to miss a minute of the fun and that the two of them would mingle with the guests as they arrived.

The other aspect of their wedding that wasn't typically Van Slyke was the guest list. Oh, all of Lauren's close relatives were here, along with her friends,

Rosalie, friends of the family, and the board members of the Van Slyke Foundation.

But not Hunter Clifton, of course. Aside from anything else, he was no longer a board member. He'd resigned after he'd been charged with conspiracy to commit a felony and with counseling a youth to commit a crime—both very serious charges, according to Elliot, which were going to result in a jail term when Hunter was convicted.

Sully glanced around again, making sure his kids were all behaving. They, of course, were part of what made this an unusual guest list for the Van Slykes. And in addition to the boys, Grace and Otis were here, along with a goodly number of Sully's friends and neighbors.

A few of them, like old Zeke Scrouthy, were wandering around wearing stunned expressions. Not long after Zeke had arrived, he'd taken Sully aside to ask him why the Van Slykes would want to rattle around in a two-story apartment that was bigger than the Newcomb Hotel.

Looking across the living room to where Roger and Susannah were talking with Marisa and her boyfriend, Sully couldn't help thinking that things had gone far better with Lauren's family than he'd dared hope. Marisa and Elliot had been great right from the start. And once Roger and Susannah had quit fighting the fact that Lauren was determined to marry him, they'd made an obvious attempt to accept him.

He forced his attention back to the moment and tuned in on what Lauren and her great-aunt Dorothy were chatting about.

Aunt Dorothy, whom he'd guess was about eighty years old, was wearing a dead fox around her neck.

He didn't think the animal heads Lauren had made him take down from the lounge had looked any worse than that, but he knew better than to voice his opinion.

He listened for a couple of minutes, while Aunt Dorothy talked about her problems with getting exactly the right accommodations on her upcoming cruise, then his thoughts drifted to the painting.

It had been three days, now, since the art experts had declared it an authentic van Gogh, but he was still having trouble believing it really was.

As for the question of ownership, Lauren had suggested waiting until they were certain that it was genuine before asking Elliot to look into that. She'd had a feeling they might jinx things, otherwise. At any rate, while Elliot had promised to have one of his friends, a top-notch estate lawyer, check into the specifics, he hadn't gotten back to them yet.

Until that happened, Sully knew he wouldn't be able to stop worrying. It would hardly be the end of the world if the painting wasn't legally his, but he'd feel a lot better if it was. Because as hard as he'd tried he just hadn't been able to shake his uneasiness about marrying money when he had none himself.

He looked at Lauren, thinking how much he loved her and how much he wanted her to be happy with him. He intended to do whatever it took to ensure she was, and if that came down to shoving his uneasiness into the dark recesses of his mind and forcing every last one of his concerns to stay there, he'd just have do his best to manage that.

Lost in thought, he didn't realize Elliot and Ursula had arrived until they were standing in front of him. Elliot shook his hand and kissed Lauren and Aunt

Dorothy. Ursula kissed all three of them, then dragged Aunt Dorothy off, saying she wanted to tell her what the children had been up to.

"I've got something for you, Sully," Elliot said, taking a fat envelope from his inside pocket. "It's an opinion letter on the issue of ownership."

His chest suddenly felt so tight he could hardly breathe. He told himself Elliot wouldn't give him bad news fifteen minutes before the marriage ceremony, but he was still afraid to reach for the envelope.

"Sully?" Lauren murmured, lightly poking him in the ribs.

He made himself stick his hand out and take the letter, made himself open the envelope and unfold the pages inside, made himself read.

Dear Mr. Sullivan,

Mr. Elliot Van Slyke has asked me to provide you with an opinion as to the ownership of a painting you recently discovered at Eagles Roost. Further to this instruction I have examined:

    a) the 1960 Agreement of Purchase and Sale between Frank Watson (purchaser) and Hettie Russell (vendor) under which title to the property commonly known as Eagles Roost passed to Frank Watson; and

    b) the Last Will and Testament of Frank Watson, executed April 7, 1988, and submitted for probate on February 3, 1990.

    In addition, I have researched relevant statutory authorities and the case law.

    Under the Agreement of Purchase and Sale, Hettie Russell sold the land, buildings *and all their contents* to Frank Watson. The contents are not in any way itemized but would, in my view, be deemed to include the painting. I stress, however, that this is my opinion only. Photocopies of three recent rulings bearing on this issue are enclosed for your information.

Subsequently, Frank Watson bequeathed the Eagles Roost land, buildings *and their contents* to you. No items were excluded or bequeathed to any other legatees.

After careful consideration and absent, unfortunately, of any directly relevant decided cases, it is my opinion that title to said painting passed to you pursuant to Frank Watson's will.

Should you require further advice or assistance in this matter, I would be pleased to help you.

Yours truly,
Marcus Westerby, Attorney-at-Law

Sully silently handed the letter to Lauren, desperately trying to contain his excitement—because part of what was in that letter made him extremely anxious.

"Elliot?" he said as Lauren read the letter. "Why does he stress that it's only his opinion? That sounds as if he's not certain."

"Is he, Elliot?" Lauren said, looking up from the letter.

When Sully glanced at her, her face was so pale that his heart sank. He'd been right to be anxious. The painting wasn't definitely his. When he took her hand she squeezed his so hard it hurt.

"Elliot," she said again, "your friend thinks the ownership will be contested, doesn't he?"

"No, although it's always possible." Elliot smiled, then added, "But I think it's awfully unlikely. And all Marcus is saying when he stresses it's only his opinion is that he can't state it as a legal certainty. But there really doesn't seem to be anyone to contest anything. The Russells never had children. And when Hettie died, she left everything to a hospital."

"Then," Lauren said, "the hospital board will—"

"Uh-uh," Elliot interrupted, still smiling. "The hospital no longer exists. It was torn down ten years ago, so in *my* legal opinion, Sully is home free."

Sully wasn't sure which of them moved first, but Lauren was suddenly in his arms, half laughing and half crying against his chest. He felt like both laughing and crying himself, but she seemed to be doing a good enough job for both of them so he simply held her—feeling happier than he'd ever felt before in his life. He was about to marry the woman he'd never expected to find. The woman he loved more than life itself.

"You know," he finally whispered to her, "I've been thinking a lot about what I'd do if the painting *did* turn out to be mine."

"And what did you decide?" she whispered back.

"Well, I was wondering if you could handle being director of *two* foundations."

"Maybe. If I had enough staff. Why?"

"Because I'd like to use the bulk of whatever that van Gogh's worth to set up The Frank Watson Memorial Foundation. And have it fund all kinds of programs for kids. Maybe award scholarships, too."

"I think that's a wonderful idea. But could you use a bit of the money to add a new wing to the lodge?"

"You mean expand the Eagles Roost program?"

"Well, we could, but what I actually meant was that you're so wonderful with kids it would be a crime not to have some of our own."

"Dammit, Lauren," he said, tilting her face up so she'd see he was teasing, "first you rush me into marrying you and now you want to rush me into having a family. I'm afraid to think what will be next."

"You know what I'm afraid of, Sully?"

He shook his head, worried that she suddenly seemed so serious.

Then she smiled one of her fantastic smiles and said, "Absolutely nothing. As long as I've got you, I'm not afraid of anything in the world."

"Ditto," he whispered, forgetting all about the apartment full of people and proceeding to kiss her breathless.

Fall in love all over again with

This Time... **MARRIAGE**

In this collection of original short stories, three brides get a unique chance for a return engagement!

- Being kidnapped from your bridal shower by a one-time love can really put a crimp in your wedding plans! *The Borrowed Bride*— by **Susan Wiggs,** *Romantic Times* Career Achievement Award-winning author.

- After fifteen years a couple reunites for the sake of their child—this time will it end in marriage? *The Forgotten Bride*—by **Janice Kaiser.**

- It's tough to make a good divorce stick—especially when you're thrown together with your ex in a magazine wedding shoot! *The Bygone Bride*— by **Muriel Jensen.**

Don't miss THIS TIME…MARRIAGE, available in April wherever Harlequin books are sold.

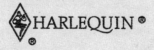

HARLEQUIN ®

HARLEQUIN®

Don't miss these Harlequin favorites by some of our most
distinguished authors!
And now, you can receive a discount by ordering two or more titles!

HT #25645	THREE GROOMS AND A WIFE by JoAnn Ross	$3.25 U.S./$3.75 CAN. ☐
HT #25648	JESSIE'S LAWMAN by Kristine Rolofson	$3.25 U.S.//$3.75 CAN. ☐
HP #11725	THE WRONG KIND OF WIFE by Roberta Leigh	$3.25 U.S./$3.75 CAN. ☐
HP #11755	TIGER EYES by Robyn Donald	$3.25 U.S./$3.75 CAN. ☐
HR #03362	THE BABY BUSINESS by Rebecca Winters	$2.99 U.S./$3.50 CAN. ☐
HR #03375	THE BABY CAPER by Emma Goldrick	$2.99 U.S./$3.50 CAN. ☐
HS #70638	THE SECRET YEARS by Margot Dalton	$3.75 U.S./$4.25 CAN. ☐
HS #70655	PEACEKEEPER by Marisa Carroll	$3.75 U.S./$4.25 CAN. ☐
HI #22280	MIDNIGHT RIDER by Laura Pender	$2.99 U.S./$3.50 CAN. ☐
HI #22235	BEAUTY VS THE BEAST by M.J. Rogers	$3.50 U.S./$3.99 CAN. ☐
HAR #16531	TEDDY BEAR HEIR by Elda Minger	$3.50 U.S./$3.99 CAN. ☐
HAR #16596	COUNTERFEIT HUSBAND by Linda Randall Wisdom	$3.50 U.S./$3.99 CAN. ☐
HH #28795	PIECES OF SKY by Marianne Willman	$3.99 U.S./$4.50 CAN. ☐
HH #28855	SWEET SURRENDER by Julie Tetel	$4.50 U.S./$4.99 CAN. ☐

(limited quantities available on certain titles)

	AMOUNT	$
DEDUCT:	10% DISCOUNT FOR 2+ BOOKS	$
ADD:	POSTAGE & HANDLING	$
	($1.00 for one book, 50¢ for each additional)	
	APPLICABLE TAXES**	$_____
	<u>TOTAL PAYABLE</u>	$_____
	(check or money order—please do not send cash)	

To order, complete this form and send it, along with a check or money order for the
total above, payable to Harlequin Books, to: **In the U.S.:** 3010 Walden Avenue,
P.O. Box 9047, Buffalo, NY 14269-9047; **In Canada:** P.O. Box 613, Fort Erie, Ontario,
L2A 5X3.

Name: _____

Address: _____ City: _____

State/Prov.: _____ Zip/Postal Code: _____

**New York residents remit applicable sales taxes.
Canadian residents remit applicable GST and provincial taxes.

HBACK-AJ3

Bestselling authors

ELAINE COFFMAN
RUTH LANGAN

and

MARY McBRIDE

Together in one fabulous collection!

OUTLAW
Brides

Available in June wherever Harlequin
books are sold.

HARLEQUIN ®

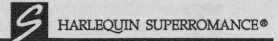

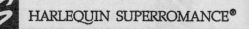

HARLEQUIN SUPERROMANCE®

Emotional, daring, adventurous—a stunning new novel
from the award-winning author of *The Third Christmas* and
The Keeper. **Margot Early** has been called "an author whose
talent will carry her to the top" and "one of the brightest
rising stars of contemporary romance." This book proves it!

Waiting For You

According to family legend, golden-haired Christopher was
born with a mission—to break a family curse. Only he, it is
said, can end the history of miscarriages, stillbirths and
maternal deaths.

Christopher, a doctor living and working in Colorado, isn't sure
he believes all this. But now Dulcinea—the first and only
woman he ever loved—is pregnant. With his brother's baby.

She comes back to Christopher, begging him to take the risk,
to break the curse. *How can he refuse?*

Waiting For You will be available in June wherever
Harlequin books are sold. Don't miss it!

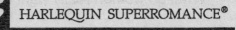

HARLEQUIN SUPERROMANCE®

Showcase

Not Without My Child

by

Rebecca Winters

A very contemporary and deeply emotional story of love, family and second chances. By the award-winning author of *The Wrong Twin*.

Tessa Marsden. Her marriage was a mistake; her son, Scotty, was not. She loves her child with all her heart and soul. She's tried hard to make the marriage work, but this is a marriage that can't be saved. She knows now that she has to get out—before it completely destroys her *and* her husband, Grant.

But when she files for divorce, Grant—for reasons of his own, reasons she doesn't understand—demands full custody of Scotty. Tessa can't live with that. *She can't live without her child.*

Alex Sommerfield. He's the lawyer handling her divorce. He defies all the rules by falling in love with his client. But he's determined not to put her custody case or her happiness at risk....

Watch for *Not Without My Child* in June wherever Harlequin books are sold.

SHOW8

What do women really want to know?

Trust the world's largest publisher of women's fiction to tell you.

HARLEQUIN ULTIMATE GUIDES™

I CAN FIX THAT

A Guide For Women
Who Want To Do It Themselves

This is the only guide a self-reliant woman will ever need to deal with those pesky items that break, wear out or just don't work anymore. Chock-full of friendly advice and straightforward, step-by-step solutions to the trials of everyday life in our gadget-oriented world! So, don't just sit there wondering how to fix the VCR—run to your nearest bookstore for your copy now!

Available this May, at your favorite retail outlet.

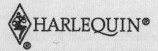

HARLEQUIN®

FIX